Checked In

BOOKS BY TEYLA BRANTON

Unbounded Series
  The Change
  The Cure
  Protectors
    Ava's Revenge
    Mortal Brother
    Set Ablaze
  The Escape
  The Reckoning
  Lethal Engagement
  The Takeover

Other
  Times Nine

Imprints Series
  First Touch (prequel)
  Touch of Rain
  On The Hunt
  Upstaged
  Under Fire
  Blinded
  Street Smart
  Hidden Intent
  Checked In

Colony Six Series
  Insight (prequel)
  Sketches
  Visions
  Travels

UNDER THE NAME RACHEL BRANTON

Lily's House Series
  House Without Lies
  Tell Me No Lies
  Hearts Never Lie
  Your Eyes Don't Lie
  Broken Lies
  No Secrets or Lies
  Cowboys Can't Lie

Town Called Forgotten
  Kiss at Midnight
  This Feeling for You

Finding Home Series
  Take Me Home
  All That I Love
  Then I Found You

Other
  How Far
  Royal Quest

Picture Books
  I Don't Want To Eat Bugs
  I Don't Want to Have Hot
    Toes

Checked In

TEYLA BRANTON

WHITE
STAR
PRESS

This is a work of fiction, and the views expressed herein are the sole responsibility of the author. Likewise, certain characters, places, and incidents are the product of the author's imagination, and any resemblance to actual persons, living or dead, or actual events or locales, is entirely coincidental.

Checked In (Imprints Book 8)

Published by White Star Press
P.O. Box 353
American Fork, Utah 84003

Printed in the United States of America
ISBN: 978-1-948982-22-1
Year of first printing: 2020

This book is once again dedicated to my family.
Without out them life wouldn't be nearly
so interesting. (Although, to be honest,
I'd get more sleep.) Love you guys!

Chapter 1

The sight of the bed and breakfast belonging to Shannon's parents made me forget, at least for a moment, the strange circumstances bringing us to Jacksonville Beach, Florida. I'd been expecting Haven Retreat to be a nice place, maybe even something special, but the lovely red-bricked Victorian mansion set in a copse of lush trees swept my breath away. The hanging baskets of cascading white and pink flowers set at regular intervals along the wide wraparound porch beckoned welcomingly, and the attached gazebo made the place look like something from another time.

"That's strange," Shannon said as we climbed from our white rental sedan. "They usually rush right out to meet me, or at least Mom does. I texted her when we landed."

"Maybe she's making dinner." My stomach rumbled at the idea. Part of our agreement with Holt and Bonnie Martin for coming here was that they provided meals. Shannon had bought lunch on our flight from Portland, but I was pickier with my food choices and had to content myself with snacks from my carry-on. Even though it was only two o'clock in the afternoon back in Oregon versus five in the evening here, I was famished.

"Maybe." He went around the car to open the trunk.

I tore my eyes away from the gray-roofed, three-story turret on the right and reached into the back seat to grab our carry-on luggage. For all of three seconds, I considered donning the white jacket I'd been wearing on the plane over my red tank top and flowy red and white skirt but decided I cared more about relief from the August heat than I did about making a good impression.

Shannon hefted the suitcases, and we started up the flower-lined walkway toward the porch. The cement walk felt warm on my bare feet—not nearly as hot as I'd expected. Perhaps because of the many trees, bursting in bright pink and ivory blossoms, that arched partially over the walk. Someone here had a green thumb, and I was betting it was Shannon's mother.

"There's a parking lot around the side," Shannon said, "but it's easier to dump the luggage here first. At least it is if we're in the Wedding Suite instead of the cottages."

He'd told me that each of the seven rooms inside the house had theme names, like Royal Chamber, African Safari, Space Walk, and Sea Scape. They sounded nice, but I was personally crossing my fingers for one of the three cottages instead. I'd met his parents at our wedding and liked them, but I wasn't sure how I felt about spending the second week of our honeymoon under the same roof.

We arrived on the porch, where none of the bed and breakfast guests were in sight among the inviting clusters of wrought iron furniture. I hoped their absence didn't tie into the reason we were here, because we still had no clue as to why his parents had insisted that we come.

I was leaning toward a mystery we could solve quickly with the combined advantage of my psychometry ability and

Shannon's homicide detective skills. For free flights and a week at the beach, it would be well worth our time, even if they hadn't been family. But an uneasy feeling in my gut had me wondering why his parents would go to such costly measures and interrupt our honeymoon—certainly not for something easy.

Shannon's father, who was a retired beat officer with the Portland Police Bureau in Oregon, should have skills and connections enough to solve a casual mystery, even if he'd hated police work and had left the force the minute his twenty years had been served. But maybe I had it all wrong, because Shannon suspected financial woes, health problems, or structural issues with the bed and breakfast itself.

This last seemed unlikely as we entered the unlocked house and stood in the wide, vaulted entryway under an enormous gold chandelier. Not one but two sweeping staircases led to an upstairs floor. Two kinds of vibrant paper decorated the walls, from the elaborate chair rails clear up to the thick, ornate crown molding. An amazing free-standing coat rack stood to the left of the door, and an antique wall table that I envied sat next to it. Several nice paintings, one of which I was sure was an antique, completed the entryway.

"Wow," I murmured, feeling torn in every direction. I wanted to pull off the thin polyester gloves I'd worn to protect myself from stray imprints, as I usually did now in public places, and explore the house, reading all its secrets. But I'd remove them soon enough, depending on why we were here, and what I could do to help his parents.

Shannon chuckled. "I knew you'd like it. Of course, it didn't always look this way. My parents did all this wallpaper and trim work themselves." He set the suitcases on the marble floor. "No point in taking these further before we know what room we're in."

I dropped my bags and sniffed deeply. "Smells like heaven. Your mom has to be in the kitchen."

He took my hand, and we followed our noses into the kitchen—or I followed my nose because Shannon had obviously been here before. Soft singing reached our ears as we entered the large kitchen, where a huge island and off-white cupboards greeted us. A lovely bronze-skinned woman with curly, black hair pulled back in a loose ponytail was behind the counter, chopping vegetables and singing in a language that sounded somewhat like Spanish but definitely wasn't. She wore jeans, topped by a bright orange tee.

She stopped singing as she noticed Shannon. "You're here. Good!" She looked a little too relieved to see us, especially since we were expected.

"He's here! He's here!" shouted another voice, the tone higher and a little muffled. An instant later, two heads with short, black hair popped up behind the counter, one on either side of the woman, each belonging to a boy that looked exactly like the other, their skin tone a shade lighter than their mother's. They rushed around the counter and threw themselves at Shannon.

"Whoa," Shannon said as he bent to give them a simultaneous hug. "How've you guys been, huh?"

"Will you play hide-and-seek with us?" asked one of the boys. "Mom's too busy working."

"Not now, he won't," the woman said, picking up a towel to wipe her hands. "Remember what I told you? He's on a honeymoon. And he has to help Vovô."

"That stinks," the boy retorted.

"Dimas Eduardo da Silva de Carvalho de Santos Ribeiro!" his mother said. "Say you are sorry right this minute." The part of her sentence that was in English was as good as my own; the boy's name sounded like fluid music.

Dimas hung his head. "Sorry," he muttered, obviously not sorry at all.

Shannon grinned. "That's okay. Everyone, this is Autumn Rain, my wife. Autumn, this is Micaela Ribeiro and her boys, Dimas and Lucio. Micaela has worked here for at least ten years, before the boys were even born."

Micaela came around the counter to hug Shannon and shake my hand. "So pleased to meet you," she said. If she wondered why I was wearing gloves and no shoes, she didn't bring it up.

"You too." I grinned at the boys to include them, but they were poking each other and seemed to have forgotten us.

"I'm sorry I couldn't come to the wedding," Micaela added. "It looked beautiful from the pictures. But someone had to take care of our guests."

"Our fault for marrying on such short notice." Shannon motioned to the counter and the vegetables. "But since when do you cook anything besides breakfast here? And what did you mean about helping Vovô?" To me, he added, "That's what the boys call my dad. It means grandfather in Portuguese." Looking back at Micaela, he added, "My mom hasn't given me any details about why we're here, and this whole thing is a little strange. My dad's not sick, is he?"

Micaela shook her head, her forehead creasing. "I was preparing one of the guest rooms when your mom called me down to watch the food because the police were here. They wanted to talk to your dad."

Shannon gaped at her for several long seconds before questions rushed out: "Why? How long ago? Where are they?" The fact that the police were here on a Saturday wasn't a good sign.

"They went out to Rose Petal Cottage. That's where your dad is. You just missed them."

"But why do they want to see my dad?" Shannon demanded.

Micaela turned her attention to the boys and snapped her fingers. "Saiam! Esperem por mim lá fora." The boys straightened immediately, alerted by the tone in her voice, and hurried from the room.

When they were gone, their mother heaved a sigh. "You know about Welby Carr, right? The owner of Magnolia Inn next door?"

"That he died?" Shannon nodded. "I was sorry to hear."

"Well, his granddaughter, Lyndia, was supposed to inherit the inn—she's been running it all this time with him since her parents died. But Welby's other son, Nigel Carr, showed up out of nowhere a few weeks before Welby died. He's been terrorizing Lyndia ever since, trying to steal the inn from her. Then a week and a half ago, he went missing."

"Maybe he went back to whatever gutter he crawled out of," Shannon muttered.

Micaela snorted. "I doubt that. Lyndia says he plans to sell Magnolia Inn to a big developer who will make more of those box-sized retirement apartments, or maybe a high-rise hotel. He wouldn't have gone anywhere without a big pay-off."

"But what does all that have to do with Shannon's dad?" I asked, sensing Shannon was growing more frustrated by the second.

"Nigel claimed that the land one of our cottages is on actually belongs to Magnolia Inn, even though Holt and Welby had an agreement. Holt was furious when he learned about it, and he confronted Nigel at Magnolia Inn the day before he left to attend your wedding. No one has seen the man since. And it looked suspicious that your dad was out of town when the police started searching."

"But that's got to be old news now," Shannon said. "Something else must have happened to bring them here again."

Micaela nodded. "That's what I think. But they would only talk to your dad."

"Don't worry. We'll clear this up." Pursing his lips, Shannon turned on his heel to head back the way we'd come. I hurried to keep pace with him.

"You might as well take your luggage out in a golf cart," Micaela called after us. "Your mother put you in Rose Petal Cottage. That's why your dad's out there, making sure it's ready."

"Well, that's something, at least," Shannon said to me as we hefted our luggage once again. "Once we figure this out, we'll have all the privacy we want."

"I don't know," I said, keeping my tone light. "You were really looking forward to that heart-shaped tub in the Wedding Suite you told me about."

We were out on the porch now, and Shannon stopped short, turning to me, suitcases still in hand. "We shouldn't have come. This was our time. I'm really sorry."

"Of course, we had to come. I'm part of your family now, bad timing and all."

He stepped closer until our bodies were tantalizingly close. "I'll make it up to you."

"We'll make it up to each other." With a wink, I hurried down the steps ahead of him.

As Shannon promised, there was a small parking lot on the side of the house, partially hidden by more flowering trees. An unmarked police cruiser was there, clearly recognizable by the state license plate and the light bar embedded in the front grille. There were also two golf carts, and we loaded the suitcases into one of these. Shannon started it up with a code he typed into a tiny touch screen.

From the parking lot we could see a tiny bungalow with a swing set, slide, and play area. "That's Family Chalet," Shannon said, steering onto a wide cement path cutting through the yard. "Rose Petal Cottage is next. It's the prettiest, so I'm not surprised Mom put us there." He allowed himself a smile. "She likes you."

I wasn't sure we'd spent enough time together in the two days they had been in Portland to be sure of that, but I was determined to do what I could to encourage a relationship with his parents. How I'd eventually tell them I could read emotions imprinted on certain objects, I had no idea. Shannon hadn't believed I was anything but a fraud for months, even when he was half in love with me, and they'd raised him, so I figured my chances of them easily accepting my strange ability wasn't strong.

"Frontier Cabin is the closest to Magnolia Inn," Shannon said into the silence. "That's the cottage on the disputed land Micaela was talking about. It was derelict for years before my parents talked to the neighbor and took it over. I can't believe the guy's son is trying to steal it from them. I remember hearing he was the black sheep of the family."

"Maybe his past has caught up with him."

"If it has, this could very well be a homicide my dad's stumbled into. My parents should have told me earlier."

"I agree." I removed my gloves, stuffing them into my bag,

and reached to take one of his hands from the wheel, holding it in mine. "But I'm kind of glad they didn't." The private week we'd spent alone in the Oregon mountains had been a slice of perfect.

His heated look sent a shiver through me. "Yeah. You're right."

After passing Family Chalet, the sidewalk turned sharply to the right around a bush, revealing the next cottage. Roses grew all around the small, tan structure, climbing up trellises against the house. Dark brown trim and a thatched roof gave it a quaint look, as if Snow White lived there with her dwarf companions.

"It's amazing," I said, drinking it all in.

Shannon chuckled as he stopped the golf cart, but it sounded forced. "Door's open. Looks like they're still here." Leaving the luggage where it was, he vaulted from the cart and hurried toward the house. I went after him.

Inside the cottage, short Bonnie Martin stood in the center of a room that was not only a sitting room but a kitchenette and dining nook as well. She stood with her hands on her ample hips, her pale, freckled face tinted with heat, and her strawberry-blond hair matted to her head with humidity.

Two people stood near her: a thin, wiry man with blond hair, whose dress pants, white button-up shirt, and shoulder holster screamed detective, and a wide-set woman with close-cropped hair and skin as dark as midnight, who loomed over both of them. They were all staring away from us at a loft that jutted out over the kitchen and dining area.

"Are you just about finished?" Bonnie called up to the loft.

"Almost," Holt answered. "Don't get your panties in an uproar."

"Whatever that means," she grumbled. "How long does it take to put one little gift basket up there? The officers need to talk to you, and our son will be—" She broke off as she glanced in our direction and noticed our arrival.

"Oh, sweetie." Bonnie rushed toward us in a flurry of gray and yellow floral, throwing her arms around Shannon. "I'm sorry I wasn't at the house to meet you. Dinner's almost ready. Are you hungry?"

Shannon stared down at her with a frown. "No, I'm not hungry. Why don't you tell me what's going on here?"

Ignoring her son's question, Bonnie stepped over to hug me too. "How was your flight?"

"Long." I smiled to soften the response. "We read, though. I even dozed off. I can sleep anywhere."

Shannon blew out an impatient breath at the small talk. "You should have told us about this," he said to his mother. To the detectives, he added, "Is my dad a suspect? If you're planning to arrest him, you'd better have solid evidence."

"You must be the homicide detective son." The female detective strode over to meet us and extended a hand to Shannon. "I'm Detective Nisha Wallace, and this is my partner, Detective Remy Burke." Wallace's black dress pants and short-sleeved, wine-colored shirt could belong to any civilian, but the badge and large gun clipped to her waist said otherwise.

"I'm Shannon Martin." Shannon shook her hand and that of her partner.

"Autumn," I said, reaching for Detective Wallace's hand as I hadn't her partner's. She wore a ring, and I was curious to see what might be printed on it. The scene came in a vibrant flash, pulling me instantly into it. For that moment of the imprint I was Detective Wallace, experiencing all her feelings and seeing through her eyes.

"*If the chief wants an arrest to shut up the ex-wife, I say we give him one,*" Detective Burke said to me from the passenger side of our vehicle. "*The blood shows that Martin guy knows more than he's told us.*"

"*Maybe,*" I said with a glance at him, my fingers clenching the wheel so tightly that my ring dug into my flesh. "*But without a body, it's all circumstantial. If we mess up, we'll be passed over for the next promotion.*"

"*Well, we can at least bring him in for questioning.*"

I frowned. If we brought him in, the chief would make us arrest him. I had more time on the force, and I was a woman besides, so I'd be blamed if someone else ended up being guilty, or if the missing man turned up unharmed.

A new imprint was beginning as Wallace drew her hand from mine. She was staring at my eyes, so she'd noticed my heterochromia—my left eye was blue and my right hazel, a genetic condition I shared with my sister and biological father—but she didn't ask about it.

I wished I could tell Shannon what I'd seen from her ring. Knowing that these detectives were under pressure to make an arrest, even if it wasn't the right arrest, might help him know what to say to them.

"You've known about my father's argument with the missing man for more than a week," Shannon said, not catching my intense stare. "What's changed?"

Detective Wallace opened her mouth to say something, but Holt spoke from the loft, drawing her attention. "Glad you two got here safely." He stood next to the small railing which appeared to be more for decoration than security. In his hand he carried a large wicker basket stuffed high with items I couldn't identify. "Guess our surprise is ruined, though," he added good-naturedly, lifting the basket. He frowned at the detectives. "Why are you here again? Did you find Lyndia's uncle?"

"Mr. Martin, if you'll please put that down," Detective Wallace said, tipping her neck back to see him better. "We need to ask you a few more questions." It didn't escape me that her hand now hovered near her big gun. What did she think Holt was going to do?

"Oh, sure." A line of puzzlement appeared on his brow. "I'll put it on the bedside table, I guess. I already tried the bed, but it tipped over and all the stuff spilled. That's what's taking so long." He disappeared again and returned seconds later on the left side of the loft without the basket and began his descent down a steep, narrow staircase that hugged the wall.

Holt reached us in seconds, his curly blond hair and broad shoulders reminding me of Shannon, even though he was a head taller than his son. "I already told you I don't know where Nigel Carr is," he said to the detectives. "That isn't going to change."

"We're here because forensics came back on your hoe." Detective Wallace approached Holt warily. "Nigel Carr's blood was found on it. We need you to come to the station for another chat about his disappearance."

"Wait, what!" Bonnie hurried to Holt's side, flushing an angry red. "This is ridiculous! Just because my husband argued with the man, it doesn't mean he whacked him over the head with a hoe."

A shocked silence filled the room—or at least Shannon and I were shocked. The detectives didn't appear fazed.

"Where was this hoe found?" Shannon demanded.

"Here on the property," Detective Burke said, shifting uncomfortably. "We found it in here during our initial search after we learned about the altercation between your father and Mr. Carr."

Shannon's chin raised an inch. "That doesn't mean a thing, and you know it. Who else has access? Everyone in the house and probably half the neighborhood."

"Nevertheless, it was Mr. Carr's blood," Detective Wallace said. "We need to know how it got there."

"Of course it was his blood," Holt interjected, pulling the attention back to his annoyed face. "Darn fool kicked my hoe himself when I was out weeding the flowerbed at Frontier Cabin. He was wearing those ridiculous flipflops we used to call thongs in the old days. Ridiculous footwear, even for the beach."

Detective Wallace glared at him. "And you're just telling us this now?"

Holt shrugged. "I didn't spend twenty years as a police officer for nothing. I knew you'd think some dumb thing, especially when what happened was so lame."

"And what exactly did happen?" Detective Wallace asked.

"I just told you. I was out weeding, and he comes along and asks me why I was bothering when the land was his, and he was going to sell it to some big developer. It was the first I'd heard of that, so I explained that Welby and I had an agreement, and it was in his most recent will that he wouldn't dispute my claim." Holt's bottom lip curled in disgust. "Nigel just laughed and said there wasn't a will, even though I saw it myself at least two years ago. And I didn't slave over at Magnolia Inn for the better part of two years for nothing, so I said I'd see him in court. He tried to kick the hoe from my hands, and it sliced him good. Blood went everywhere. Then the jerk said he'd make sure the new development cut off our easy access to the beach." He gave a sharp shake of his head.

"We have a leeway," Bonnie protested. "Everyone uses it."

"It doesn't have to be in that exact spot, though," Holt said. "And making our guests go around to something that's not as nice will eventually force us to lower our rates."

"So you knew it was his blood?" Detective Wallace was like a dog with a bone.

"Yeah, and he probably had to go to the hospital for stitches." A note of satisfaction tinged Holt's voice. "It was his own fault, and my hoe certainly didn't make him disappear."

Wallace jerked her head toward the door. "Can you show me where this happened?"

Holt sighed. "Guess so."

We followed him outside and down the cement path a short distance to the next cottage, nearly invisible behind a thick stand of palm trees and vegetation. Bonnie and Holt were in the lead, then the detectives, with Shannon and me bringing up the rear.

"It's all circumstantial," Shannon said as we closed in on the detectives. "For all we know, he got gangrene. Have you checked the hospitals?"

"Of course we have." Detective Burke gave him a sour look. "He's in none of them. That's why we suspect foul play."

"If you arrest Holt, the attorney will have him out by morning," I said. "And when we find out where Nigel really is, you'll both look bad." Playing on Detective Wallace's imprint might not be fair, but this was Shannon's father we were talking about and fair didn't weigh into it.

Wallace slowed her steps, turning her head to meet my gaze. "We'll wait to see if there's anything at the site before we decide what to do."

"But you already searched here, right?" Shannon pressed.

Detective Burke rolled his eyes. "We miss things all the time, especially when we aren't sure there's been a crime."

"And you still can't be sure." Shannon spoke as if trying to hold in a snarl. I didn't blame him. "No body, no way to prove a crime." The detectives didn't respond.

We arrived at Frontier Cabin, which was a tiny, rustic-looking log structure. Like everywhere else on the property, the trees gave it an air of seclusion, though I doubted the entire Haven Retreat was more than three-fourths of an acre, which was still a small fortune in this location.

"Right here." Holt pointed down at an expansive flowerbed that burgeoned with wildflowers and small pine trees. I wasn't sure how he could tell weeds from the wildflowers, but the terrain looked realistic.

We all stared, with Detective Wallace squatting down and getting close to study the dirt. "Nothing here now," she said.

"We've watered every other day," Bonnie said.

"When was the incident?" Wallace asked.

Holt shrugged. "Tuesday, I think. Yeah, that was it, a week ago last Tuesday. I stewed about it all night before I went to confront him at Magnolia Inn the next morning." Holt took a step back. "That's proof he was fine afterward. Lyndia was there and saw the whole thing. Look, do I have to call my attorney?"

Detective Wallace, who was still crouched down in the flowerbed, glanced up and shook her head. "I guess not. But I want you to write out a detailed description of what happened.

And I want to know if anyone can vouch that your neighbor gave up his claim to this cabin."

"Lyndia should be able to verify," Bonnie said. "She's the one who scheduled all the work Holt did on their property in exchange. Didn't she tell you already?"

"Not that I recall." Wallace arose.

I moved back to give the detective room and stepped into a rush of cool air. I turned to it, hoping to feel it on my face, but not a breeze stirred the trees.

That doesn't make sense, I thought. Then I saw it—a patch of aqua blue showing behind a spray of yellow wildflowers that poked out from under one of the squat pine trees. As I stepped in that direction, the cold became more apparent.

Cold.

I'd felt a similar thing before in my last case, but that had been nearly a month ago now. My birth father thought it signaled a recently deceased person, and maybe it was. Or maybe I'd just stepped into the shade.

I bent and reached for the object. *A baseball hat,* I had time to note before I was swept up into a vivid imprint.

Dear old dad was good for something, after all. Anticipation shuddered through me as I stared at the tiny cabin in the darkness, the only light coming from its small windows. Soon there would be a huge high-rise hotel here, and I'd be sitting on the beach drinking. I could appease the ball-and-chain with a cut and get her off my back. Even that no-good son of mine would have to admit that I'd done good. Too bad I couldn't tell him the truth about how it came about. That would be signing my own death warrant.

Of course the girl was something I'd have to take care of, but she'd served her purpose for now. Maybe she wouldn't have to end up like her grandfather.

A rustling sound made me look around, but all I saw were a few palm trees that looked out of place so near this little rustic cabin. Well, now that I'd had my smoke, it was time to get back to the inn.

A glimpse of something in my peripheral vision made me hesitate. I turned.

Too late.

Pain burst into my skull, zipping across the entire right side of my head. A cry rose in my throat but stuck there without sound. I was falling, the world going dark. My face hit the ground. I smelled grass and dirt. The terrible pain ebbed until there was only numbness.

More rustling noises.

The part of me that was still Autumn knew this wasn't my reality or even my memory. I needed to release my hold on the cap. Doing so was normally no longer a problem, but now my hand refused to obey. It had been a tiring day, and this imprint had been completely unexpected. I was still inside the imprint—and might be until the imprinter lost consciousness.

Footsteps. I knew that whatever had hit me was coming again. Who are you? I wanted to scream. Wetness dribbled down the side of my face and into my mouth. Blood. My muscles clenched, waiting for the next shot.

The scene vanished as the cap was wrenched from my hand. I gave a sigh of relief and opened my eyes as Shannon gathered me from the grass and into his arms.

"You okay?" he whispered into my ear.

"Yeah." My head pounded, and my heartbeat was spiked on adrenaline, but I was all right. I was pretty sure whoever had imprinted on that hat couldn't say the same.

He held my gaze for a long moment, verifying for himself

that I was fine. This time I didn't protest. He'd saved me from whatever else had been on the cap, and I was grateful. Unfortunately for Holt, I couldn't touch the cap again—it was too dangerous.

I sat up and pulled away, noting that the others had all turned toward me, staring. *Great.*

"What happened?" Bonnie asked. "Are you sick?"

No way to get around explaining imprints to Shannon's parents now—not in front of the police, of course, but sooner than I'd hoped. I opened my mouth to speak, hoping to plead exhaustion.

Detective Wallace beat me to it. "That looks like Nigel Carr's Miami Dolphins hat. According to his ex-wife, he always wore it, and it's not in the items he left behind at Magnolia Inn." She removed a pen from a pocket and bent over to carefully pick up the cap where Shannon had tossed it. "And if I'm not mistaken, that's blood and a bullet hole."

Shannon helped me to my feet, and we moved closer to Detective Wallace. Sure enough, there was a little hole, and one side of the hat was stiff and darkly stained with what might be dried blood.

Wallace's nostrils flared as she pulled a plastic bag from her pocket and slipped the cap inside. "I'm sorry, Mr. Martin, but you'll have to come with us."

"It's still circumstantial," Shannon said. "Even if this turns out to be the missing guy's hat and his blood."

Detective Wallace straightened her shoulders. Every bit as tall as Holt, her posture gave her the impression of looking down at all of us. "Will you come with us?" she asked Holt. "Or do we have to cuff you?"

Holt's shoulders sank. "I'll come." To his wife, he added,

"Sorry to mess up dinner tonight. You better call our attorney. He'll know who to recommend for this."

Bonnie clutched at Shannon's arm. "Do something."

Shannon gave the detectives a withering glare. "I'm coming too." He leaned over and gave me a kiss. "Text me everything you saw," he whispered.

We watched them go, with Bonnie's freckled face drained of color. She looked lost and more than a little afraid.

She had every reason to be afraid, because after the imprint I'd seen, and the strange cold, I was betting that Nigel Carr wasn't missing but was very thoroughly dead.

Chapter 2

"It'll be okay," I said, placing a hand on Bonnie's arm. She tore her gaze away from her husband's retreating back. "I hope you're right." She squared her shoulders. "Well, let's get you back to Rose Petal Cottage. We shouldn't leave your suitcases on the golf cart."

We'd started walking when a voice came from behind us. "Hi, Bonnie."

I turned to see a handsome, dark-haired man with exactly enough face scruff to make him look fashionable. He was dressed only in swim trunks and sandals, and the towel draping around his neck did little to cover up the tanned expanse of his muscled chest.

"Oh, hello, Tyrus." Bonnie stepped easily into the role of host. "How was your time at the beach?"

"Very relaxing. Thank you." His eyes went to me, wandering down my figure to my bare feet and back again, his smile widening.

"This is my daughter-in-law, Autumn," Bonnie said. "She and my son are spending the second week of their honeymoon here."

He clicked his tongue. "I should have known she was taken." Which was flattering, but a little too smooth to impress me.

Bonnie glanced in my direction. "This is Tyrus Lockwood. He's staying in Frontier Cabin this summer. He writes travel guides and is doing one of this area." To Tyrus, she added, "How's the book coming along?"

"Slowly." He chuckled. "There's actually too much I want to include, which isn't a problem in the print book, but in the video version, I have to narrow it down." He shrugged. "It'll get there." He shot me a lingering smile that made me wonder if he was a flirt or if he was simply friendly. Maybe he was hoping for another book sale.

"That's good," Bonnie said. "Hey, if you have the time, why don't you come up to the house for dinner in about thirty minutes? My husband and son were called away, so we have plenty of food."

"Oh, I wouldn't want to intrude."

"No intrusion, really. It'll be just us and Micaela. It'd be nice to have male company."

Male company? Either Bonnie was a genuinely conscientious hostess, or she was angling to get her bed and breakfast listed in Tyrus's book.

His grin widened. "Okay, I'd love that. If your breakfasts have been any indication, it'll be great."

Bonnie gave him a pleased smile. "We're having cheesy rigatoni with roasted potatoes and cabbage. It's one of my specialties."

I found myself wanting to laugh at that. Of course she was serving pasta. Shannon loved the stuff, and while it wasn't my favorite, it was growing on me.

"It's organic," Bonnie said with another glance in my

direction, which told me Shannon had mentioned my food preferences. Not that I would have objected to anything they served. I was determined to do my part to grow our relationship.

"I'll be there," Tyrus said. "Thank you."

"Good." Bonnie started to turn, but Tyrus's next words stopped us both.

"Um, there wasn't any problem here, was there? Did I see those two detectives that were here before leaving with your husband?"

Only a slight tightening of Bonnie's expression betrayed her upset. "They're still searching for the man who went missing next door. I'm really sorry if your work has been interrupted by all that."

"Not at all. I'm curious, is all."

His words reminded me that I was in Florida for exactly that reason—to help Holt and Bonnie. In the imprint I'd witnessed, the cap-wearer had been staring at Frontier Cabin. Maybe Tyrus had seen him.

"Did you know Nigel Carr?" I asked.

"He was snooping around the cottage one day," Tyrus said, glancing over his shoulder. "Saw him out here a couple of times, once with a woman and once with a man."

It wasn't exactly an answer, and the way he'd spoken hinted at dodging the question. "But you didn't know him personally," I pressed.

Tyrus shook his head, frowning. "No. I do hope they find him, though." With an apologetic glance at Bonnie, he continued, "It was a little odd finding him outside the cottage, but when I heard about the land dispute, well, it made sense."

"You heard about that, huh?" Bonnie lifted her chin. "I assure you, Frontier Cabin and the land it's on are ours. I'm sure the new owner of Magnolia Inn will attest to that, if it comes to it. That man had no right to be on our property. Once they do find him, I'll make sure he stays away from you."

If Nigel was the man who'd imprinted on the baseball hat, I suspected he wasn't in any condition to return to Haven Retreat any time soon, if at all. But telling Bonnie that when her husband was in police custody probably wouldn't help matters.

"I'm not really concerned," Tyrus said.

"Did you talk to him when you saw him?" I asked. "Was he the one who told you about the cottage?"

"Um, I . . ." His hesitation told me I was on the right track. "Yeah, it's sort of my business, talking to people. I like to find out what they're about, where they like to eat locally, where they hang out. That sort of thing."

"And what was your impression of Mr. Carr?"

Bonnie chuckled nervously. "My daughter-in-law is a bit of a private investigator. She's helped the police solve quite a few cases."

I'd solved more than a few cases on my own instead of helping the police, but with her son being a detective, I understood her bias. "I work with Eli Stone Investigations in Portland," I said, calling up my new partner's name. Having a licensed PI on my team gave me more credibility that didn't involve me dropping Shannon's name or having to prove I could read imprints—which for the most part I liked to keep quiet.

"Really." One brow quirked upward, as if wondering how I'd hold up as a PI. I was only average height and a little on the thin side for a woman, but what he couldn't guess was that I'd completed my second-degree blackbelt last month and usually wore a concealed weapon when I was on a case. I couldn't do that here since my Oregon permit wasn't reciprocal in Florida, but unlike my new husband, I didn't feel limited. I'd always considered my hands my best weapon.

"That's right," I said, "and I will find Mr. Carr. In the meantime, I'd like to know what else you talked about and what you thought of him."

Tyrus stared directly into my eyes. "We didn't say much. I found him to be a very unpleasant man. He told me I'd better enjoy my stay since the cottage wouldn't be here next year." Tyrus was either a very good liar or he was telling the truth. It bothered me that I couldn't tell the difference, and he wasn't wearing anything I could check for imprints. Only items that are greatly valued and seldom washed or items touched while experiencing great emotion generally held worthwhile imprints, and his swim trunks, towel, and sandals didn't qualify.

"Did you have a drink with him? Or invite him in?" I asked. Finding an imprint from the missing man inside Frontier Cabin might be a long shot, but I had to follow the lead.

"No." Tyrus gave me a bland smile that held none of his former flirtatiousness. "He wasn't someone I wanted anything to do with."

Was that a catch in his voice? I was almost certain it was. And it might mean Tyrus Lockwood was lying. I'd have to research him and make sure he was really here to write a travel guide—and somehow get inside his cottage to touch his belongings. Maybe he had a more sinister reason for being at Haven Retreat—and more specifically at Frontier Cabin. For now, I'd let it slide, but he was going on my list of suspects.

"Well," he said, thumbing over his shoulder, "I'd better

shower if I'm going to make it for dinner. I'll see you both in a little while."

"See you soon." Bonnie smiled, and once more we turned to follow the short path to Rose Petal Cottage. I'd expected her to bring up my near fainting spell once we were alone, but she didn't. Maybe she was too busy worrying about her husband.

"So," I said. "How long have you and Holt owned the bed and breakfast? Shannon told me you opened it after Holt retired from the police bureau, but I don't really know the details." Shannon and I had spent more time in the past year knocking heads than talking about our families. With my recently found twin sister and the birth father we'd tracked down in Oregon, he knew a lot more about my family than I did about his.

Bonnie's head jerked a little as if pulling her thoughts back to the conversation. "Oh, yeah, well, we moved out here right after Shannon's first year of college." She looked up in the air, her face thoughtful. "Guess it's been about seventeen years. In another three years, we'll have been doing this for as long as Holt was a police officer."

"That long?" No wonder Shannon had been so close with his college history professor grandfather. The old man had left Shannon his house in Portland when he'd died—as well as a watch with imprints that were so loving, I felt I knew him.

"Yeah, it all worked out. Holt was at loose ends wanting to quit the department, and Shannon didn't really need us anymore. His grandfather was still in Portland then, in case of emergencies. My great-aunt who owned this house died and left it to my siblings and me, and no one wanted to do anything with it or to pay the taxes, so Holt and I got my siblings' share for a steal. It was pretty run down, though. Shannon probably told you about spending holidays here with his grandfather, helping us fix it up."

Shannon hadn't mentioned that, though I'd seen for myself in the days before our wedding that he was handy with a hammer. My antiques store had burned down after being torched as a result of my last case, and he'd helped with the demo. My biological father was in charge of the reconstruction during our absence, and after we returned, the entire new upper floor would be awaiting our sweat equity.

"He is pretty handy," I said, wondering what else Shannon hadn't told me. And why hadn't I asked? Yes, his parents had been far away, and we'd been busy with our separate cases, but those were only excuses. Maybe I'd never really thought a rule-keeping police detective like Shannon would decide to spend the rest of his life with a shoe-hating, wild child like me.

We'd arrived at Rose Petal Cottage, and I busied myself with the luggage. Bonnie jumped in to help me get the heavier bags through the door.

"Should you be carrying so much?" she asked, which confused me until I realized that was her subtle way of asking about my health.

What was I going to tell her? She'd been a good sport about my eccentricities so far, but this was way out there. Some people called me a psychic, while I believed I simply used a part of my brain that most people didn't have access to. Reading imprints had become as natural as breathing, and I'd come to a point where I loved my life with them.

"Oh, these aren't that heavy," I said. "So how far away is the beach?"

"Three blocks. The path goes by Frontier Cabin and leads between Magnolia Inn and the group of retirement homes next door, where it joins up with the city sidewalk after the entry to Magnolia Inn's parking lot. It's a direct line to the beach." She grimaced. "At least it is right now. If that Nigel Carr gets ahold of the land . . ." She shook her hand and forced a smile. "Anyway, it's not far. Please let me know if you need anything. We've stocked your mini fridge here, and of course you are welcome to eat meals with us or come to the house at any time."

Playing the good hostess, she continued telling me about the cottage and the amenities. It was really all we had between us—this visit and her son—but I hoped that before I went back to Oregon we'd become more than strangers who happened to share a love for the same man.

"Here's the key," she said, finally having run out of things to tell me. "I'll let you settle in for a few minutes before you come up to the house. Would you like me to leave the golf cart?"

"No. Thank you. It's so close."

"Okay, then." She smiled at me again. "Feel free to lie down and rest or whatever."

Another hint about my health, and I knew I'd have to tell her about imprints sooner rather than later. Maybe I'd wait for Shannon. "Thanks."

When I shut the door behind her, I beelined for my carry-on and the new laptop I'd bought after the fire. It had ten times the memory of my old desktop and was almost as portable as my phone. I sat on the rose-and-beige striped couch, settling into the comfortable array of matching throw pillows. Logging onto the Haven Retreat Wi-Fi, I pulled up a video link to my partner, Elliot Stone of Eli Stone Investigations. He'd changed his name for the business because he thought it sounded tougher, but he looked more like an Elliot to me, and that's what I called him. I'd only started working with him to get my own license, but he'd turned out to be quite useful during cases.

I wasn't surprised when his round, bearded face appeared almost immediately. Elliot was an agoraphobic who left home only a couple of times a week—and then only under specific circumstances. Before our first cases together, he'd done most of his investigating from his car or his computer, meeting occasionally with clients at a local mall eatery. What he lacked in social skills, he made up for with his technology skills, and that's what I wanted him for now.

"Hey, Autumn," he said.

"We've got a case."

He pushed up his glasses. "You mean for your new in-laws."

"Yeah, sorry, it's another freebie. I'll foot any expenses you end up needing." Not his time, I meant, but he knew that. Partners didn't charge partners. At least that's what I was hoping.

He shrugged. "Okay. But keep an eye out for other interested parties who maybe we can get onboard to foot the bill." Elliot was the king of finding someone to pay for his services, while before meeting him, I'd never charged to use my ability. He was right because I needed to pay the hours lost at my antiques store—or I would once we were up and running again.

"Don't count on it this time, but we'll see. And after our last payout, I know you have enough for another few months of rent."

He smiled. "Yeah, so what trouble are your in-laws in, and what do you need?"

"A man, Nigel Carr, is missing. He's the son of the former owner of Magnolia Inn next door to Shannon's parents' place."

I grimaced. "I can't remember the former owner's name now, but he died last month. His granddaughter lived with him and was supposed to inherit the place—until a long-lost, black sheep son showed up."

"Okay." Elliot was already typing and looking away from me at another monitor. "Looks like his name's Welby Carr."

"That's right. The granddaughter is Lyndia, I think. So I need everything you can find on those three, including other family members who might be lurking in the wings. I also need you to check on a Tyrus Lockwood, who's supposedly staying here all summer with my in-laws at Haven Retreat while writing a traveling book."

"Tyrus Lockwood," Elliot murmured, typing again. "Wow, he does have at least a dozen books to his name, it looks like."

I pushed back disappointment. "Guess he was telling the truth about that. Well, let me know what else he's into and if he has any connection with the missing man or Magnolia Inn. Someone hurt Nigel Carr. He may even be dead—him or someone else wearing a hat exactly like his."

Elliot's gaze whipped back to me. "Sounds like you found an imprint."

I told him about the police and the cap. "I think he might have been shot, and it grazed his skull. A second shot might have followed."

He leaned back in his chair, folding his hands over his wide chest. "Hmm, too bad you didn't see the rest of the imprint."

"No way." I didn't know what would happen to me if a person died in an imprint. Presumably, I'd wake up after it was over, but every time I'd come close to seeing a death, the result had been bad enough for me not to want to test my theory. "Besides, the police have it now. It'll be days before they release it, if ever. I'd be better off going over to the inn and seeing if I can touch his things there."

"Probably a smart idea. But when was the imprint?"

I thought back. When I read imprints, I always saw the date and time as if highlighted on a calendar. The closer the event, the better I could pinpoint the exact time. "A week ago last Wednesday right after eleven at night."

"Your in-laws didn't get here in Portland until Thursday, right?" He scratched his beard before adding, "What do you really know about them?"

"Elliot!"

But I'd been thinking the same thing. Of course Holt would have to go on the suspect list, but I'd be up at the main house in a few minutes, and I'd find something there to clear him.

I toned down my indignation. "Let me know when you get something. There's nothing really more I'll probably get tonight, but I'll do the same if I find anything."

"Will do. Take care." He leaned forward and severed our connection.

Out of curiosity, I typed in Tyrus Lockwood's name and saw a list of travel books with US destinations: California, Texas, New York, Washington DC, Colorado, Kansas, Maine, and more. "Okay then," I said.

Next, I texted Shannon about the imprint, as he'd requested, telling him about the timing as well, so he'd be able to ask his father for an alibi. Even if we couldn't convince the police that I knew something they didn't, the information might begin pointing everyone in the right direction. I also told him I believed Nigel was dead—because who'd shoot him and leave him alive to tell the story?

I felt a coldness again like I did during the last case, I added.

Might have been a breeze. But I think that, more than anything, made me suspect Nigel Carr was already dead.

Shannon didn't answer, so I figured he was busy inside the police station. With ten minutes before I needed to appear for dinner, I carried the suitcases up the narrow staircase to the bedroom. It was a simple, open loft featuring a quaint bed with a white headboard and a rose-colored patch quilt. It took me only a few minutes to empty our suitcases into the free-standing armoire, half of which contained drawers and the other half a pole for hanging clothes.

Finally, my attention went to the large, overflowing wicker gift basket Holt had been holding earlier. Sitting on one of the white bedside tables, it was overflowing with snacks, but there were a few movie tickets and gift cards as well, and I was sure this wasn't the typical guest gift basket. A lump grew in my throat. They were trying hard too. My own parents might be gone, and like with my biological father, Shannon's parents could never take their place, but that didn't mean we couldn't be close.

My stomach rumbled, but I ignored the contents of the basket. Better to remain hungry for dinner. Wait, was that organic dark chocolate? I'd recently started loving dark chocolate, and a few pieces would never stop me from eating a full meal. I studied the basket for a minute before sinking into the sofa mattress on the bed and pulling it onto my lap. I hadn't been expecting any imprints because it was a simple basket, one they'd probably used dozens of times for guests, but a strong imprint grabbed me at once. I relived again the scene I'd witnessed here earlier, except this time through Holt's eyes.

A sinking feeling clenched my gut as Bonnie called out that the officers were waiting to talk to me. I fumbled as I tried to set the basket on the bed, cursing under my breath as it spilled its contents over the bed. I gripped the basket tighter. My heartbeat thundered in my ears.

If they were back, it was because they knew Nigel's blood was on the hoe, and I'd become a real suspect. Now they'd dig into my entire life. They'd find out what I'd done.

"Are you just about finished?" Bonnie called.

I responded without really knowing what I said. Keeping hold of the basket with one hand, I scooped the fallen items back inside. It didn't look as nice as when Bonnie had packed it, but who was to know?

I stepped to the edge of the loft, which sported only a thin, short railing. The idea had been to leave the loft without one, but the insurance requirements had nixed the idea.

Immediately my eyes fixed on my son, who had arrived from Portland, and I experienced a rush of mixed feelings. Relief because Shannon was a good detective, and Autumn seemed to have a knack for solving mysteries—and worry for the exact same reasons. It was all going to come out now.

I should have stopped them from coming, I thought. But Bonnie had insisted, and every time I'd tried to say I could handle it on my own, she'd glared at me like the fiery US Airforce personnel officer she'd been when I first met her.

The basket felt suddenly heavy in my hands, like the guilt that weighed on my heart.

The rest of the conversation played out until Holt set down the basket. More imprints followed, but they were faint and years old. I set the basket on the bed, and as had happened with Shannon's father, the contents spilled out, the chocolate bar landing near my fingers. But my appetite for chocolate had vanished.

I'd been mistaken that Shannon's parents both wanted us here. Shannon's father hadn't because he was hiding a secret he didn't want anyone to know about. Whatever it was, I'd have to dig enough to find out if it was related to Nigel Carr's disappearance.

That doesn't mean he's guilty of anything, I told myself. The imprints I saw always came from the viewpoint of the imprinter, and that meant it was colored with their interpretation, their feelings, and their personal judgments. For instance, I'd felt guilty about a lot of things in my life, even the death of my adoptive father, Winter, but I hadn't caused the bridge bombing that had taken his life.

My hand went to the scar I would always carry under the outer side of my left eye. If only I hadn't made Winter go with me to the estate sale that last day.

I shook the thoughts away and rose to my feet in determination. I'd get to the bottom of the mystery of Nigel Carr and whatever Holt Martin was hiding. I had to trust that they weren't one and the same thing.

And somehow I'd have to tell Shannon.

Chapter 3

On my way up to the main house, Tyrus Lockwood caught up with me. His hair was still wet from his shower, and I detected the strong scent of aftershave to match his newly shaved jaw. He was even more handsome without the scruff, but I wondered who he was trying to impress. His chest was less impressive inside his royal-blue button-up shirt, but the attire was much more appropriate for dinner.

He nodded at me and then did a double-take at my eyes. "Your eyes are . . ."

"I know." I smiled to soften the words and was glad he didn't care enough to pursue the reason for my heterochromia.

When we walked into the kitchen, only Bonnie was there. "You're just in time," she said with a smile. She gave Tyrus a decorative bowl filled with salad dressing. "Will you take this into the dining room for me?"

"Sure." He took the bowl and disappeared through a connecting door.

Bonnie passed me a pitcher of juice. "For the boys." After a slight hesitation, she asked, "Did you hear anything from Shannon? I'm so worried."

I knew that already from the vague imprint she'd left on the pitcher. "Not yet, but it hasn't even been an hour. They'll have just gotten there. They'll probably be a few hours at least."

"What if they arrest him?"

"Then we'll get him out on bail." I set the pitcher down and put a hand on her shoulder over her gray and yellow flowered dress. "It's going to be okay. We'll find out what happened to Nigel Carr. We will."

She took a breath, as if preparing to speak, but closed her mouth before saying anything. Nodding, she picked up a plate of garlic bread and preceded me through a connecting door to a dining room that held one long table in the middle, with two shorter ones pressed up against the wall. Once again, the elaborate wood trim and wallpaper had me in awe.

Micaela looked up from the plates she was laying out and smiled at us. "Hi." She was even prettier than when we'd first met, though I couldn't tell what had changed. Tyrus was staring openly at her, the bowl of salad dressing still in his hands.

"You two come sit here by me," Bonnie said from the head of the table. Tyrus and I obeyed, sitting across from each other and kitty-corner to Bonnie. Micaela sat between Tyrus and one of her boys; the other boy was next to me, which I was sure was more by design than accident. Divide and conquer, so to speak.

"Smells wonderful," I said.

Micaela grinned. "It's all Bonnie's doing. All I did was to keep it from burning and make the salad."

"And you finished the garlic bread." Bonnie bowed her head. "Now let's say grace."

The boys barely waited for her to finish before lifting up on their seats to grab a piece of garlic bread, stuffing the ends into their mouths. Bonnie started with the salad, and Tyrus took a good-sized serving of the cheesy rigatoni before passing it to Micaela.

"Do I have to eat the cabbage?" the boy next to Micaela said as she put the pasta on his plate, his mouth full of bread. I was pretty sure he was Dimas, the rambunctious twin his mother had chastised earlier. That made the boy beside me Lucio.

"Only if you want to grow tall and strong like Mr. Lockwood," Micaela said.

"That's right," Tyrus agreed, lifting an arm to show off his muscle. "I always eat my cabbage." To Micaela, he said, "Please call me Tyrus."

"Okay. And I'm Micaela."

"I know."

His comment made her flush. I guess I knew now why he'd used the aftershave—and hadn't he only agreed to come after he'd heard Micaela was here? I didn't know anything about her marital situation, but by Bonnie's pleased expression, I assumed the matchmaking was her idea.

We finished dishing up and made appropriate murmurs of appreciation as we tasted our food.

"You seem familiar," Micaela said. "I've been meaning to ask you about it, but well, I'm always so busy at breakfast when you come in. Have we met before? Somewhere besides here, I mean."

"Possibly," Tyrus said. "Or maybe I have one of those faces."

Micaela laughed. "Maybe so."

"He might be on TV," Dimas said.

Tyrus leaned his head back and laughed. "Only in my dreams. But you never know. Maybe someday one of my YouTube videos will make it to prime time."

"That's it," Bonnie said. "You probably saw one of his videos."

"So, Micaela," I asked. "Where are you from exactly? I heard you speaking another language to the boys?"

"Oh, yeah. Portuguese," she said with a laugh, tearing her gaze from Tyrus. "And I'm from a few different places. I was born in Mozambique, but my mother was Portuguese. My father was half Portuguese and half Mozambican. He died when I was four, and we returned to Portugal until I was ten. Then my mother married an English man who lived here in the States. We moved to England when I was in high school, but I came back here for college, and I've been here ever since. My mother is still in England with my stepfather and my half-siblings. The boys and I go there on occasion to visit, but this is our home."

No mention of the boys' father, I noticed.

"Micaela has worked for us since college," Bonnie said.

"I love working here," Micaela said. "And I'm grateful because the boys can come here when they aren't in school. Bonnie and Holt are more like grandparents than their own grandparents."

I reached for another helping of the pasta. No one else was eating it, so I might as well. Tyrus and Micaela were too busy staring and talking to eat much, and Bonnie was mostly moving her food around on her plate, taking an occasional bite. Probably worrying. The boys and I were the only ones eating. That wasn't surprising on my part, as the only person who could match me bite for bite at any meal was my sister, Tawnia, especially when the food was this good. No wonder Shannon liked pasta. I might have liked pasta a lot more if I'd grown up eating this.

"That's sometimes the way it works," I said. "Friends become closer than family." When Shannon and I had children, I didn't know how Bonnie and Holt would play a part in their lives from so far away, and before this moment, it hadn't mattered to me. It did now.

As if reading my mind, Bonnie said, "They've filled in for us too, but we're hoping for more grandkids, of course." She smiled at me. "In time." She seemed to be waiting for me to comment on that, but I didn't have anything to tell her.

The talk moved on to how hot it was, Tyrus's upcoming book, and then to the rebuilding of my antiques store and Portland tourist sites.

"I've heard of Portland's amazing bridges," Tyrus said. "I'd love to see some of the inner workings someday." He gave a self-deprecatory chuckle. "Or at least enough to write about it. You know what they say about writers: jack of all trades, master of none."

"Except writing," Micaela said. Her dark bronze skin was glowing, and it seemed clear she was as taken with Tyrus as he seemed to be with her.

"Maybe," he said. "But that's nothing compared to the work you're doing, raising these two boys."

To me the comment sounded either awkward or insincere—and I was betting on the latter. Did he have a woman in every country and state he'd visited? He looked the type, but maybe that impression was only because I felt he'd withheld information when we'd first talked. Or maybe I was feeling protective about Micaela and her boys. If she was a single mother, life hadn't been easy for her.

"My brother-in-law is an engineer for the city specializing in over-water bridges," I said to Tyrus. "If you ever get to Portland, look me up at my shop, and I'll hook you up."

"Okay, don't be surprised if I do." He glanced lingeringly at

Micaela. "Even when I do finally settle on a place to call home, I'll still travel."

Again, I couldn't decide if his comment was clumsy or slick. But it wasn't my call.

"Can we go?" Lucio asked his mother before I was halfway finished. "Please. We're done."

"Well, we have chocolate cake for dessert," she answered, "but after you can be excused."

"Uh," Tyrus said awkwardly. "You guys play Frisbee? Be glad to throw one around with you after dinner."

Dimas snorted. "Frisbee? No way. We like soccer. We're like one-fourth Portuguese and half Brazilian, you know. That makes us natural soccer players."

Tyrus laughed. "Okay, you can teach me a few moves." He said this to the boys, but he was looking at Micaela. I wanted to roll my eyes. It was a tricky move, getting to the mother through the boys, but there was nothing I could do about it.

"Right now?" Lucio asked. "After the cake?"

"If your mother agrees."

When Micaela nodded, Tyrus started shoveling in his remaining food, avoiding pieces of cooked cabbage despite what he'd told the boys earlier.

"I'll get the dessert." Bonnie hurried to the kitchen and returned carrying a chocolate cake with ice cream in the middle. The boys inhaled their pieces with amazing speed.

"We'll be outside." Dimas jumped to his feet and rounded the table, slugging his brother before starting for the door. Lucio dropped his fork and raced after him.

We finished our dessert, and I regretted not being able to fit in more than one piece. When Tyrus left to play with the boys, Micaela began to gather the dishes.

"Leave it," Bonnie said. "I'll take care of it. You've already done more than your share today."

"I was glad to help." Micaela continued stacking dishes and scooping the remains onto a single plate. "You and Holt have been so great to me."

Bonnie stood and took a plate from her hand. "Go play with your boys. It'll be bedtime soon. And who knows, I think Tyrus might ask you out. Goodness knows it's taken him long enough."

Micaela snorted, sounding a lot like her son. "I've been avoiding him because not a lot of men want to take on two kids. He might be, you know, one of those players."

Bonnie shrugged. "Maybe not."

But I was glad Micaela had some reserve.

"Go," Bonnie urged.

"Okay. If I don't see you before I take off, I'll be back in the morning." Micaela shifted her gaze to me. "Again, I'm so glad to meet you. I've never seen Shannon happier."

"Thank you." I guess if her boys were like grandchildren to Bonnie and Holt, Shannon might be like a brother—or perhaps a stepsibling or cousin. "I'm glad to meet you too."

I began helping Bonnie clean up the table. I was itching to search the house for imprints, but I was growing more concerned about why Shannon still hadn't texted me back. I could check his location on his phone, as we were linked, but I resisted the urge. I hated it when he checked up on me.

Bonnie set the dishes in the sink and began rinsing before placing them in the dishwasher. She was like a one-woman windmill, using such hot water, I was surprised she had any skin left.

"What happened to the boys' father?" I asked.

Bonnie didn't look at me as she replied. "He was a marine. He died overseas when the boys were only one. Micaela doesn't like to talk about it much. She's still in love with him, I think. Tyrus reminds me a lot of him in looks." She sighed. "Maybe that's why I was hoping . . ." She didn't finish.

"What about their grandparents on the father's side?"

Bonnie shook her head sharply. "They send presents for birthdays and Christmas, but they live in California, so it's a bit far."

About as far as it is to Oregon, I thought. "I'm really sorry to hear it."

"Well, they have other children and grandchildren who live nearby, so for them it's not bad. And Micaela's mother was here for six months after it happened. I thought for a time that Micaela would go to England with her, but she likes it here."

We finished the rest of the cleaning in silence and had everything put away in less than ten minutes.

"I would really love to see the rest of the house," I said. "The rooms that aren't occupied, of course."

"Only two are empty right now, at least until the next guests arrive tonight and in the morning." She checked her watch. "There's time to see them now. And the other rooms will all be free at some point during the week, except for one, and Micaela can show you that one when she goes in for housekeeping."

First, Bonnie showed me the communal sitting room, library, and small meeting room, which doubled as a theater for the guests. I touched everything I could, but there were no imprints except a few strong ones of contentment from Bonnie over a vase or a picture, and only vague ones on the furniture from guests. Not surprising as none of them were likely to feel anything strongly about items that didn't belong to them.

The first unoccupied room was African Safari, and going inside was like walking into another country, though I suspected the décor was based more on a concept than on reality. The room had a mosquito net on the ivory tusk bed, colorfully-patterned bedding, and skins hanging on the bright yellow and red walls, but the bed was far too large, the blankets too soft, and the ivory and skins were definite fakes. The jacuzzi tub resembled a watering hole, but its dark base was plastic and the jets were modern. I loved every bit of it.

Sea Scape was next, with a shell bed hidden behind a curtain of strung shells, blue walls covered with different ocean scenes and shell wall hangings, and several enviable statues of sunbathing mermaids. The large tub squeezed into the bathroom was big enough to hold at least two real mermaids.

In either room, I found no imprints more interesting than an argument from a couple who had quickly made up, and another from the former owner of the mermaid statues—regret at no longer having room for them. I was glad Bonnie washed and dried the bedding between guests. Extremely high heat, I'd recently learned, was the only way to remove imprints. The clothes dryer, while not hot enough to remove everything, did dull imprints over time, and the actual washing also removed bits of the cloth itself, which added to the fading. That meant cloth generally didn't hold strong imprints, a good thing when you were checking out rental rooms.

"I love what you've done," I said. "And now that I've seen some of your themes, I can keep an eye out for items for you, if you want."

Bonnie's worried smile became real. "That would be great. I go to yard sales and such when I can because I'm always needing to replace items when they become worn or if they break." She laughed. "Besides, switching things up makes guests eager to return to see what else I've found."

"I marked a few estate sales we could go to next week." Presuming the case was finished before then and we had the time.

"That would be nice. Maybe we could invite Lyndia next door. She probably needs to get out. You'll really like her. She's sweet."

"Sure. The more the merrier."

Outside in the hallway, Bonnie grabbed my hands. "I know I told you this at your wedding, but I'm really happy about you and Shannon. He's so passionate about his work, and I was beginning to worry he would never make time for a family."

Shannon was thirty-six, so I understood what Bonnie was saying. She also didn't mention but had to be thinking about the female officer he'd once dated, who had left the force to work with a PI and had been killed. Years later, the same PI had almost caused my death. After that case, Shannon had asked me to marry him.

"Thank you," I said. "That means a lot."

"I hope we'll be good friends." Her grip tightened, and I could feel her wedding ring, which brought a series of dizzying flashes—both scenes and emotions. Apparently, even the searing water she used in the sink wasn't hot enough to destroy imprints. I tried not to pull away. One flash that came from the morning of our wedding was more vibrant than the others.

"Maybe you should tell him," I/Bonnie said, clutching my hands tightly together. "Maybe it's time."

On the bed in the guest room at Shannon's house, Holt hung his head. "No."

"Well, we still need him to come. Once the police find out

about the blood, you know what's going to happen. And we can't lose Frontier Cabin. Not after all the work and money we've put into it. Don't you dare tell him not to come."

Bonnie gave my hands a final squeeze and pulled away. I released a silent breath of relief. Apparently, Bonnie knew Holt's secret, whatever it was, but so far I hadn't found anything related to his feelings of guilt in the entire house. I had to be looking in the wrong place.

"Are you okay?" Bonnie asked over her shoulder as she began walking down the hall toward the staircases.

"Yes." I hurried to catch up. "What about where you and Holt sleep? I hope you have your own private suite—it could be difficult not having somewhere to retreat on occasion."

"Oh yeah." Bonnie motioned to me. "Come on. I'll show you. All the rental rooms are up here, and our personal rooms are beyond the public ones downstairs. We do keep them locked, and we do hide out there sometimes."

"I'm also thinking about going over to Magnolia Inn and having a chat with your neighbor. You said her name's Lyndia, right?"

"Yes. But are you sure you're feeling up to that? You've had a long flight . . ." Her eyes searched mine as if asking a question I couldn't decipher.

Maybe she was back to the fact that I'd almost passed out. I was going to have to answer to that before she decided I had some terrible illness. "I'm really fine. It's just a lot hotter here than I'm used to." That was the truth—at least part of it.

Her eyes dropped. "Okay. If you wait until my guest arrives, I can walk you over and introduce you."

Too late, I realized I shouldn't have brought up going next door, because testing for imprints under one watchful eye was difficult enough and having her there would make it more difficult. I'd have to weigh that against the advantage of being introduced as a family friend. On the whole, I'd rather have Shannon with me. I took out my phone and sent him a single question mark in a text.

We went down one of the wide staircases, passing a hand-holding couple who smiled and greeted Bonnie but didn't stop to chat. "They're in the Wedding Suite," Bonnie said after they passed. "They leave in three days, if you and Shannon want to move in there for a few nights. But the only advantage is the jacuzzi tub, and the one in Rose Petal Cottage is almost as nice. In fact, we've installed similar ones in all the rooms."

"So I've noticed. Really, we're good at the cottage. It's incredible."

"Thank you. It is my favorite."

She stopped in the kitchen to put in a batch of chocolate chip cookies. "I like to have some waiting for guests, and there's almost none left in the cookie jar I leave out for everyone, especially for Dimas and Lucio."

After setting the timer, she led me back to near the theater room, where the hallway ended in a door with a code lock. She typed on it quickly and opened it to reveal a modern room with a television and a comfortable-looking leather sofa with the largest matching ottoman I'd ever seen. No theme here, except slightly upscale comfort.

"This is really nice." I preceded her into the room.

"I think so, and we double-insulated all the walls and ceilings, like we did in the bedrooms upstairs, so we have a decent amount of quiet as well as privacy. I even have a little kitchenette because Holt likes his morning coffee before he showers, and he doesn't like to run into anyone else."

"I don't blame him."

There was also a sliding glass door in the sitting room that led out to the back patio where a fenced pool beckoned. Three groups of people were out there now, enjoying the evening. No one had ventured into the in-ground hot tub, however, which steamed in isolated preparedness.

I let the curtain fall back over the glass doors as she continued through it to a master bedroom and connected bath that was larger than each of the rooms upstairs. Again, no theme. The huge, comfortable-looking, four-poster, mahogany bed, covered with a deep purple bedspread, matched the lovely mahogany furniture. I was glad to see they were taking care of themselves.

"I love it," I said.

Bonnie let her gaze scan the room. "We've worked really hard to get to this point, and it's taken a long time to finally turn a corner. It's tough keeping people happy so our reviews stay high. That's why this whole land dispute and the cloud hanging over Holt is so serious. It would only take a handful of bad reviews, and our bookings could start hurting."

"We'll figure it out," I said. Unfortunately, I couldn't exactly start touching things under her steady gaze unless I told her why.

Bonnie was already going back through to the sitting room. I followed her but paused near the leather couch, calculating what I might get away with touching. "I'm thinking of buying something like this for the house in Oregon."

"Good. I've been telling Shannon he needs new furniture to match the new paint. Go ahead and try it out."

I sat and leaned back, sinking into luxury. I had never thought about having a couch this nice in a room with a television, but I was rethinking that now.

"Nice," I murmured. A feeling of contentment came through my hands, splayed on the leather, but no imprint that brought a scene to mind. "I have a Victorian sofa I refinished that's in my apartment, and I put in extra padding, but it's nothing compared to this. I'll probably end up moving it and the other stuff from my parents' place to the new apartment above my shop once it's finished. You know, things I don't want to leave for the renters."

"I can't tell you how glad I am that you're putting an apartment up there." Bonnie folded her arms under her ample chest. "I worry about Shannon driving home some nights with the hours he keeps."

"We're both trying to work on that." Looking around, I finally spied the remote on the small table next to the couch.

"It'll be important. Especially once you have kids." She didn't look at me as she said the words, but I could feel the hope in them. It was a hint that Shannon and I weren't getting any younger, and at thirty-four—thirty-four and a half, to be exact—I'd be lying if I didn't admit my biological clock was ticking like crazy. Being close to my niece, Destiny, only made me that much more ready for a child. But the whole kid discussion was one Shannon and I had both agreed to shelve until after my shop was up and running and my PI license finished.

"Right," I said, leaning sideways with the plan of reaching for the remote. Surely if anything in this room contained Holt's imprints, it had to be this, right? "That's another reason why the apartment over the shop is a good idea. I can have a sitter come during rush hours at my shop."

Bonnie beamed as if I'd given her a million dollars. "I can send Holt to help you with the trim. He could probably do it all in a weekend as long as his back doesn't act up."

"Thank you." My hand closed casually over the remote. At first I felt only the vague impression of humor, but that was quickly replaced by a vivid emotion from Bonnie, who was upset that yet another bachelor had ended things with the woman he'd supposedly chosen to marry. All the other imprints that followed told me Bonnie was the one who controlled the remote, and mostly she watched alone while Holt snored with his head on her lap. This wasn't his domain, so what was?

Maybe wherever the hoe had been found by the police detectives. Maybe he was the one with the green thumb.

Bonnie pulled her phone from the pocket of her floral dress and read something on the face of it. "Oh, I've got to go. Looks like my new houseguest has arrived."

Chapter 4

I jumped up and peered at Bonnie's phone to see a live stream of a woman approaching the front door of Haven Retreat.

"We have cameras on all the public doors," Bonnie explained, pocketing the phone again as she hurried to the door of her suite. "When a guest is about to arrive, I make sure to send notices to my phone when the motion sensor activates. All too often, I'm busy and lose track of time." She cast a rueful glance at me. "I set it for you and Shannon, but I was a little occupied at the time."

"We did wonder where you were." I followed her down the hallway and into the entryway. "So does Holt have a workshop then? Where he makes or fixes things?"

"Yes, well, it's in the garage."

"A garage?" I hadn't seen one so far.

"The door is off the main hallway to the left before you turn into the kitchen."

Our conversation ended as we neared the entryway door, which was opening. "Welcome," Bonnie sang out.

"The sign on the door said to come in," the woman said. "I hope that's okay."

Or at least that was what I think she said. The rest of her was so much larger than life, it was hard to concentrate on her words. Everything about her called for attention, from her heavy makeup and thick eyelashes to her vivid orange top and flowing green culottes. Her bright blond hair was piled high on her head—either a hairpiece or her real hair with a heavy amount of ratting. She was pretty and voluptuous in a way that was both brassy and sweet at the same time.

"Of course," Bonnie said. "I always put that up when I'm awaiting a new visitor. You must be Freddi Dottson. So glad you're here. I'm about to take some fresh cookies out of the oven. Would you like some? Or would you like me to take you up to your room first?"

Freddi dropped her fat, wine-colored suitcase on the floor. "Cookies, of course! It's only an hour's drive from Palm Coast, but I had some errands to do before I arrived here, and I could do with a snack."

"Well, come on back, and I'll give you a tour before I take you up to your room."

"That would be lovely," Freddi said. "Do I just leave my suitcase here?"

Bonnie looked around as if searching for Holt and then remembering where he was.

"I can take it upstairs," I said.

Freddi inclined her head at me, and the pile of hair barely moved. "Thank you so much." Her hand whipped out to mine, gripping it quickly. As two of her many rings touched my flesh, I experienced a flash of white-hot anger, but she withdrew before I saw more than a mere sideways glimpse of a woman's pale face. Today, not more than thirty minutes ago, this new guest had been furious at someone.

I tightened my fist, only to find that Freddi had slipped me a five-dollar tip. I stared at it for a second before lifting my gaze to see Bonnie smirking at me. "You sure you can carry it?" she asked. At my nod, she added, "She's in African Safari. I left the door ajar when we were up there earlier. Just pull it shut when you leave. It's self-locking."

I nodded and watched the women leave, Bonnie asking Freddi something about Palm Coast. My gaze dropped to the suitcase. If it had more imprints like her rings, I was going to need my gloves. I held my hand over the handle, waiting for the tingle that would signal imprints. Only a faint tingling registered, so probably not as powerful as those on her rings, but I still touched the handle gingerly. Instantly, I saw a brief but clear imprint from this morning:

I'd resolve this once and for all, I thought with determination. He's cheated me out of my money for far too long. If I'd known, I'd have married Alberto instead of living with him. Alberto would have at least paid alimony.

This was followed by more imprints of a vacation to Paris two years earlier with said Alberto, and nothing more. At least the imprint explained the white-hot anger from her rings—or could explain it. Divorce and alimony was one thing that seemed to be a hot button with a lot of women in their late forties, which was what I judged Freddi to be.

Picking up the suitcase felt a little like lifting a pregnant cow, and I was glad for all the heavy lifting in my antiques shop. But I got the case up the stairs and into the African Safari room, which I was pretty sure the colorful Freddi Dottson would love.

I'd barely left the room when I received a text from Shannon. *On my way back. They're holding my dad, but his attorney will get him out in the morning.* It wasn't good news that they were keeping Holt, but I was sure Shannon had done all he could.

Back down in the entryway, I walked close enough to the kitchen to hear Bonnie and Freddi chatting like old friends. I also identified the door to the garage, but the door had a code lock like their bedroom, so I wouldn't be getting inside. Retracing my steps to the entryway, I went into the front sitting room and took the opportunity to run my fingers along some of the trim, paintings, and furniture. There were many imprints—some dating back more than twenty years on items Bonnie must have bought at secondhand shops since the bed and breakfast hadn't been opened then. Some of the imprints were touching (a granddaughter opening a gift of a candlestick from her grandmother and a woman pouring tea for her guests), some upsetting (a man selling a painting he loved to pay for his son's funeral and an old disagreement over a family heirloom). None were important to my current case until my finger touched a picture of Bonnie and Holt standing on either side of a twenty-three-year-old Shannon at his graduation from the police academy. All of them beamed, and the pride on Holt's face was almost tangible. The imprint shocked me.

I stared down at the photo in my hands. If he knew I'd killed someone that way, my son would never look up to me. Better to have him think I couldn't hack the job.

The imprint was from ten years ago, more recent than the photo, and I was pretty sure the work-roughened hands I glimpsed belonged to Holt Martin, but I didn't have any context for the information. Did "job" mean the police job he'd retired from? Had there been another job in between? It didn't seem to have any bearing on the current situation. Unless something from Holt's past had caught up to him. I waited for more, but there was nothing else to shed more light on Holt's emotions.

Should I wait for Shannon or head over to Magnolia Inn? I didn't have to decide at that moment, because my phone rang. Checking the caller ID, I saw it was Elliot.

"Hey," I said, going out the front door to the wraparound porch. "What's up?"

"I've still got my programs digging, and I have a few feelers out to my contacts, but I've got enough to get you started. I emailed you what I have so far, but since you didn't answer, I wanted to make sure you knew it was there."

"Thanks. It's been busy here, but I'll check as soon as I can. In the meantime, can you give me a summary?" I sat on one of the black, padded wrought iron chairs and leaned back to listen.

"Nigel Carr is the second son of Welby Carr. Nigel was the typical black sheep of the family, and he served a little time for boosting cars before he was kicked out of his father's house at eighteen. He was married for ten years, and it looks like they were divorced five years ago, at least from what I've found so far, though I don't have the official decree yet. But for sure they haven't been living together during that time. In my email I've included details, pictures, and last known addresses for both. She's a looker for her age, by the way. Don't know what she saw in that Nigel character. All his pictures make him look scrawny and wrinkled and mean."

"Any children?"

"Not for them, but there's a mention of a son with another woman. No name yet. Still tracking that down."

"There's two people right there who might be better off if he's dead," I said.

"My thoughts exactly. Except Nigel Carr barely has two dollars to rub together. He's a day worker for a construction company and lives in an apartment with half a dozen other men."

"Until Nigel's father died without a will."

"Estranged father," Elliot corrected. "But that's right. He's suddenly worth a lot more, and that means his heirs would benefit by his death. I haven't been able to track down exact numbers, but he was trying to sell Magnolia Inn to a couple different individuals."

"Probably right out from under his niece."

"Looks like." Elliot paused before saying, "Lyndia Carr is a little bit of an interesting person herself. Her mother married Nigel's older brother, Leon, and he adopted her shortly after when she was one. Then Leon and her mother were killed in a car accident when she was twelve, and her grandfather, Welby Carr, took custody. She was in and out of therapy for several years."

So Lyndia wasn't blood related to the old owner of Magnolia Inn. Would that make a difference in Nigel's claim if there wasn't a will? "Poor thing," I said. "What happened to her biological father?"

"That's another thing I'm tracing. There doesn't seem to be any information about the father. Maybe he was never identified."

"And what about Tyrus Lockwood?" I looked around a bit guiltily as I said it. He might still be playing somewhere on the property with Micaela's twins, if they hadn't already gone home to bed. It would be eight soon.

"He seems to be exactly what he appears. He's the only child of a Thomas and Katrina Lockwood, who both live in Tampa. There really isn't much about them available—they don't even do social media. Only Tyrus does, and it's all about his work. So that's another thing I'll look into."

"Any connection between Tyrus and Nigel Carr?"

"Why do you ask?"

"A gut feeling."

"Then I'll do more research, but so far, no. I've bought ebook copies of all his books—eleven of them to be exact—so I'll search them for any connection to the case. Looks like he's writing two to three a year."

"I'll pay you back," I said.

He laughed. "I know. But that reminds me, he has a book about Florida already out. It was actually his first one that released five years ago."

"That's odd," I said, feeling vindicated. "Then why would he be doing another one?"

"Well, he could be doing an extended version, a revision, or maybe a book focusing more on northern Florida. His other book was based on Miami and the surrounding area, according to the title. The state is a huge tourist attraction, so maybe it's his best seller, and he wants to capitalize. Plus, he still lives in Tampa, though not with his folks. Must be less expensive to write about his home state."

"That doesn't explain paying for a whole summer here at Haven Retreat."

"I guess not." He paused. "Well, if there's nothing else . . ."

"There is one more thing." I looked around me again. "I want you to do a search on Holt Martin."

"Shannon's father? Are you kidding?"

"I want to find out why he left the police force in Portland. Shannon said he hated being a police officer, but I think there's something more. From what I can see, Holt is proud of Shannon. He doesn't act like a man who thinks being a police officer isn't worth the time."

"Maybe it was different for him. You don't have to love something like your kid does to be proud of him. At least that's what I hear."

I thought of the pride on Holt's face in the picture with Shannon and in his touch on the frame. "Maybe you're right. I still want you to check, okay?"

"Sure. But Shannon could probably dig up more. Or his partner could."

"For now, let's keep it quiet. I know you have a connection in the PPD."

"Okay." Elliot paused. "But keeping things from Shannon— that's not a way to begin a marriage."

I groaned. Just what I needed—marriage counseling from a single man who didn't date. "I'm going to tell him when and if I know there's something to say."

We hung up quickly then, as we always did, without dragging it out. For a moment I thought about calling my sister. Seeing her and baby Destiny on my phone would make me miss them both less. But Tawnia only knew that we were here on the second half of our honeymoon, and she'd take one look at my face and realize something was wrong. I didn't want to worry her, and there was nothing her own special gift could do this far away to help me.

My mind turned once again to Magnolia Inn. Besides Holt's garage, that was the place I wanted to go next. But I was suddenly sleepy, probably because I'd eaten too much at dinner. Yawning, I forced myself to my feet just in time to see our rental car entering the front circular drive in front of the bed and breakfast. Shannon must have seen me because he slowed the sedan and parked in front of a tiny, metallic blue car that had to belong to the new guest. He climbed out and met me with a hug.

"Well?" I asked.

His arms loosely circled my body. "It is blood on the hat, but they won't know if it matches Nigel's until they finish testing. The good news is that because there's no body, the police will be letting my dad go in the morning. The attorney and I convinced them that charges at this point would be over-turned, and they don't want to look bad."

"Then what's the bad news?"

"There's been no movement on any of Carr's credit cards, he doesn't seem to have a car, and his roommates and employer haven't heard from him, though he was supposed to be back on the job this week. The roommates told the police that he said he'd come into some money and would only be back for his belongings, but he never showed up for them. Then the ex-wife was at the station today, claiming he owed her five years of payments, and she wanted to lay claim on his estate—namely Magnolia Inn—for over fifty thousand dollars plus interest. When she finds out the cap she told the police her ex-husband always wore was found here with a bullet hole in it . . ." Shannon blew out a sigh. "Even worse, some woman called in a tip about seeing my dad with Nigel near Jacksonville Beach Pier the Wednesday night before my parents left for Portland. They say he gave Nigel an envelope that looked like cash."

I shivered. "That's the night imprinted on the baseball cap."

He nodded. "They featured Nigel on the news last night, and the call came in this afternoon."

"And the caller identified your dad by name?"

"No, just by description. The caller wouldn't come in for a lineup."

"I guess that explains the captain's pressure to arrest someone. They couldn't track the caller?"

"They tried and failed. Which is good for us because if the witness could be substantiated, it might constitute probable cause."

"It's still all circumstantial," I said. "There's no evidence of foul play."

"Except the blood on the hoe and the baseball cap, and my father's admission about their argument."

Right. We couldn't forget about the cap or the blood. "Did your dad say anything about meeting Nigel at the beach?"

"He denies it. But now the police are threatening to get a warrant to search the entire place, regardless of the inconvenience to the guests, with the expectation of finding something they can use to charge him. The attorney and I got them to delay for a few days with the threat of a harassment lawsuit, and because I promised to find Nigel, but we need to get some idea of where he is." His eyes strayed to the porch. "I'm going to have to tell my mother all this, and I'm worried about how she's going to take it. The only good thing is that my Dad didn't test positive for gunshot residue, though he normally goes to the shooting range every week, so that couldn't really prove anything without a match from his gun to a bullet."

That made me wonder. "The bullet could still be around. At least the one I experienced in the imprint. It seemed like it skimmed through the side of his head, so it might have come out."

"I think my dad has a metal detector. We could try to find it."

"Why are they even holding him tonight?"

"Because they can—and I think they're hoping to find something that will stick before they have to release him." His tone held a hint of bleakness.

I took his hand as we started for the house. "I do have some suspects." I told him about Tyrus, his unease at my questions, and his obvious play for Micaela. "Plus, there's the ex-wife and the missing son, and whoever his mother is."

"Nice. That's a good start." Shannon smiled at me. "Any idea how old the son is?"

"Elliot's working on identifying him, but maybe Lyndia knows. Her uncle was staying at her inn, right?"

"I think that's what they said." Shannon paused on the porch in front of the door. "The police told me Welby hadn't seen his son in twenty years, and that Lyndia only called him when Welby was at death's door in an attempt to have them reconcile."

I saw where he was going with this. "And then Nigel tries to steal the inn from her."

"Exactly. Good deeds never go unpunished."

I wasn't a believer in that—the universe would exact her dues—but I understood the feeling. "I just need to touch the right things," I said.

His hands tightened on mine. "That's exactly what I was thinking as I stood there watching them lock my father away." He shook his head. "I've never seen him so defeated. So ashamed. He couldn't really even speak for himself. It was almost like he thought he deserved it."

Because he was guilty about something, I thought but didn't say because I didn't have real proof. People were their own worst judges.

"I'm really sorry," I said. "We should have come last week."

He shook his head. "No. I'll never regret that." He leaned forward and kissed me, long and slow. His touch reminded me that whatever happened in our lives, we would always have the memories of last week. Hopefully there would be many others.

"We're going to have to tell your mother about the imprints," I said. "I think I've already weirded her out about touching things. She's beginning to look at me very strangely. I need to be free to touch everything without her wondering why."

He somehow managed a chuckle. "Well, that's not a conversation I'm looking forward to."

"Me either." We laughed again, and it made things feel better.

We found Bonnie alone in the kitchen, her fresh batch of cookies mostly gone, which hinted that either she and Freddi had indulged a little too much, or she'd gone outside with a plate for her guests who might still be lounging around the pool. Her face lit up as she saw Shannon, but as her eyes went past us and didn't see Holt, her worry returned.

"I'm picking him up in the morning," Shannon said, hugging her. "It's going to be okay. They won't be charging him." He recounted everything he'd told me, including the phone call from the anonymous tipster.

"Your dad was working in the garage the night before we left for Portland, not at a beach meeting that horrid man," Bonnie said.

"You were with him?"

Her face fell. "No. I guess I can't prove he was here."

"Wait," I said. "There are cameras, right? Does the feed save anywhere? We might be able to prove Holt didn't leave."

"The feed is saved for a month," Shannon said, "Unfortunately, the cameras are only hooked up to the public entrances, and those only encompass parts of the front and back yards."

"There are a lot of paths the cameras don't cover," Bonnie added. "Holt could get out of the house without being seen if he wanted to."

"What about cameras at the cottages?"

"No cameras there," Bonnie said. "The residents are the only ones there, and they're responsible for any damages. Not like here where people are actually in our home among our personal belongings."

I stifled a grimace. The part of me that eschewed government overreach was happy to hear my comings and goings at Rose Petal Cottage wouldn't be observed, but the investigator in me wished for an easy answer.

The talk moved on to what they might be able to do to mitigate the guest fallout if a thorough search of the house and grounds became a reality.

"If we could get the police to go into the rooms during cleaning time and not make a mess, we could probably downplay it with the guests," Bonnie said. "I mean, they can't think we have him tied up there, right?"

Shannon sighed and sat down on one of the four cast-iron stools at the counter. "Oh, they could make an argument for anything, if they choose. It depends on how positive they are that you're hiding something. I just wish Dad hadn't volunteered how the blood got on the hoe. We could have at least argued that others had access. He always leaves the garage open while he's working."

Bonnie stared at him for a moment before giving her head a sharp shake. "Of course he had to be honest. That's who we are, and they asked him a direct question. Anyway, that's a problem for tomorrow. Are you hungry? I put a plate of food away for you." Without waiting for his response, she busied herself with heating up his pasta.

I sat next to Shannon and downloaded a few email attachments from Elliot on my phone, wishing I had thought to bring my laptop to the house. At least this way, I'd get a start on weeding out the useless information from the things I'd want to follow up on.

In seconds, I was peering at the pictures Elliot had sent of Nigel Carr—and understood why the caller of the anonymous tip had recognized him. His skin was darkened to a leathery reddish brown by the sun, and if he had any hair left, it was completely covered by an aqua blue Miami Dolphins baseball hat. His large ears jutted out on each side on top of the cap, so big they looked almost fake. His face was wide at the top, narrowing to a sharp, hairless chin. Thin, deep wrinkles spanned the visible part of his forehead and above his prominent cheekbones next to his flat, wide nose. His bushy eyebrows drooped, and the gap between his two front teeth was accentuated by the fact that the two teeth on either side were missing. He looked several decades older than his fifty years. Definitely he was memorable, though maybe not so much here in the land of retired people and sun worshipers as he would be in Portland.

I scrolled down, and a familiar face was suddenly staring back at me. I pulled my phone closer to my face, though it wasn't necessary. The poofy blond hair and grinning, overly made-up face were clearly recognizable. This was Nigel Carr's ex-wife, the woman Elliot had said was a looker.

"You got to be kidding," I muttered. The others stopped talking and stared at me expectantly. I set my phone in the middle of the countertop for them to see. "Your mom's newest guest, Freddi Dottson, is Nigel Carr's ex-wife."

Bonnie gasped. "What? You mean the woman Shannon said is after part of Lyndia's inheritance?"

I nodded. "The one and the same."

"Why that little—" Bonnie came from around the counter in a hurry. "She's going to answer a few questions right now."

Shannon popped up and stepped in her path. "No, Mom. The last thing you should do is go banging on her door. She's a suspect, and Autumn and I will take care of her. And that includes questioning her before she realizes we know who she is. You need to let us do our jobs."

Bonnie stared up at him, her brow creased and mouth pursed. Slowly, she let her rigid body relax. "Okay."

Shannon nodded. "I'll need a master key. Once we're sure she's out, Autumn will need to check out the ex-wife's things."

Bonnie stared from him to me and back again. She walked to the hallway as if checking to make sure no one was in the public areas of the house. When she returned, she handed him a key from her pocket. "Be careful about using it. I can't just let anyone into the rooms, you know."

"We'll be careful, of course. And discreet. If it makes you feel better, we can go in with Micaela when she cleans the room in the morning."

Bonnie waved the words away. "I know you'll be careful. But why does Autumn need to check out the room and not you? If this woman is a suspect, wouldn't your training be better for that?"

Shannon's gaze touched mine briefly. At my nod, he set a confident hand on his mom's shoulder. "Mom, there's something I need to tell you—*we* need to tell you. Come sit down."

Inexplicably, Bonnie brightened. "I think I have an idea of what you're going to say." She held her fists up to chest level as if getting ready to jump to catch a prize. "And I couldn't be happier. Oh, I'm too excited to sit!"

Shannon blinked, and his next glance at me was not as confident. "You really should sit, Mom."

"I suspected when you got married so quickly," she rushed on. "And when I saw Autumn today—well, it's obvious she's glowing. Then when she fainted, well, that sealed it." She squealed and her arms shot out, going around her son. "Thank you, thank you both. I'm finally going to be a grandmother!"

Chapter 5

o wonder she'd been so solicitous of me all afternoon and through dinner. I was usually intuitive about these sorts of things, but I'd missed her suspicions completely.

"Autumn isn't pregnant," Shannon said bluntly.

Bonnie's expression was so crestfallen that I hurried to add, "We both want children, and my niece is already a year old, and my sister's thinking about having another one, so naturally, we want our kids to grow up with cousins."

Bonnie put a hand to her mouth, flushing a bright red. Her freckles stood out on her face like dark bits of pepper. "I'm so sorry. I guess I saw what I wanted to see."

"That's normal." I gave her a tentative smile.

Her brow furrowed. "But why did you get dizzy?"

Shannon explained while I tried not to watch Bonnie's face too closely. I was glad he talked about me using a part of my brain to activate a sense that others might also feel but were unable to interpret instead of going straight to "psychic." After the brief rundown, he told her about the hat and what I'd witnessed.

"So that's how she solved all those cases you told me about," she said almost accusingly. "No wonder your department pays her consultant fees."

"Right." This time Shannon didn't look in my direction—probably because he knew I'd want to know how long he'd been talking about me. He'd had a thing for me for months before he believed in my ability, which had been a dealbreaker for any kind of a relationship. He'd almost watched me fall into another man's arms to put space between us—until he'd come around. He was that stubborn.

Bonnie turned in my direction. "Oh, Autumn, I think a psychic is exactly what we need here. Holt doesn't believe in such nonsense, of course, but I always read my horoscope."

Psychic. Yes, she'd gone there. Just wait until she knew that my sister also had an ability I considered far more psychic. "Like father like son," I murmured, half under my breath.

"What?" Bonnie asked.

"I'll need to check Freddi's room," I said louder. Would it be too much to ask her to let me go through Holt's personal drawers in their bedroom? Probably. "And I'd like to see the garage." To make sure she didn't object, I added, "To look for clues. Sometimes people see things that don't seem important at the time, but they end up being crucial."

"You mean like knowing who Nigel's ex-wife is before we let her settle into one of our rooms."

"Something like that. If Holt does the yard work here, he might have witnessed something he doesn't even remember."

Shannon sat back down and picked up his fork. "We'd also like to borrow Dad's metal detector."

"Sure thing." Bonnie motioned in the general direction of the kitchen door. "It's in the garage. It was working the last time one of the guests used it. Your dad always keeps it plugged in." Her attention came back to me. "Is that why you wear gloves?"

I'd used them at the wedding because of the jewelry people had been wearing, and it hadn't been strange because they matched my outfit. But I'd also worn other gloves the day before as we made preparations, and she must have noticed.

"Yes." I waited for the inevitable—for her to ask me to read something.

Instead, she looked at her phone. "I'd better go gather up the towels by the pool. I think everyone is finished there for the night. Go ahead and help yourself in the garage when you're ready."

"Mom," Shannon said as she started to turn. "I meant what I said about not talking to the ex-wife about the case. Remember that something happened to him, and she has fifty thousand reasons to want him gone."

Bonnie nodded. "And it was a woman who called in the tip to the police, wasn't it?" With a tight smile, she was gone.

Shannon stood and dumped the remains of his dinner into the sink, washing the food into the garbage disposal before setting the plate into the nearly full dishwasher. "Let's go," he said. "We might as well look for the bullet tonight before it gets any darker. The three-hour time difference is going to make it hard for us to get up early."

All my former tiredness vanished, and I beat him to the garage door, where he punched in a code. Only one car was inside the three-car garage, the other half taken up by a riding lawn mower, a push mower, a grass trimmer, two worktables, several large saws, a big drill, and many other smaller tools. One wall was filled with perfectly organized and adjustable metal shelves, and cupboards ran around the top of the entire garage.

"He's organized," I said. "I think I want shelves like these metal ones in my shop. Only wood instead of metal. I could move them to whatever height I need and still have the floor open for furniture." Better yet, they were something I could put in myself.

"They'd be easier to match than free-standing shelves, though you're going to need those for the middle aisles," Shannon agreed.

Elliot had already located used bookshelves and cases, so my shop would be ready for reopening a few weeks after we arrived home, but it would mean twelve-hour days of setup that I wasn't exactly looking forward to.

While Shannon tested the metal detector, I was busy touching everything else. Most of the large yard items barely tingled, and I guessed Holt must wear gloves during his yard work. That meant even if I had the hoe, I probably wouldn't be able to relive the scene between him and Nigel Carr. I moved to the saws and then the worktables. Still nothing that related. Only on some of the smaller tools did I begin to find imprints: satisfaction about a job well done, excitement about the upcoming trip to attend Shannon's wedding, and sadness last month as he used a paintbrush to finish a frame he'd made for Lyndia that would contain a picture of her and her newly deceased grandfather.

Whatever Holt's secret, he wasn't dwelling on it on a daily basis. At least not here in the shop—which I understood. I often let my mind wander away from important things as I worked on my antiques, letting the imprints on them ease me into a sense of well-being. Holt did the same thing with his work.

"Anything?" Shannon asked.

I shook my head. "It was a long shot anyway."

He hefted the metal detector. "Well, this battery looks good. And there's an extra."

I hadn't tested the metal detector, so I touched it now. Fleeting imprints rushed over me. Casual ones that were alternatingly hopeful and bored. After the date on the impressions went back a few years, I withdrew my hand and shook my head. "Let's go try to find a bullet."

We went out the back door of the garage that led to the pool area. Bonnie was nowhere to be seen inside the pool fence, which wasn't surprising as we'd been in the garage for over twenty minutes. The garage itself blocked the parking lot from sight, and we started around it, presumably to get back to the path leading to the cottages. I was going to ask why we hadn't left by way of the automatic garage door that opened directly to the parking lot, but then Shannon cut across the lawn, passing a basketball court and volleyball pit.

"The path from the parking lot curves," he said. "Cutting across the grass will lead us straight to Frontier Cabin."

We heard talking before we saw the people standing outside the cottage. Bonnie was there too, looking furious. Seeing us, she hurried in our direction. "Look," she said, shaking a paper at us. "They have a warrant."

"To search the B&B?" Shannon asked, his voice disbelieving.

"I think that's what they said." Her voice rose on the last note. "This is a terrible time. Most of the guests are in their rooms already."

Shannon eased the metal detector to the ground and took the paper, skimming it quickly. "Looks legit. But it's only for around this particular cottage. They must have decided to try for a narrower warrant after they verified it was blood on the hat. If they find a bullet, they'll want dad's guns next for comparison." He looked at me. "You're sure it was here that he was shot, right?"

I nodded. "But I have no way of knowing if that bullet grazed him and went out or if it was at enough of an angle to lodge in his skull. But he was still coherent. And I can't say for sure that it was even Nigel. He wasn't looking in a mirror, and no one said his name." It was a moot point, but I thought I should mention it.

Shannon's jaw clenched and unclenched. "I'll take care of this," he told Bonnie. "You go back to the house."

"Should I hide the guns?" she asked.

"No. Dad didn't shoot anyone." His forehead wrinkled. "He still keeps them in the safe, right?"

She nodded. "We haven't gone shooting for over a month."

"Good. Don't open it then, and don't go shooting until this is over."

"Okay." With a bleak smile, she said goodbye and started back to the house.

"Well, let's get this over with," Shannon said.

We walked over to the CSI team who was searching the area, not only with metal detectors but with spotlights and other equipment. Detective Wallace nodded at us as we approached.

"I thought you were going to give me a few days," Shannon said.

Wallace shrugged. "With gunshot residue and blood on the cap," she said, "it probably means a homicide, and this is the logical next step. We'll know soon if the blood was Nigel's."

"It's still not a homicide without a body," Shannon reminded her.

"Maybe, but if we can find the gun, we can find someone who knows something about the shooting." This came from Detective Burke, who stepped out from behind his partner, surprising me because I hadn't noticed him there.

Shannon had nothing more to say, so we watched them work. "It could be anywhere," he muttered. "Where exactly was he standing?"

I was torn between wanting the police to find a bullet and worried that they would. If it ended up that Nigel Carr had been killed here, his body might still be nearby. "Let's see." I thought back, almost wishing I could touch the cap again. I never saw new information when rechecking imprints, but my memory was as fallible as anyone else's.

"It was close to the house," I said. "Really close to where I found the cap, but not close enough for it to have fallen there." My gaze met his. "And I don't think he was in any condition to hide the cap where it was. I mean, he might have found the strength to get up and run, but I don't think he'd run to the side of the cottage in the shrubbery. I think he'd try to go around to the front and bang on the door."

"It could have been planted by the murderer."

"Or it fell off when he ran. I wonder if there was a storm or wind that night."

He sighed. "We'll have to check. Look, it's probably too late to do anything more tonight except research on the Internet, which Elliot seems to have well in hand. Let's drop the metal detector off at Rose Petal Cottage and take a walk. I'd like to check out the place on the beach where my dad and Nigel were spotted by that anonymous caller."

"Sounds good. I'd also like to see how far Magnolia Inn is from here."

"It's close."

"Probably too late to stop in, though, right? It's after nine." The sky was already beginning to darken.

"I don't know. It's summer, so maybe not. Depends. But you've been reading a lot of imprints. How are you feeling?"

Truthfully, I was tired, though I believed that was a result of the imprint from the cap rather than from the plane travel and all the other imprints combined. Good imprints strengthened me while negative ones drained me.

"The inn might better wait until tomorrow," I admitted. "I don't want to miss anything."

"Want to bring the golf cart?" he asked. "We can go much of the distance in it."

"No. It's only a few blocks, and it might get in the way."

We went back to the cottage and used the key Bonnie had given me to let ourselves in. We filled a couple of water bottles and put them in a pack before heading down the path once more. Behind Frontier Cabin was the end of Haven Retreat property with a short bar gate that covered the wide path, so only someone with a key to the padlock could take the golf carts further than the property. A smaller footpath cut away from the main one, diverging around a decorative boulder, and it didn't have a gate. Once we'd passed the gate, I realized how unique Haven Retreat was with all its flowering trees. There were still palm trees on the surrounding properties, but after the lush vegetation of the B&B, everything seemed too open and afforded little privacy. No wonder people were willing to spend hundreds of dollars a night to stay there.

Directly after leaving Haven Retreat, Magnolia Inn was on the left side of the path, a pale pink, three-story box affair, featuring a huge sign with a pink magnolia on it. A fluorescent

NO VACANCIES flashed underneath the sign. Across from the inn was a settlement of small, one-story houses set close together. If whoever planned to buy Magnolia Inn from Nigel managed to also buy those, I could see how stealing away the land under Frontier Cabin could add hundreds of thousands, if not more, to the bid.

I stared doubtfully at the plain walk going up to Magnolia Inn. "Not a very pretty place, is it?"

"No, but if you overlook that, it has all the amenities. And it's got a nice pool and covered parking around the other side. My father actually restored their pool at the end of last summer."

"Was that part of the deal for Frontier Cabin?"

"Yeah. And from what Dad told me last night, that was supposed to be the last of it. But old Welby couldn't do as much this past year, so my dad continued doing maintenance and repairs. They were friends, and friends pitch in when they're needed. That's why all this has been so hard." He paused and stared up at the inn. "Welby was always such a strong man. I thought he'd live at least ten more years. He used to walk for hours on the beach. Even last year when I visited."

"What did he die of?"

"Actually, I don't know. Old age, I think. No one ever said."

"Hmm."

"What?"

I started walking again. "I don't know, but two deaths in a family this close together is weird."

Shannon's hand slipped into mine. "So far Nigel is only missing."

That's when the cold slammed into me, as if I'd passed

through a portal to another dimension or some such crazy thing. I stopped, feeling it all around me. "Tell that to whoever is here," I said.

I dropped Shannon's hand and reached out—and felt nothing.

"Nigel?" I said, though I wasn't sure why. If I started hearing ghosts, I was going to have to rethink my idea of being psychic, and I really didn't want that.

"Come on." Shannon grabbed my hand again and pulled me out of the cold. The sudden heat of the sidewalk beneath my bare feet and the heavy, humid warmth was almost a shock. But the cold was still there at my back as I walked. I didn't tell Shannon.

"I don't like this," he said. "I've barely come to terms with the fact that something I can't see can hurt you when you touch objects and now this . . . this cold . . ."

"Presence," I said.

"An unhappy one, according to your dad—I mean Cody."

Shannon had never known my adoptive father, and I didn't blame him for thinking of Cody as my dad. As my biological father, Cody was the closest thing I had to a parent now, and the fact that he shared my gift bound us more strongly than our blood.

"Cody only felt his mom after her death. And it was a warm feeling."

"But he tries not to use his ability," Shannon said. "You're always using it. Your ability must be growing. It's got to be related."

My turn to agree. "This feels unsettled, and that's why we're here, right? To find out what happened."

The cold followed as we reached the end of Magnolia Inn

property, where a public street and a proper city sidewalk began. We walked past houses and businesses, crossed a few streets, and finally wound our way to the red stone, cobbled sidewalk near the Jacksonville Beach Pier. Partway down the wooden pier, looking down near where the ocean met the sand, a lone figure in a blue rain jacket leaned on the northern side of the railing. *A woman,* I thought, though it was hard to tell at this distance.

"It's over there." Shannon pointed not toward the pier but further north up the cobbled sidewalk where we stood. "The caller said they were in front of the wooden path to the left of the pier that goes down to the sand."

We walked over and examined the wooden walkway that jutted out like a bridge over the vegetation growing next to the beach, I felt the railings, pulling my hand back as a mixture of imprints shuddered through me—glimpses of times and people and emotions.

"Nothing here from him that I'll be able to decipher," I said. "Too many imprints from too many years. Besides, I doubt he would have held onto it long enough, if he touched it at all."

Shannon looked around. The parking lot to our right was almost deserted, but a few diehards were still on the beach below. The cold pressed against me, urging me toward the wooden walkway, and for the first time that day, I wished for a jacket like the one worn by the woman on the pier. I stifled a shudder and stepped forward onto the wood path, which ended in a few stairs to the sand.

"Might as well dip our feet, right?" I said.

Something in my voice alerted Shannon. "What's wrong?"

"I'm wondering how long a body might take to wash back up on shore is all."

Shannon surprised me by chuckling and pulling me close. His lips landed on mine. "That's one of the reasons I love you so much, you know?"

"Because I'm morbid?" I smirked at him.

"No, because you're willing to follow your intuition even if it ends up in a place you don't want to be."

"Then let's go." I kissed him once more, deeply, before pulling away. I didn't tell him about the cold because it wouldn't have made any difference.

Instead of a body, we found Micaela on the beach with Tyrus Lockwood. Her boys were kicking a soccer ball near the water while Tyrus stood close to her on dry sand. She wore a jacket that looked like it might belong to him, which made sense with the strong breeze coming from the ocean.

I started forward, but Shannon stopped me. "I haven't seen her smiling like that in a long time."

My heart sank because the cold was still propelling me forward. "He might not be everything he seems," I reminded him. "By the way, does that master key open his cottage?"

"It should." Flat determination had entered his voice. "I'll have Paige do a background on him." Paige was his partner in Portland, and we both knew she'd jump at any chance to help us after our last case when we cleared her boyfriend of murder charges. But I wondered if Shannon wanted to track Tyrus more because the man was interested in Micaela than for his possible involvement in Nigel's disappearance.

As we watched the group under a darkening sky, they seemed like any other family who had stayed late on the beach. The cold pressed against me, counteracting the push of the breeze from the ocean, but I didn't continue forward. The sensation was so real, it was a wonder Shannon couldn't feel it. If anything, it was more concentrated near him.

As if it knew him. I couldn't help the thought.

Looking up, I saw the woman on the pier. Even as I watched, she pulled away from the railing and started toward the shore. Had she been watching the boys play soccer? Not that it should be a concern.

Tyrus chose that moment to leave Micaela and run to the boys, stealing their ball. They ran after him on the sand, and he led them toward their mother, finally letting them have the ball when they drew close to her.

"Time to go," Micaela announced, swooping down on the ball as one twin kicked it to the other. "You should already be in bed."

"Aw, Mom," one boy said.

We resumed our trek across the sand toward them, and when the boys spied us, they gave up trying to get the ball from their mother and ran toward us.

"Can we play hide-and-seek? Can we play hide-and-seek?" they shouted together.

Shannon laughed and opened his mouth—probably to agree—but Micaela beat them to it. "Nope. It's past your bedtime already. Tell Mr. Lockwood thank you for playing soccer, and let's get going."

The boys chorused their disappointment, but I sensed there wasn't a lot of effort behind the protests, just as there hadn't been when she'd captured their ball.

"We'll play soon," Shannon said. "We're here for a week."

Tyrus nodded at me. "Hi again." He offered Shannon his hand. "Congratulations on your marriage."

"This is Tyrus," Micaela said to Shannon. "He's staying in Frontier Cabin for the summer. He writes travel books."

"Nice to meet you," Shannon said as if we hadn't already thoroughly discussed him.

"Micaela told me about the boys' Uncle Shannon," Tyrus said. "You're a police detective?"

"Yep. Portland Police Bureau, Violent Crimes Unit."

"Fascinating."

"Usually," Shannon agreed. "If you don't count the paperwork."

Tyrus laughed. "That's what I'm good at."

We laughed politely, and as Micaela began herding the boys to the stairs, we all followed.

"We're actually here to help my parents," Shannon told Tyrus. "We're looking for Nigel Carr."

Tyrus pursed his lips. "I heard about that, but I'm sure the guy's around somewhere."

Micaela snorted. "He's probably trying to figure out a way to get the inn away from poor Lyndia."

"There has to be a will," Tyrus said. "Welby knew he was ill. He would have made sure things were taken care of."

Shannon gave him a sidelong glance. "He did have one, according to my father. But I didn't know you knew Welby."

"Not as well as I'd have liked to." Tyrus's expression was solemn. "We played a lot of checkers together."

"Tyrus talks to everyone," Micaela added. "That's how he finds all the fun things to write about."

"I guess Florida is a popular tourist destination," I said.

Tyrus grinned. "I hope so."

I noticed he didn't mention that he'd already written a travel guide about Florida.

We fell silent as we crossed the wooden path to the cobbled walkway. By unspoken agreement, Shannon and I kept pace with the others as they walked back to Haven Retreat. I was relieved that the cold presence I'd felt had dissipated. Whether it was my imagination, or I was doing what the cold wanted, I couldn't say.

Dimas amused himself by bouncing the soccer ball like a basketball in front of his mom and Tyrus, while Lucio dropped back to walk with us. The boy glanced at me shyly. "Do you play hide-and-seek too?"

"She's the best at it," Shannon said before I could answer. "She always finds everything, even if I don't want her to."

"Thank you." I gave him an ultra-sweet smile. Obviously, he was still a little put out that I'd read an imprint about the keys to a new car he'd bought me as a wedding present before he presented it to me at the cabin last week. "I'm good at hiding too," I added, lifting my chin a bit mockingly at Shannon. "No one finds me unless I want them to." He'd tried in the past, but I knew how to give him and his men the slip, even if I wasn't trying to do that often these days.

Shannon laughed. "That's for sure."

"Then I want to be on your team," Lucio said. "Dimas is always too noisy."

"Sure." I wasn't aware hide-and-seek required teams, but I was happy to agree.

"Great!" With a bright smile, Lucio raced forward to take a turn with the ball.

As we passed Magnolia Inn, something called my attention to one of the lower windows. Was that a movement? I stopped to look, and the others paused with me.

"It's a beautiful old place," Tyrus said, seeing my gaze. "Or it was once. I've seen pictures. The stucco wasn't always pink, and there were magnificent trees before they pulled them out for the covered parking. Now it's sort of barren."

"Pink is for girls," Dimas muttered.

Tyrus rumpled his hair. "I definitely agree."

We continued walking and in two minutes arrived at Frontier Cabin, where it looked like the police were still searching with their equipment. The boys ran ahead to check it out.

"What's going on?" Tyrus asked, looking between Micaela and us. She shrugged and Shannon didn't answer, so it was up to me.

"They found a baseball cap today that might have belonged to Nigel Carr," I said. "It had a hole in it, and the material was stained with blood, so they're looking for a bullet."

"A bullet?" Tyrus paled visibly.

Was he nervous that a shot might have happened outside the cottage where he was staying, or was it something more?

Micaela turned toward him. "I'm taking the boys home. I really don't want them talking about blood and a bullet all night. Thanks again. It meant a lot to them."

"Well, uh . . . I had fun," Tyrus said awkwardly. Or insincerely? Once again, I couldn't tell which. Or maybe he was simply concerned about the police. "I . . ." he started, taking a step toward her before seeming to remember us. "Uh, I'll see you at breakfast."

"Sure. See you then." Micaela jogged off after her sons.

"I think there's an empty room up at the house, if you'd rather sleep there tonight," I told Tyrus.

"Oh, no. It's fine. I'm not worried." That's not what his face said, so I wasn't sure he was telling the truth. He gave us a wave and disappeared inside Frontier Cabin, shutting the door firmly behind him.

"What do you think of him?" I asked.

"He's hiding something. I'm still wondering how he played checkers with Welby if the old man was so sick this summer. Something's off." I was glad he agreed with my assessment.

The darkness among the many trees was cloying, as if the humidity itself had fingers that clamped down on our skin. For how long we watched the police work, I couldn't say, but eventually a few of the lights began to click off and mutters from the team told us they might be giving up for the night. We'd started moving along the path again when a shout went up from investigators. Shannon, his face rigid, hurried over to see what they'd found, and I, of course, tagged along.

Detective Wallace held up a clear plastic bag containing a misshapen bullet as we approached. "It was hiding under one of the little pines," she said, her face triumphant. "Looks like maybe a nine mil or a three eighty."

"The question is how long has it been there?" Shannon countered.

"I think there's blood on it. Even after a week, we should be able to lift something. And we'll be taking your father's guns now."

"I'll let my mom know."

Not sure whether we should be encouraged or disheartened at the progress, we walked away. Shannon called his mom and told her to show the police the guns when they came to the house.

"They haven't opened the safe in a month," I said as we arrived at Rose Petal Cottage. "So the bullet won't match. And there's still no body."

Shannon shook his head. "If they find Nigel's blood on the bullet, this will no longer be a missing persons case, but a murder with a missing body, and my dad will be the prime suspect."

"Come on," I said. "Let's get to bed. We'll need to get up early if we're going to question Nigel's ex-wife at breakfast."

He raked a hand through his hair. "I don't know if I'll be able to sleep."

"That's okay. It's still our honeymoon, and I've got a better idea." I put my arms around his neck and kissed him until we both forgot about Nigel Carr.

Chapter 6

"Even if Nigel's blood is on the bullet," I said the next morning as we walked up the paved path to the main house for breakfast, "why should that mean your dad is the prime suspect?"

"Because he had motive and opportunity."

"If he didn't do it, that means someone else had a better motive," I countered.

He stopped walking. "What do you mean *if?*"

The early morning sun angled in a way that made his hair look even more blond. It was just beginning to curl at the ends the way I loved it. At that moment, I was glad for every bit of my past, even the horrible sadness of losing my father that triggered my ability, because all of it eventually led me to Shannon.

"Of course he didn't do it," I said.

We continued walking. Even at eight o'clock in the morning, it was humid and hot, causing a light sheen of moisture to form at the base of my neck and in the hollow between my breasts. I was happy to be wearing the long, flowy, multi-colored sundress I wore, and that my dark hair, dyed red on top, was short.

After a few more seconds, I said, "What do you know about why your dad left the force? He seems so proud of what you do."

"He said that?"

"Imprints."

"Oh. Well . . ." We'd reached the parking lot, but instead of going around to the front, he angled around the garage to the back of the house. "He was there barely twenty years. A beat cop. If he'd liked it, he would have stayed, right? But he got in and out as quickly as possible."

"That's all you know?"

"I was only nineteen when he left, and he doesn't talk about it much. I ran into one of his old partners once at another precinct, and he only had good things to say, but they worked together early in Dad's career."

"Maybe you don't know everything."

Shannon laughed. "If there had been another reason, he would have told me."

"Would he?" I asked as we passed the pool. "If he hasn't talked about it since, maybe there's something more."

"He spent the last year of his career there at a desk. That tells me a lot."

I wasn't sure where he was going with that. "What does it say?"

"That he didn't enjoy it anymore. Or maybe he started to believe he wasn't doing any good. For every criminal I put behind bars, there's a dozen more needing capture. And with all the vilifying of the police of late, it's discouraging. Sometimes police work is a hard, thankless job."

I'd seen that up close, so I knew he was right. Thinking of the imprint on the basket, and the others I'd read, I said, "Maybe you should ask him."

Shannon opened his mouth to speak but shut it as his mother came out onto the patio from the double glass doors on the dining room side of the pool. "Come on! I just put out a fresh batch of Sunday pancakes."

"Sunday pancakes?" I asked.

She grinned. "We serve them every Sunday. Luckily, Holt is back to help because I'm not nearly as good at making them. He's hurrying so we can make it to church on time. You guys coming?"

Shannon shook his head. "We're on a honeymoon, Mom. I'm not sharing Autumn with any more people than I have to. Especially strangers."

She laughed. "Point taken. Well, come on and get your food. I'm going upstairs to change."

The pancakes were works of art, with different cartoon characters and shapes. I had no idea how Holt made the designs, but I intended to find out before I left Florida so I could make them for my niece, Destiny.

In the dining room buffet, we loaded our plates with pancakes, bacon, eggs, and fruit. I had fresh-squeezed orange juice and Bonnie's special hot chocolate while Shannon had a double dose of extra strong coffee. He hadn't slept well, and the time difference was affecting him more than it was me.

Unfortunately, Freddi Dottson, the main reason we'd come to breakfast this early, didn't make an appearance. When Micaela came to refill our drinks, she told us Nigel's ex-wife had requested a tray in her room.

"We'll have to talk to her later," Shannon said to me in an undertone. "And check out her room."

We ate at the long banquet table I'd eaten dinner at the night before, watching Micaela as she went around the room, nodding at the few guests, pouring drinks, and refilling serving dishes. When Tyrus Lockwood appeared in the dining room doorway, her smile widened.

"It's only a matter of time between those two," I told Shannon.

He finished draining his coffee cup. "Then we'd better find out what he's hiding. Let's go talk to Lyndia."

"Okay." We took our empty dishes to the sink in the kitchen, though the guests were leaving them on the table for Micaela and Bonnie to clean.

Holt didn't look up as we entered the kitchen, his tall frame bent over the pancake griddle on the counter. I stared with interest as he "drew" lines with dark pancake mix from a squeeze bottle before filling it in with two different lighter ones. When he turned it, he had a perfect triangle pizza with dark spots that were obviously pepperoni.

"Nice," I said.

He grinned at me. "Took me years to make anything you could recognize. I still can't do faces. I stick mostly to food items and easy cartoon characters."

I'd eaten a pancake banana, a shell, a crab, and a Mickey Mouse face, so I knew he was understating his ability. "I'd love to try."

Holt grinned and handed me a squeeze bottle of dark batter. "Be my guest."

A subtle imprint came from the bottle, but it was of contentment and gratitude to be home, which vitalized me. Carefully, I drew out the simplest little fish—the outline, the gills, an eye, and half a smiley face. Then I filled it in with another color.

"Not too bad," Holt said, flipping it. "Maybe make the lines a little thinner next time and the fish bigger."

"My niece is going to love this."

We became aware of Shannon hovering in the background, and we turned to him. "Want to try?" Holt asked.

"No. I want to know what they said this morning when they let you go."

Holt glanced around to make sure no guests were within hearing range. "Nothing new, if that's what you're asking."

"There is something new." Shannon stepped closer and told him about the bullet, while I tried to make a pancake mermaid—and utterly failed.

Holt's face creased with concern. "Yeah, your mother told me. I believe they'll be testing my guns, but it's the weekend, so unless Wallace can pull favors, that won't be happening today."

A frustrated grunt escaped Shannon's lips. "Still, this means whoever was wearing the cap was shot on your property. I wish you hadn't confronted him. That's not like you, especially when you knew Welby put it in his will."

"Which conveniently can't be found." Holt straightened, seeming to tower over both of us. "I'm not letting that weasel steal my property."

"Well, you don't have to worry about that now, do you?" Shannon retorted, his voice low but tense. "You just have to worry about going to prison."

"I didn't do anything to him. Besides, that's why you're here, right?" There was a catch in Holt's voice now. "You and Autumn."

Yet he hadn't wanted us here. I wanted to ask why, but not in front of Shannon. I didn't want to put a wedge in their relationship. Shannon looked ready to say something he might regret, and whether that was to call into question his father's sanity or to ask why he'd really left the force, with guests in the dining room, now wasn't the time.

I grabbed Shannon's hand and met Holt's gaze. "I hope you'll give me another lesson soon. Right now I need a walk."

"Before you leave, for sure," he said. "You'll need them once you start having children." His gaze dipped midway down my colorful sundress, and I guessed he hadn't gotten the memo yet that we weren't expecting.

"She's not pregnant," Shannon muttered.

Holt snorted. "Well, son, that's not my fault."

I pulled Shannon in the direction of the dining room once more. "You weren't kidding about your parents being glad to see you married."

"Tell me about it."

"They mean well," I said as we went out to the pool area.

"Yeah, but it doesn't make sense that my dad would have gotten so angry about Frontier Cabin. It's been in use for over a year, and it's obvious Welby knew about it and was okay with it. Possession is nine-tenths of the law, after all, especially if Lyndia backs them up."

I didn't answer but breathed in the scent of the flowering trees and heat. Everything was so well-kept and beautiful. We'd have to visit more often because I could see why his parents wouldn't want to give all this up to move to Portland.

Shannon cut across the lawn this time, and I followed him. "It can only mean one thing," he said as we approached Frontier Cabin. "He's hiding something."

I sighed. "Yes."

Shannon stopped walking and faced me. "What do you know? Is this why you were asking about his leaving the PPB?"

I nodded because I wouldn't lie to him, even if I had been able to do it with a straight face, which was hard for me—probably my greatest drawback as a private investigator. "But I don't know anything concrete, which is why I didn't say anything yet. I did pick up an imprint that he was worried you'd look into his past and find out everything. He feels guilty about . . ." This was going to be the hard part. "He thinks he killed someone."

Shannon gaped, his face flushing. "Why didn't you tell me?"

I put my hands on my hips, lifting my chin. "Because it was only yesterday and there hasn't exactly been time. And because what I see on imprints isn't always the truth—it's only what the imprinter believes. You know that. Your father was a police officer, and there could be a million reasons why he feels guilt over someone's death. I'm not causing trouble between you two until I know there's something valid to pursue."

He didn't look appeased. Turning on his heel, he headed in the direction of our cottage.

"Where are you going?" I asked.

He glanced over his shoulder. "To call in a few favors. I'm going to find out what he's hiding."

"Why don't you just go ask your dad?"

He gave his head a sharp shake. "If he had anything to say to me, he would have already. Besides, Paige might have finished that check I asked her to run on Tyrus." He started forward once more.

If he thought I was going to run after him and beg for

forgiveness, he'd married the wrong girl. "I'll meet up with you then," I called to his back. "I'm going to Magnolia Inn."

Shannon's steps faltered, but he looked around again and nodded. "We'll trade info later. *All* of it this time."

Yes, he was annoyed, but it wouldn't be the first time, and maybe going on my own would be better. That way I could control the questions without interference.

"And Autumn," he said.

I turned around. "Yeah?"

"Be careful."

I stifled a grin. My husband—the super tough, homicide detective—couldn't stop himself from worrying about me. I lifted my hands. "I'm carrying, even if you aren't."

He laughed, despite his anger, and I knew we would be okay once he calmed down. We'd had enough practice over the past year with fighting and making up. I couldn't stop following my intuition because I was married now, and he'd realize that. We'd agreed we would support each other as we pursued our jobs.

I continued across the grass, thinking about how I'd introduce myself at Magnolia Inn, provided Lyndia Carr was there and caring for her guests. Bonnie had explained that the inn was basically like her bed and breakfast, except they had more rooms—fifteen rooms, to be exact—business services, covered parking, and more amenities like vending machines and extras you could buy.

As I rounded Frontier Cabin, I hesitated. Tyrus had been in the dining room hitting on Micaela not that long ago. Which meant I could at least check out his doorknob and maybe the tiny patio that was probably around the back like at Rose Petal Cottage.

Glancing over my shoulder to make sure no one was in

sight, I ventured onto the flat, mishappen stones that served as a walkway to the door to the tiny log cabin. The door handle was an antler—plastic, though. I touched it gingerly with a fingertip and was glad I had exercised caution when a vivid imprint from last night held me in place.

If the police find out, it could ruin everything. Why did it have to happen now? I hoped Nigel Carr burned in hell. I'd have to convince Lyndia to do what I needed and soon.

A gasp escaped my lips. Tyrus definitely meant hell as in the place. Did that mean he suspected Nigel was dead? I didn't have time to consider that as an earlier imprint manifested from shortly before dinner last night.

Maybe this time I could catch Micaela's attention. The glimpses of her every morning weren't enough. I needed to make my move before it was too late.

Again.

The word "again" seemed to indicate that he'd failed once before, but there wasn't enough context for me to extrapolate anything more. Micaela had mentioned he looked familiar from somewhere besides Haven Retreat. Was that possible?

No time to dwell on the idea. The next imprint was one of fury—hot, blinding fury. *I'll kill him. I will. No one would blame me.*

My gut tightened. The imprint had occurred a month earlier than the previous one. The emotion felt so logical and right—killing the person I was mad at was not only justified but necessary.

Murder was necessary.

The Autumn portion of me rejected the idea, but it was such a small objection as to be almost negligible.

Another imprint followed, this time from almost six weeks

earlier. *The old man was dying, that was sure. I could see it in his slow movements and in the dullness of his eyes. I hoped Lyndia would be strong enough to do what she had to do.*

What would Lyndia need to do? Was it related to the first imprint and what Tyrus would try to convince her to do? Or was it simply referring to running the inn? I waited for more, but the imprint ended as the imprinter—Tyrus, I assumed—pulled his fingers from the antler.

Why did everything seem to lead back to Magnolia Inn? Presumably because Nigel had been staying there. I'd need to check there for imprints, especially where Nigel had slept.

Another imprint began, but before I had the chance to see it, a sound came from behind me. I pulled my hand away and turned to see Tyrus paused on the path in front of the cottage. No trees shaded the path where he stood squinting at me.

"Do you need something?" His tone was stiff, and I wondered if he'd somehow heard about my ability. I hadn't exactly asked Bonnie to keep it quiet from Micaela, who in turn might have mentioned it to Tyrus this morning. If he did know, it could make my investigation of him that much harder—especially if he really was capable of murder.

"Oh, there you are," I said rather lamely, going to meet him on the cement path.

Tyrus thumbed over his shoulder. "Just finished breakfast. What can I do for you?"

I'd already come up with a good reason. "My husband had a little work to do this morning, and I wanted to go over to Magnolia Inn to talk to Lyndia. Since you used to know the owner, I was hoping maybe you could give me an introduction."

"Okay." He cocked his head. "But may I ask why you need to see her?"

Why? Right. I hadn't thought that far—or considered that he would be protective of her. I racked my brain for a few seconds before finding a good answer. "I do have some questions related to my investigation into Nigel Carr's disappearance, but mostly it's a social call. Bonnie and I are going to a few estate sales next week, and we thought she'd like to come along. If not, I can at least look at her décor and see what she likes."

"That's kind of you, but I don't know if she plans to continue with the inn."

"What?" It was the first time I'd heard this.

Tyrus frowned. "It's a hard thing to run on your own, and Lyndia is only twenty-five."

I'd started my antiques shop at twenty-four. Winter had been alive then and had helped me set up and had pushed his own customers from his Herb Shoppe to support me, which had probably ensured my success. But the inn was already set up with many paying customers, so why couldn't Lyndia continue?

"How long have they owned the inn?" I asked. "Do you know?"

He shrugged. "I'm not sure exactly, but I think Welby had it for several decades. Maybe even when his wife was alive."

"When did she die?"

"Thirty years ago, I think. Long enough that he didn't talk about it much." He gestured to the path. "I can go with you now and introduce you. Wait just a minute, though. I need to grab something I want to show her."

"Sure." I followed him back over the stepping stones to the cottage, hoping to get a glimpse inside, but he very firmly shut the door behind him. Did he have housekeeping, or had he been the only one in the cabin all summer? If Nigel Carr's blood was found on the bullet, would they get a court order to search in there too?

Well, it wouldn't matter because I'd get inside first—as soon as I got the key from Shannon.

Tyrus was out in less than two minutes, a printed paper in his hands. I wondered what it was, but I'd wait to see if he'd volunteer information.

"So, what's the most interesting book you ever wrote?" I asked as we started up the path toward Magnolia Inn.

"Ah, that's easy," he said. "Portugal."

"Oh, yeah? For some reason I thought you only did locations in the United States."

"Mostly. There's a lot less competition for really good guidebooks that focus on a single state. Too many books encompass the entire country, and America is just too big for that. Or they go into too much history, which bores many of the younger generation. So I like to summarize, hitting the highlights and linking to additional information if they're interested. But I also finished one on France earlier this year. It's being edited right now."

"And you have a lot of readers?"

He laughed. "Not really. My real job is on YouTube. I have a bunch of ten-minute segments I produce myself, and I get enough views that the ad revenue is my main income. The books help, but they're more to add credibility."

"What are the videos about? The same stuff that's in the guidebooks?" I'd have to tell Elliot about the videos, if he didn't already know.

"Well, I do produce an hour-long video with the same title of each book," he said. "But the shorter ones are about short trips, travel tips, even sponsored ad-type videos—just about anything you can think of. I put up four to seven every week, and there are several different series, like hour trips, day trips, stuff for kids, a weekend getaway. The possibilities are endless."

"Sounds like a lot of work."

He shrugged. "It's mostly deciding what to cut and post. I video everything and keep thorough logs so I remember what I have available. I still try to limit my work to forty hours a week, though. That wasn't possible in the beginning, but now it is. I can produce a ten-minute segment in about two hours."

He sounded eager and so normal while talking about his work that I'd forgotten he was a suspect. I needed to steer him back to my case.

"So, you've been here the whole summer?" I asked as we passed the boulder that marked the disputed Haven Retreat property line.

"Yeah. Bonnie gave me a deal, and I sublet my own apartment in Tampa, so the difference isn't that much. Saves driving."

"So what was your first book?"

He laughed. "Actually, it was Florida. Mostly the Miami area. I'd been doing short travel videos for years—filmmaking was my major in college, and that book was my first attempt at legitimacy. You won't believe how many more people will watch my segments when they learn I'm a published author."

I gave him credit for frankness. "I think I'm seeing the same thing with my antiques business. I recently started selling online, and because I have a physical store, more people seem willing to take a risk on larger items. Probably because they know where to find me if the object isn't as described."

"Plus, they think you must know what you're doing since you run an actual physical store," he added. "That's the legitimacy I was talking about. Eventually, you'll probably make more online. That's the trend these days."

Magnolia Inn now loomed in front of us in all its pink glory. We nodded at two women in beachwear who passed us as we entered the front doors. Inside, the inn resembled more of a small hotel than a bed and breakfast, complete with a front reception desk that was currently unmanned.

Tyrus rang a push bell on the counter, but the sound didn't bring anyone. "She must be upstairs or outside."

I looked with longing at the bell, wishing I could test it for imprints, but I would read it later when I wasn't under Tyrus's scrutiny. "Let's try looking around," I said.

He led the way through the open entry to a serviceable dining room, which held none of Haven Retreat's charm. Only two guests were still eating, and a woman with a short ponytail was sucking up spilled cereal on the counter with a tiny hand vacuum, her back toward us. I thought it might be Lyndia Carr, but when the faint whirring of the vacuum stopped and she turned a tired face toward us, I realized she was at least two decades too old. She was slender everywhere except around her waist, where a small roll of fat mushroomed above the pants of her pink uniform.

"Hey, Deanna, is Lyndia around?" Tyrus asked.

She thumbed toward the double doors on her right. "She went outside a little while ago. She has a headache." Was that a little roll of her eyes? I couldn't be sure. I wondered if Lyndia normally helped with the breakfast clean up. Breakfast for fifteen rooms of guests would be a big job for Deanna alone.

"Thanks." Tyrus nodded and turned toward the doors.

Once again, I was itching to touch everything in the

breakfast room, but that would have to wait. Besides, Nigel's personal belongings would be more likely to hold useful imprints.

The back doors opened up to a large deck and a choice to continue right to a covered parking lot or forward to a fenced pool area. A third option to the far left led to a narrow walkway circling the entire fenced pool area, where large bushes lined the border with Haven Retreat. Tyrus headed to the pool. Unlike at Haven Retreat, a key card was required to enter the pool area, but this morning the gate was open, held in place by a metal bar.

A family of four were playing in the water, even this early in the morning, never mind the beckoning of the nearby ocean. Far to the left, near a round, stone table, a solitary woman lay in a white plastic lounge chair, the top only partially reclined and a small white towel over her face. She was using the only lounge chair near the table, which she must have brought over from the others around the pool.

We headed toward the woman, leaving the smooth cement around the pool for the circle of decorative flagstones that didn't quite match the rest of the décor.

"Lyndia?" Tyrus called when we were a few feet away from the resting woman. "Is that you?"

The woman threw off the towel and turned, pulling her feet from the lounge to the ground. "Tyrus! How good to see you!" She jumped up, surprising me with her enthusiasm. She was about my height, and her hair every bit as short, but hers was blond and far spikier. She wore no make-up, very tiny jean shorts and a halter top, and her bare toes were painted a bright blue. She looked about fifteen, not twenty-five. She was curvy in all the right places, and her legs longer than they should have been for her height. Her pinched, smallish face kept her from model-type beauty, but her large, beautiful eyes went a long way toward mitigating that effect.

She hugged Tyrus, and he hugged her back, though with decidedly less excitement. "Lyndia, this is Autumn. I think you know her husband, Bonnie and Holt's son."

Lyndia turned to me, her blue eyes opening wide. "Oh, yes, Shannon's wife. Bonnie has told me all about you." She rushed forward and shook my hand, her grip firm. "Congratulations. I love Shannon—he's such a sweet guy. And I'm so glad you came over. Is Bonnie or Shannon with you?" She looked past me, searching for them.

"No, Bonnie went to church, and Shannon had to make a few calls. But I wanted to meet you. Bonnie said you might want to go to a few estate sales with us next week, and I'm interested in what kind of things you might be looking for."

"That would be awesome!" Her arm swung out to the other chairs around the stone table—no, not a table but a firepit with wide stones on the outer edge and tiny fire stones in the middle under which I suspected was a gas ring. "Please, have a seat. Would you like something to drink?"

"Not now," I said, choosing the chair closest to her, tucking one bare foot up under me and resting my hands on the armrests. No imprints that weren't faded and more than a year old, but immediately, I was engulfed in a sensation of cold, as if I'd sat in a snowbank. I stifled a shiver and remained where I was. Getting up and moving wasn't something I could explain.

And then I felt it—an imprint that was not days old or one that had been left even an hour ago, but an emotion that was being imprinted that instant on the armrests. Not from me, but from someone else.

What's he doing here! I thought. Helpless rage bubbled up inside me.

I tried to rise, but this woman with the short red hair—something about her pinned me in place. Pinned me to my helplessness.

More anger. I would do something. Somehow.

Wait, I knew this woman. I'd seen her before. She'd found the cap—with a little help from me.

The emotion was strong, but the accompanying view of Tyrus and Lyndia was faded as if I were seeing it through water or in a dream. But I was sure it was an imprint from the cold presence, and that was more frightening than anything I'd ever experienced.

Which meant my gift hadn't changed, not really. I was still reading imprints, but this time the imprinter was dead.

Chapter 7

"I brought you what I want to say about the inn in my new book." Tyrus handed her the paper in his hand. "That is, if you decide to keep it. I don't want my information to be out of date, so if you're selling, let me know as soon as you can."

Lyndia looked down at the paper, her eyes moving along the text. "Oh, this is so sweet. Thank you so much." She hugged him again.

"Anything I can do to help." Tyrus moved to the other side of the firepit and sat in a chair.

I didn't know if the cold was paying attention, but the imprinting had stopped and was starting over as imprints always did. I put my hands in my lap, so it wouldn't replay. For now, I needed to focus on the living.

"So you're an antiques dealer, right?" Lyndia folded the paper and set it on the ground next to a phone before settling back onto her lounger. "And you help your husband solve cases."

I laughed. "I sometimes consult when the bureau needs my expertise."

"I remember Bonnie telling me about an estate sale company that was knocking off old people." She sputtered a laugh before frowning. "Not that it's funny, or anything. Seriously, I don't get these people who go to so much trouble to do bad things. They're evil."

"Or they think they won't get caught," Tyrus said from the other side of the firepit where he'd chosen to sit.

Lyndia folded her legs, hugging them to her chest. "They really are stupid, aren't they?"

Tyrus nodded in agreement and then bounced to his feet. "I need some water. Why don't I get us all some?" When Lyndia started to rise, he said, "No, I can do it. You wait right here and continue your chat."

"Okay," Lyndia said with a laugh.

"You should drink a lot of water for headaches," I told her when he was gone.

Lyndia stretched her legs out again and covered a yawn with her small hand. "What I have today isn't a headache but laziness. This inn is so much work, especially without my grandpa—but you probably already know that from Bonnie. She's always busy."

I nodded. "We were sorry to hear about your grandfather. Shannon has good memories of him. Said he liked to jog on the beach."

"Yeah, he'd be gone for hours." With a sigh, Lyndia put a hand over her eyes. "I miss him so much. I mean, I knew he was going downhill this past year, but I still can't believe he's gone." She dropped her hand, revealing glittering tears in her eyes. "He was the glue that kept this place together. I can't do it without him."

"You could get another partner." I was thinking maybe Bonnie and Holt might be willing. They seemed fond of her.

"Maybe." She looked behind her at the back door to the inn where Tyrus had vanished. "If it could be someone like Tyrus, I might be all over that."

"You and Tyrus?" I said. "I didn't know."

"We've only been on a few dates." Her eyes dipped modestly. "I guess it might be wishful thinking on my part. He's so gorgeous—kind of out of my league in that respect, I know. But he seems to like me, and if I sell the inn, well, maybe I could go with him on his research trips."

Her words were spoken with a naivety that made my heart ache for her. "How long have you known him?"

The answer surprised me. "At least ten years." She laughed. "I had an even bigger crush on him when I was fifteen, I'll tell you that. But anyway, he comes out and stays with us for a few days every now and then. Maybe once a year."

"But not this time?"

She frowned. "I guess we didn't have a long-term rental available. Come to think of it, Bonnie and Holt must have had a cancelation. They usually fill up before we do, even at their prices."

How strange was it that Tyrus had chosen to stay at Haven Retreat this year—especially in the same cottage near where the missing man was shot? The reservation time was at least a lead I could follow up on with Shannon's parents.

"Right before my grandpa died, Tyrus was over here almost every day playing checkers. And even now he still checks up on me. It feels different between us this time." She looked at me, and for an instant I could see the glitter of a remaining tear on her upper lash. "But I'm not holding my breath or anything." She giggled. "Lyndia Lockwood—could you imagine that? No one would ever take me seriously with all that alliteration."

I smiled politely, though I wasn't amused. "You know, I started my antiques shop when I was about your age," I said, my voice harder than I'd intended. "You learn to do things on your own pretty fast."

"I guess I'm not really sure what I want to do with my life now that I have the choice to leave." A half smile played on her lips. "It's all I know, but what if something else is better for me?"

I was all for following your dreams. "It's something to think about."

"Yeah. But anyway, I have done some things here on my own." She pointed at the firepit. "I did all this."

"Really? Good for you." But then I had an awful thought about how new the firepit area looked. "When did you do it?" The idea that someone might have used Lyndia's construction job to hide her missing uncle's body was more than distasteful.

"Right before my grandfather died. It means a lot to me that he was able to play checkers here at least a few times."

That was a relief. "The firepit is gas?"

"Yeah. There used to be a wading pool here for kids, but when we replastered the pool last year, we put in a wading section at one end for kids, and we filled this with sand. My idea, but a big mistake." She laughed in self-deprecation. "The sand kept ending up in the pool, and the neighborhood cats kept coming in and using it as a litter box. So I hired a guy to rip out the cement, install a gas line, and lay these flagstones in this circular pattern. So when I say I did it, I really mean I made it happen."

"That's usually how it works with big things." My burned-up shop was a great example.

"I did buy the firepit myself and secure it here on top of

a cement ring. I had to hook it up to the gas line and use some cement glue, but it was pretty easy. It's not real stone; it just looks like it, so it's not super heavy. I chose a taller firepit because I wanted it to double as a table for Grandpa. There's an inset that goes on top of the firestones. But it's inside right now."

She seemed proud of the firepit, and it was nice, if you didn't count how the color and circular design didn't match up with the pool area itself. "I bet your guests love it."

"Some of them have been roasting marshmallows every night since I got it finished."

Silence fell, and I began to wonder what was taking Tyrus so long. The cold I'd experience before had receded, or maybe it couldn't compete with the increasing heat of the sun as it rose higher in the sky. It had to be near ten now.

"Look," I said, "the police did find a bullet last night outside Frontier Cabin. And your uncle's baseball cap. It's looking like something serious might have happened to him."

She gasped. "That's terrible. Do they know who did it?"

"They suspect Holt."

"No way." She sat up straight, her back stiff. "No freaking way. Holt is the sweetest man. He helps me with anything I need."

"What about your uncle? Did he help after your grandfather died? When did he get here?"

"Nigel *never* helped," she practically spat, lying back again on her lounger. "He was a lazy butt during the day and a drunk by night. He came about two weeks before my grandfather died—but that was my fault."

"How so?"

A huge sigh rushed from her like a leak from a hot air

balloon. "My uncle and grandfather had a falling out years ago. But when I realized Grandpa was dying, I wanted to make sure he had a chance to mend his bridges, you know? Only it didn't work out that way. Grandpa didn't want to see him, and when they did talk, all they did is argue, and Nigel wouldn't leave."

"He was staying here?"

"Well, I let him have a guest room when we had one empty for the night. Otherwise, he'd sleep on the couch in our suite, and I thought when Grandpa died, he'd leave, but he didn't."

"He claimed the inn was his?"

She nodded. "Or at least half of it. Because even though I'm not related to Grandpa by blood, my dad did adopt me, so Nigel couldn't cut me off completely."

"What about the will?"

She shrugged, tears once again welling in her eyes. "Nigel must have taken it when he left." She chewed on her lower lip for a moment before adding, "Maybe that bullet was old—or maybe he put it there to make Holt a suspect. They fought, you know."

"Is your uncle the type who would leave before things were settled with the inn?"

"No, I guess not." She bent over and picked up her phone from the ground. "But speaking of that, some investors he was working with are coming by in a bit. Hopefully to make me an offer."

"Do they know Nigel's missing?"

"Yeah. I told them." She glanced behind her at the inn again, and this time Tyrus was emerging with full glasses of ice water balanced on a tray.

"Bonnie says you were aware of the agreement between your grandfather and Holt about the land their Frontier Cabin is on," I said, finally getting to that question. If Lyndia was serious about selling the inn, the Martins needed to know where she stood on the issue.

Her eyes snapped back to me. "I'm not sure what you mean. Holt did help us out a lot, but I thought it was because they're friends. I didn't know there was payment involved."

A shiver ran across my shoulders. "You never saw the will? Because Holt said he saw it."

"Only the part where he left the inn to me."

"But you *will* back up their claim to the land, right?" I asked as Tyrus reached the gate.

"Well . . ." She hesitated. "I do worry the developer won't buy my inn without it. That's what Nigel said would happen, and he's in the construction business."

"Are you saying Holt's lying about the arrangement?"

Eyes opening wide, she shook her head vigorously. "No, of course not. I simply don't know anything about it. But if I decide to sell, I'm going to need enough to start over somewhere. And now that I'm thinking about it, the developer might be willing to pay them a bonus for the land as well."

I didn't know what to make of that, but once more cold suffused me, propelling me up from the chair. The cold presence was furious—at least that's how I was interpreting it. But was it because of what Lyndia had said or because Tyrus had returned? I surreptitiously touched the armrest to see if more imprints had been added, but only one stark thought met my effort: *Find the will.*

"Here we go, ladies," Tyrus said. "Sorry for the delay. Apparently, something is wrong with your ice dispenser, so I had to dig a bit to get this ice out. But don't worry. I think it's working now."

"That's so sweet of you," Lyndia gushed. "Every time I call in a repairman, it's hundreds of dollars. It's like they look at the inn and automatically mark up their services."

"No problem." He set the tray down on the faux stone edge of the firepit, and I used the excuse of picking one as a reason to be out of my seat. No imprints on the glass except for the impression of hurry.

Still sitting on her lounge chair, Lyndia shook her head at the glass Tyrus offered her and stared up into his face with a wide smile. "Hey, I wanted to ask you to come over tonight to roast hot dogs and marshmallows? It'll be fun."

"I wish," he said, picking up a glass. "But I've got plans tonight."

"Oh, that's too bad." Lyndia's shoulders slumped, and her eyes took on a mournful expression. "I was really hoping. What are you doing?"

Tyrus downed half his water in a single long draw. "Just helping Micaela with her kids."

"That's so sweet of you," Lyndia said. "They've never really had anyone but Holt, and he's a little old for beach soccer. I really do need to get back in touch with her. We used to be such good friends as teens."

If that was a hint to invite Lyndia tonight, Tyrus didn't take the bait. Was he merely being nice to Lyndia, his friend's granddaughter, or was he playing both her and Micaela? The cold presence was no longer pushing at me, so there was no hint from that direction. The way I saw it, Lyndia couldn't begin to compete with Micaela in looks, or in sophistication for that matter, but she was an heiress now—especially with the greedy Nigel out of the way.

Eyeing her still-slumped shoulders, Tyrus relented. "Maybe

I could stop by for marshmallows after. But it would probably be late."

Lyndia's smile was back. "That would be fabulous. Text me when you're on your way, okay?"

"Sure." Tyrus finished his water. "I have to take off."

"Okay. I've got a meeting myself in a bit." Lyndia jumped up from her chair, spreading her arms as she looked down at her very short shorts. "You think this is okay for my meeting with real estate developers?"

Tyrus's gaze ran down the length of her bare legs with undisguised approval. "You look great."

I gave him a flat stare. "It depends on what kind of impression you want to make."

Lyndia's gaze dropped to my bare feet. "And what kind of impression is it if you don't wear shoes?"

Touché. I might think shorts weren't business attire, but most people would wear shoes to their important meetings. "It says I'm more comfortable without shoes that always hurt my back, and I don't care who stares because of it."

Lyndia laughed. "You are my kind of person. I'm going to wear the shorts. They'll be too busy underestimating me to see what hits them."

She might have a point.

Tyrus chuckled as he moved away. "See you later."

I barely noticed his leaving as my gaze focused on the lush bushes along the property line, heavy with clusters of tiny, deep purple berries. "Hey, those are black elderberries." I took a few steps toward the fence to be sure. My father had used the ripened berries to make tinctures to stave off sickness, but the uncooked fruit and the rest of the plant were poisonous to humans.

"My grandpa made elderberry wine every year, and we also keep them for the birds. Our guests loved to watch the birds." She gave a little groan. "Of course, the bushes have to be trimmed every year and the shoots cut, or they creep clear up to my pool fence."

"That could be bad if any of your guests are children." It wasn't likely anyone would die from the amount of raw berries they might accidentally ingest, but they might need a hospital, and sick guests wouldn't be good for business.

"That's what I always told my grandpa, but he was careful." A wistfulness had entered her tone, and I stifled a rush of pity. I had a job to do.

"So, about Nigel," I said, pausing to take another sip of water. "Now that the police are looking at Holt as a suspect, Shannon and I are doing our own searching. If your uncle wouldn't take off on his own, who besides you would have a reason to want him gone?"

She blinked at me. "Me? Oh, you can't think that. Sure, he was an evil creep, but I'm the one who brought him here. And there's no way a judge would give him half the inn just because he showed up, right?"

"I've seen worse things happen. Nigel was Welby's son, after all."

"If you ask me, Nigel's ex-wife has to be behind his disappearance. She's the only person I know who hates him more than my grandfather did. He owes her a ton of back alimony and for a car she claims he stole from her." She stepped closer to me as if making sure no one would hear, though the family that had been in the pool was leaving. "She came here yesterday and yelled at me in front of three guests, screaming that she was going to get her money. It was frightening. I knew I was right not to let her stay here when she called last week asking for a free room."

"I think you're right, but unfortunately, she ended up at Bonnie and Holt's."

Lyndia shook her head, her expression pained. "Oh, I'm so sorry. She's horrible. Nigel was right that she's a money-grubbing, two-timing . . . wench!"

Wench? That was far out of her generation's vocabulary, so she must be quoting Nigel. "What about children?"

"Children?"

"There's a rumor that Nigel has a child."

She shook her head. "Not that I know of. And I was around him constantly for weeks, so he probably would have mentioned it. But you could ask his ex-wife. Maybe that's why they broke up. I wouldn't be surprised. He seems the kind who would cheat."

"I will. But while I'm here, can I take a look at whatever belongings Nigel left behind? There could be a clue in his stuff."

"I'm sorry, I gave it all to the police. I went through everything first, looking for my grandfather's will. I was sure he'd hidden it. But there wasn't anything. It was only two suitcases." She made a face. "He wasn't big on personal hygiene."

I held back a groan. I'd have to see if Shannon could get me access, and if I didn't find any imprints in the common areas here at the hotel, I'd have to let Lyndia in on my ability so she'd give me access to the rooms where Nigel had stayed.

"When he was here, where did he mostly hang out?"

She shrugged. "Always under my feet, it seemed. Seriously, that man was scary. Like he was afraid he wouldn't get his money if he let me out of his sight too long. I know this sounds awful, but I'm glad he's gone."

I didn't blame her.

Footsteps drew our attention to two people coming toward the inn from the side parking lot. They were thirty-something men with power suits that made Lyndia seem young and inexperienced. I hoped they wouldn't eat her alive, shorts and all.

"Looks like my appointment is here," Lyndia said, coming to her feet. "Really, it was so nice meeting you."

"You too." I fumbled in my dress pocket for a card with my cell phone number on it. "Please call me if you find anything of Nigel's that you forgot to pack, okay? It could really help Holt."

She didn't glance at the card. "I absolutely will. And please come back before you leave Florida—and bring Shannon so I can catch up with him." She grinned and lifted one bare shoulder, shutting her eyes halfway in a manner that unfortunately emphasized her pinched face. "We could roast hot dogs."

"Sure," I said, smiling back. "And I can take the tray and glasses inside for you. I don't know where they go, but I'll put them on the counter in the dining room."

"I'd appreciate that. Anywhere is fine."

Something about her made me want to protect her from the shark-like investors. "Uh, you might want to let Holt and Bonnie know about the offer—if you get one. They might have good advice about how to proceed."

"They've been so supportive. I'll absolutely do that."

I bent down to pick up the tray, which felt cool to my touch. Instantly, a recent imprint captured my attention.

If it wasn't in Welby's office—and I was pretty sure I'd searched the whole thing—where would he have hidden it? The safe had been the logical place, but there had been nothing there either. I had to find it.

What if it was destroyed? A brief moment of helplessness filled me at the thought.

No, I'd find it. I had to.

Balancing the tray carefully, I pushed open the back door. The women glanced over at me, and I pasted a smile onto my face. I couldn't talk to Lyndia with Bonnie's daughter-in-law here. It would have to wait. But I would somehow convince her.

"Are you okay?" Lyndia's hand touched my arm.

I looked into her concerned face, trying to separate my thoughts from those of the imprint. "I'm fine. Sorry. Just looking at the firepit. I think I'll put one on my patio." At Shannon's place, I meant.

"Oh, you'll love it!" Lyndia said. "I wanted mine three feet wide, so I had to do a special order, but if you want the standard size, you can get them at any home improvement store. They have a bunch of different kinds. Some of the table ones even have a base large enough to hide a bottle of propane if you can't run a gas line."

"Thanks. I'll look into it." I drew away as more imprints played from the tray, but they were muted and unimportant. I could finally think again.

What had Tyrus Lockwood been looking for in the Magnolia Inn office? Did it by chance have anything to do with the missing will? Any doubt I had of him being connected to the case was gone. I had to figure out what he was up to before he hurt either Lyndia or Micaela and the boys.

Chapter 8

I passed the real estate investors on my way out of the pool area, their eyes sliding over me in calculation. Maybe they thought I was here to make a competing offer, or possibly that I was someone they would have to fire once they bought the inn.

I took the tray through the dining room to a kitchen where the employee Deanna was putting away the breakfast items. "Hi," I said. "Can I put these somewhere?"

"I'll take them," she muttered with a sour look, grabbing the tray from me and nearly toppling the glasses as she set them on the counter near the sink.

I pasted on my best smile. "Sorry to add to your work. Tyrus told us about the icemaker. I hope it's good now."

She glanced toward a huge, stainless steel box on the counter. "What's wrong with my icemaker?"

"It wasn't giving you trouble today?"

She motioned to the ice water in Lyndia's untouched glass. "Does it look like it's giving me trouble?"

Okay. So Tyrus's story had been a complete coverup, which I'd already guessed but wanted to verify.

"Anyway, I'm Holt and Bonnie's daughter-in-law, Autumn," I said, extending a hand for a direct approach.

"The one who married their son, the police detective?"

"That's right. They asked us to look into Nigel Carr's disappearance. Do you have a moment to answer a few questions?"

Her eyes narrowed. "What kind of questions?"

"What did you think about Nigel Carr?"

"Him!" Deanna flushed, her already ruddy skin darkening further. "He was a leach. If you ask me, it's good riddance to bad rubbish!"

"I take it you didn't like him."

She snorted. "Not at all. Welby was a kind and decent man. He didn't deserve such a son. And right now I'm doing the work of two people, but I'm doing it because he needs me to carry on until his heir can take over."

"Lyndia may be selling the place, unfortunately."

Sudden tears welled in her eyes. "I know. It's a downright shame." She tucked a strand of hair that had escaped the ponytail behind her ear before glancing downward. "It would break Welby's heart to know that. He loved this place. And he always thought the inn would be a good way for Lyndia to support herself when he was gone."

I began reassessing my original impression of her. Underneath her brusque nature, she had cared about her employer, and all these changes probably made her worry about the future. If the inn were sold, she'd be out of a job, for one thing. Was that enough motive to also make her a suspect in Nigel's disappearance?

"The police think Holt is a suspect, so we need to find him."

Deanna clicked her tongue. "The police are idiots. They're

probably buying into the ex-wife's claims. But I'm pretty sure Nigel is off plotting a new way to steal the inn. Especially after he and Lyndia had words."

My interest peaked. "When was this?"

"About two weeks ago."

"So two weeks after Welby died? And less than a week before Nigel went missing?"

She thought a moment. "Sounds about right."

"What did they talk about?"

"Oh, it wasn't talking, it was screaming. Lyndia said she wasn't going to let him steal her birthright, and Nigel said he was Welby's son, but if she didn't do what he wanted, he'd do something . . . I didn't hear what. They stopped when I came into the office to let them know someone needed help at the desk. But they were both angry, and there was something burning in the garbage can."

"Any idea what?"

She shook her head.

"Did you tell the police this?"

She nodded. "Of course. I also told them something was wrong with the way Welby died, but they said it was old age." She snorted. "If you could have seen him two years ago, you'd know what I was talking about."

Shannon had said the same thing, so maybe I shouldn't dismiss the idea so easily. "Was there an autopsy?"

"No." She rolled her eyes. "He was old and had been sick for a year." Her lips pursed and her chin wobbled. "He was a good man. A good friend to me and my late husband."

"I'm really sorry." I paused a moment before continuing. "So where did Nigel spend most of his time while he was here?"

"Out in the pool mostly, or in the office playing solitaire.

He was lazy. Wouldn't even go to the desk if someone rang the bell."

The office again. I needed to get in there. Was it locked? If Tyrus had gotten in, maybe it wasn't.

"What about Tyrus Lockwood?"

"What about him?"

"What's your impression of him?"

She frowned. "Welby liked him, but I think he's a liar."

Exactly my own thoughts, especially in light of his most recent imprint. "You ever see him with Nigel?"

She shook her head. "No. But Nigel was only here a few weeks before Welby passed away, and they mostly avoided each other. Tyrus would always come to play checkers with Welby early, before Nigel got his lazy butt out of bed. Since Welby died, Tyrus hasn't been around much."

That didn't seem to go with what I'd seen between Lyndia and Tyrus, but it was good to have another perspective.

"Can I see the office?" I asked. "I'm looking for something in particular that Nigel might have left behind."

"Like what? The police already took his stuff because Lyndia was threatening to throw it out." Her eyes widened. "Unless . . . I think his deck of cards might still be in the office."

Cards he'd played with often might be exactly what I needed. "Can I see them?"

"Sure. But wait a minute. I need to do something first." She turned and picked up a drawstring pouch from the counter and strode with it to a door, which opened to a large pantry. She tried to hang the drawstring on a hook, but she was missing it by an inch. I went over to help her.

"Thanks," she said. "We must have another dead mouse in the wall. It happens at least once a year, but this pouch will get rid of the stench. If the health departments smells it, they'll give us a warning. I don't know how the mice get into the wall, because they aren't in my pantry. I make sure of that. We probably need to check for holes from the outside to make sure they aren't getting in that way."

I looked around the neatly organized shelves with every single package in its own plastic food container or in original glass jars. There *was* a faint putrid smell, however.

"What's in the pouch?" I asked.

She shrugged. "Some kind of charcoal smell absorber. They're good to have around. We sometimes have to use them in the rooms after certain guests." She cracked a smile at that, the first I'd ever seen. "We get people with weird diets and that often creates awful smells."

"I've used baking soda quite a bit on antiques."

"Right, it's the same principle. We use that too in the rooms on occasion. It's always better to eliminate the smell instead of covering it up with fragrances."

"I agree."

She started to leave, but I hesitated. There were no holes in the wall or anything that looked out of place, but in light of the bullet and the blood the police had found on the hat, I had to ask. "Are there any hidden doors, or places in the inn? Big enough for a person?"

Her laugh was derisive. "You mean for Nigel to hide in?"

"Or someone to hide him in."

She stared at me, her jaw dropping an inch, but she seemed to consider the possibility. "I know this inn better than Lyndia or even Welby because I'm over the cleaning crew, and I can't think of a single spot, except the attic, which I was just in yesterday. Besides, you'd need a lot more than a little bag of odor absorber to hide something like that. Believe me, Nigel is not here, alive or dead, and as I said before, good riddance. Wherever he is, I hope he doesn't come back."

That seemed to be the universal opinion of Nigel Carr.

"Come on." She motioned for me to leave. I touched the light switch on the way out, after she turned it off, but there were no related imprints. "I've got to make sure the maid has finished her rounds," she added, "but I'll show you where the office is."

Either she really didn't care what Lyndia might think about my investigation, or she was the one really running things around here. After meeting Lyndia, I suspected the latter. Welby might have protected the young woman too much for her own good in these past years.

I touched other things along the way to the front desk—a lamp, a book, a chair, a reading table—dawdling enough that Deanna was beginning to show frustration. But if Nigel had touched these things, he hadn't cared enough about them to leave imprints. Neither had Lyndia, though I picked up a few imprints of gentle pride that I suspected might have been left by Welby before his death.

The office behind the reception desk was hot and muggy compared to the rest of the inn. "You don't keep it locked?" I asked.

"Not during the day. But we usually have a reception clerk. Lyndia doesn't schedule one on Sundays unless we have a change-over in guests, which we don't today. She or I usually man the desk."

By which I suspected she meant that *she* manned the reception desk, though maybe Lyndia would be in here if not for her meeting.

She strode to the desk and began opening drawers. "Now where did he put those cards?"

"There's no computer?" I asked.

"Not in here. We only have a laptop in a drawer at the front desk, and it's mostly for scheduling and for certain orders. Welby was old school. We have a printer in one of the cabinets out front too."

While she looked, I let my hands trail over knickknacks, the filing cabinet, and even the books on a beautiful bookcase next to the door. I suspected most of the imprints belonged to Welby, many of which were years old.

Must show Lyndia this.

The new couple will love to hear about the festival tomorrow.

The fresher food was definitely more expensive, but all the satisfied guests made it worth it. Word of mouth made sales.

How was I going to pay that bill? I'd have to cut up the credit card and tighten our belts for a few months.

Holt is a good friend. I'd have never been able to finish the covered parking or the pool without him.

More followed, all similar. I had the impression Welby was a calm, loving person who had learned over a lifetime that slow and steady and honest were the best ways to run an inn and win friends.

Two imprints stood out to me. The first was six months ago when Welby was worried about his health: *I can't understand it, he thought. I've always been as strong as a horse.* The other from two months earlier in which he was thinking about his son Nigel, and his desire to see him: *Maybe Lyndia can find him for me. She's good with the computer.*

That made three people who were puzzled about Welby's sudden decline, and while Lyndia had indicated she'd found and brought Nigel here, it appeared maybe Welby had prompted the action. Yet Lyndia had said all they did was argue. About what? I wished I could go into Welby's things to relive some of the confrontations.

"Here they are." Deanna pulled out some papers from the bottom drawer of the desk. "Do you need to put them in a sack or something?"

"Do you have one?" It was more of an opportunity to get her out of the way than to take the cards.

"Be right back."

I moved around the desk, sitting down in the chair and checking it for imprints. I half-expected to find the cold presence there waiting for me, but I felt only the moist heat of the room. Faded imprints flooded through my fingertips, mostly good ones. This was Welby's domain until six months ago. That must have been when he'd started spending more time in his bed.

I leaned over to touch the cards. Imprints came, but sluggishly as if seen through a haze of alcohol. Lyndia had been right about Nigel and his penchant for alcohol. Then, almost as if a curtain had suddenly risen, I experienced a clear, vivid imprint from the week before Nigel went missing.

I stared at the burning paper inside a trash can. Bold handwriting appeared along the top stating that it was the last will and testament of Welby Carr, dated two years earlier.

The body of the text quickly darkened and burned, followed by the title and date, until it was all ash.

Anger burned through me. I couldn't use the will now, and the poison wasn't working fast enough on the old man. I needed a payday after all these years.

The imprint ended abruptly as the imprinter's hand left the cards. Earlier ones were more of the muted, alcoholic ones.

Poison. Did that mean Nigel had something to do with Welby's death? If so, maybe we weren't looking at one murder, but two.

I lifted my finger and checked it again in order to watch more carefully. I couldn't see a hand on the cards, so it was possible someone besides Nigel had imprinted the scene of the burning will. If this was the day of the argument between Lyndia and Nigel, either it hadn't begun yet, or there had been a pause.

And was this the will Holt had seen? I wasn't sure of the timeline for the agreement between him and Welby, but the timing seemed to fit.

Footsteps sounded in the hallway, and I quickly ran my hands near the pens in the cup on the desk. Pens often held good imprints, and these buzzed with them, but there wasn't time to investigate each individually.

"Here we go," Deanna said, appearing in the doorway and extending a gallon zip bag.

"Thank you." I carefully worked the deck of cards inside them—and not just for show. If Welby had been poisoned, maybe there was residue. Though now that I was removing them, the police might take issue with any evidence they contained.

"Will that be all?" Deanna asked.

"Yes, you've been a big help."

She turned to go, and I swept up the entire batch of pens from the cup and slid them into the bag, tucking it under my arm. Deanna turned back to wait for me, and I passed her, probably looking guilty, hoping she didn't catch sight of the pens.

We walked away from the desk together, where she paused

as if waiting for me to head out the front doors. "I'm going to make some calls," I said. "Do you mind if I sit in the lobby for a bit?"

"Of course not." She gave me a sharp nod. "Ring the bell if you need anything. I can hear it upstairs for the most part. Unless I have a vacuum on."

"Thanks again."

She took two steps away before turning back to me, her thin shoulders curled forward. "I hope you find that horrible man, but only for Holt's sake."

"Speaking of that, Holt said there was some debate as to whether the land one of his cottages is on belongs to Magnolia Inn or Haven Retreat. Do you know anything about that?"

She nodded. "Two years ago, Welby agreed that Holt could restore the cottage on it and do the landscaping. In return, Welby wouldn't contest his claim to the land. Welby didn't have the time to do anything with the land anyway, and he needed Holt's help—though if you ask me, Holt would have helped him anyway. Holt and Bonnie were his best friends, and even before that, Holt was always coming over to work on one project or another with him. Welby had more than his share of work since he was running the inn practically alone before I came." She glanced over her shoulder in the direction of the back door, which I couldn't see from my position. "Lyndia could grow into it, I suppose, but she's not very good with money or service, so she wasn't involved in the actual day-to-day running of the place until Welby got sick last year." She shook her head. "Frankly, I don't know if she'll be able to do it long term."

I understood the concern after meeting Lyndia. But maybe Bonnie and Holt could help her as they had Welby.

"Would you be willing to testify that Welby intended to retract his interest? If it comes to that?"

"Of course. Anything to help Holt and Bonnie. And I bet Lyndia would too."

I wasn't as sure about Lyndia. "Thank you." I nodded and started for the set of couches near the entry but changed my mind when she disappeared. Going back to the reception desk, I touched the edge of the bell to read the imprints.

Hurry.

What is taking so long?

Wasn't like this when the old guy was alive.

This place used to be the best. I'm going to have to find a new place to stay.

All the brief imprinted thoughts came from the past month, and if they were any indication, Magnolia Inn was quickly losing popularity. But Tyrus hadn't imprinted on the bell today, and none of the other imprints were useful.

I dumped out the pens on the reception desk, sighing when I realized a camera above the desk, pointed at the entrance, probably picked me up too. Oh, well, if anyone looked at the footage, they would have to wonder for themselves about the pens.

Spread out like this, I could find the ones that buzzed the most—and I quickly narrowed it to two. The first held nothing of importance, but on the last was an imprint from four and a half months ago that captured me.

My hand shook as I tried to write. It was wrinkled and knobby, almost unrecognizable with all the weight I'd lost in the past six months. I didn't have much strength these days, so I had to do this quickly.

But my hand shook too much, and an urge to vomit overtook me. This isn't normal, I thought. Something is wrong.

Dear Grandson, I wrote. So much effort for two words.

The door to the office opened, and Deanna stood in the doorway. "There you are. I've been looking for you all over. Why don't I help you back to bed? This can wait. Come on. I've made a glass of iced tea for you."

"You're too good to me," I said.

She laughed. "Better than you deserve."

It was our customary exchange, and one that was actually true. Deanna had been a godsend these past two years. My wife was long gone, and so was Deanna's husband, though only recently. If I weren't so sick, maybe she would overlook the twenty-five years between us. No . . .

I let the thought go. I needed more time.

The imprint was over, and I still knew nothing more, except that I liked Welby, and that nearly five months ago, he'd had a crush on Deanna. Was the grandson the child we suspected Nigel had tucked away somewhere?

I turned from the counter with a sigh. Unless we knew Welby had been poisoned, it was all pointless speculation. Except for the imprint about poison on the cards, I had no new information and nothing about Nigel's disappearance. I thought of going back to the firepit to attempt further communication with the cold presence, but the buzzing of my phone in my dress pocket stopped me. Hoping it was Shannon, I answered without looking at the caller ID.

"I have news," Elliot said without a greeting. "And I didn't want to send it over text."

I headed toward the front door of the inn, lowering my voice even though no one was around to hear me. "Did you find Nigel's child? Because I'm pretty sure Welby Carr knew about him."

"No, I'm banging my head against privacy laws at the moment, so I have to do more research. If we knew a general age, it would be easier."

"I'll talk to Nigel's ex-wife. She might know more. But what's so important that you couldn't text?"

"It's about your new father-in-law."

My heartbeat quickened. "What?" I demanded, knowing Elliot's way of getting bogged down by details. "Just spit it out." I pushed open one of the inn doors and stepped out into the bright sunlight, blinking at the sudden change.

"A year before he retired, he shot a seventeen-year-old boy in a drug bust. He claimed the boy pulled a gun on his partner, but when they searched the body later, there wasn't one. Even though the drugs and the buyer were taken into custody, another suspect got away and was never identified. There was a huge backlash from the media because of the missing gun. The mother publicly accused him of police brutality and setting up her son."

"That's terrible."

"It was—for both Holt Martin and the mother. My source says Holt was exonerated of all charges, but he asked for a desk job and stayed off patrol for the last year he was on the force."

"Ah," I said, heading up the sidewalk in the direction of Haven Retreat. "That explains a lot."

"I thought so. You'll have to tell Shannon."

"If he hasn't already learned it himself."

"I'll send you the information—unless you think it'll get me in trouble with him."

"Send it. I got your back."

He laughed. "Good, because he can be kind of scary."

"It's why I love him so much." I couldn't hold back a smile.

"I hope the police there don't somehow twist Holt's background as a motive for your missing man."

"There's no way it could be connected—unless Nigel Carr knew about it." I thought of the witness who had claimed to see Holt meeting with Nigel by the pier. "Holt doesn't seem to want Shannon to know, though, so I guess they might make an argument for blackmail. But without proof, it would be circumstantial."

"Right. What about you? Any leads?" he asked.

I paused as I passed the boulder marking the Haven Retreat property border. "Yes," I said, dropping into a decorative bench under a tree that grew on the other side of the path. "A few, actually. Tyrus Lockwood was searching for something in the office at Magnolia Inn, and he has plans to convince Lyndia to do something before the police ruin his plan. He's also been angry enough to want someone dead. Then there's a puzzling imprint about him losing his chance again with Micaela. I have no idea what that means, but she's been working for the Martins for the past decade or so, and he's been coming to Magnolia Inn for about that long. They could have run into each other."

"I'll have to check if there's a connection between them."

"Do that, but there's more. I found an imprint about someone burning a will Welby Carr wrote two years ago. And another indicating that someone might have been poisoning him. My first guess is that his son Nigel was trying to cash in, but I don't have proof."

"Really. Wow, that's an unexpected twist."

I forgave his eagerness. "That's what I thought. I asked about an autopsy, but I don't think there was one."

Elliot snorted. "Of course not. You're talking about an old

man who'd been sick. Many insurances, including Medicaid and Medicare, don't pay for them. And even with an autopsy, they normally only test for certain things that might not uncover a deliberate poisoning, unless it's suspected. Many poisons damage the liver and other organs, which can make them look worn or maybe caused by alcohol consumption."

I didn't ask how he knew. "I guess what I need to know next is how can I get a body exhumed?"

"The police would have to be involved, or you'd need permission from next of kin, and you'd need a way to pay if the police don't order it themselves."

Would Lyndia agree to an autopsy? She seemed to be grieving for her grandfather, and I didn't know what I'd do in her place. After all, it wouldn't change the fact of his death, even if it might shed light on her uncle's disappearance.

"I'll have to bring this up with Holt and Bonnie. They might be able to convince her."

"In the meantime, I'll keep researching. Do you have any more suspects for me to pull backgrounds on?"

"Not really. The only new people I've met since we last talked are Lyndia Carr, and you already knew about her, and her employee, Deanna something. She's a little strange, but she seems to have admired Welby."

"Did you say Deanna?" Elliot asked.

"Yeah. She's worked at Magnolia Inn for about two years."

Silence reigned except for the *click-clack* of a keyboard. "Would it be Deanna Lowe?"

"I don't know her last name. She's fifty-something, slender, and blond."

"I'll send you a picture."

It came through a minute later, and despite the shade

overhead, I had to brighten my screen all the way to see a young woman with dark hair staring back at me. I squinted at the picture. "If it's her, she's aged a lot."

"Let me send you another one."

The next photo was familiar, even though her hair was still dark. "That's definitely her. Only she's blond now."

"Uh-oh."

I didn't like that sound.

"Deanna Lowe is the mother of the boy Holt shot," Elliot rushed on, his voice tight. "And if she's there so close to Holt, I'm betting it's not a coincidence."

I didn't think so either. Which made me reevaluate everything she'd said. Was her apparent admiration of Holt a ruse? How she felt about her former employee was also now in doubt, though I didn't know how his possible poisoning might connect with Holt's past.

Deanna had prepared iced tea for Welby in the imprint, and she likely had many other times after that day. Maybe she'd made him tea every day until he died. If so, what had really been in the glass?

Chapter 9

I knew even before opening the door to Rose Petal Cottage that Shannon wasn't there because the invisible thread connecting us didn't thicken.

For as long as I could remember, I'd been able to "feel" my adoptive parents through a tiny thread connecting us, one that grew thicker with proximity. I'd felt it with my sister even before we knew we were related, and then later with her daughter and my biological father. Shannon was the only non-family person I could feel, the attachment growing slowly over the past year. I still couldn't feel the connection with him nearly as well as with my sister, but I did feel it.

I opened the door, wondering where he'd gone. It wasn't far because the invisible thread connecting us was still tangible to me rather than a faint sensation. He'd need support if he'd already uncovered his father's secret. If not, maybe he still needed time to cool down.

His wallet was on the counter in the kitchenette, along with the rental car keys and the master key Bonnie had given us—more signs that he hadn't gone far. His laptop was also on the counter, opened to a search with Holt Martin's name. A quick look told me the entries were all reviews of the inn or about other Holt Martins, of which there were plenty. That suggested Shannon might not yet have discovered his father's past.

My sundress already felt sticky from my morning's activities, so I changed into camouflage hiking shorts and a tank top. The shorts went almost to my knees, but they were snug—no chance of anyone thinking I was pregnant in these. After Holt's comment that morning about it not being his fault I wasn't expecting, maybe that was the real reason for my change.

I rubbed myself liberally with a copious amount of my best sunscreen before heading to the door of the cottage, going back at the last moment for the master key. I needed to find out what Tyrus had been looking for and also check out Nigel's ex-wife. If I had the key, I wouldn't have to pester Shannon.

Or wait for him to give approval.

Outside, I walked a few feet, looking around for Shannon. Or rather, feeling for him. I cut across the grass instead of following the path and was surprised to deviate around a bush and run into a group of over a dozen people. I recognized Tyrus, Micaela and her boys, the honeymooners I'd passed on the stairs yesterday, and Freddi, the missing man's ex-wife, along with others I hadn't seen before—probably all guests at Haven Retreat.

Craning my neck and standing on my toes, I caught sight of the two police detectives I'd met before, along with a crime scene investigator and two uniformed officers. One of the latter held the leash of a dog while another was digging into the grass with a shovel. I spied Shannon, Holt, and Bonnie at the edge of the group, slightly apart from the others. Holt and Bonnie were dressed up as if they'd recently arrived from church. Bonnie's face was red with fury, which Shannon mirrored, but Holt's mouth quirked with an odd smile. I passed the people, who must be guests, and came up on Shannon's left side.

"What's going on?" I asked him.

"They got a warrant for a cadaver dog." The words radiated his disgust. "And now it has found something."

"I take it Nigel's blood was on the bullet?" I asked.

Shannon gave a short nod. "And on the cap. They must have called in a million favors to get the results so quickly."

I gave Holt a sidelong glance. He was still grinning in the direction of the police officers—no, almost smirking. I'd seen the same expression on his son's face, and whatever this was, it didn't bother him. The grass where they were digging looked a little newer and thinner than the grass around it, but did the police actually believe it could grow that much in the ten days Nigel Carr had been missing?

Bonnie spied me and leaned over in front of her son to say, "They're destroying the new grass. We had to take a section out here because of the crabgrass, and now we'll be back to where we started."

That seemed to galvanize Holt. He stepped forward, his hands outstretched. "Here, give me that shovel," he demanded. "Let me show you how to do it. The least we can do is save the grass."

The uniformed officer looked over at Detective Wallace, who nodded. "Give it to him," she said.

Holt cut a long horizontal line in the grass and then a vertical line from the side of the first line. "This big enough for you?" he asked as he started on a second vertical line. He finished cutting the rectangle and began slicing through the dirt under the roots and rolling the sod back. Shannon and I went to help—Shannon with another shovel that was lying on the ground and me to hold the roll of grass. Tyrus also stepped forward, so I relinquished my spot. No doubt he wanted to impress Micaela.

They'd only gone a foot or two when Holt stopped and grimaced with pain, his hand going to his lower back.

"Shoot," Bonnie muttered. "The darn fool has hurt his back again."

Shannon said something to Holt, who gave his shovel to Tyrus and stood back to watch as the two younger men continued working. When they'd moved a wide swath of sod away from the spot in a single, huge roll, Holt took the shovels from them and handed them to the uniformed officer. "Be my guest. We're not doing all your work for you."

The officer began digging again, his face unhappy, and his partner joined him. I hoped whatever they found wasn't deep, or they'd have a backhoe in here soon, which might further damage the beautiful landscaping.

"What are they hoping to find?" one of the guests asked.

Holt chuckled, and Shannon looked at him. "What is it, Dad?"

Holt drew away from the crowd, motioning to us to follow. "Remember that dog we used to have?"

Shannon thought a moment. "Buster? What ever happened to him?"

"He got old." Holt nodded at the bald spot of dirt. "I buried him here a few months ago. I chose this spot because the crabgrass was taking over, and I needed to fix it anyway."

"Oh, for Pete's sake!" Bonnie said. "You go tell them right now. Here I was worrying about what they'd find." She gave him a shove.

"Hey, it's not my fault," Holt told her. "Well-trained

cadaver dogs are supposed to differentiate between animal and human remains. I'm guessing this one isn't out of training yet, which is why they were able to get him here today on such short notice."

"Well, tell them anyway," she insisted. "Come on. I'll go with you." She dragged him away.

We couldn't hear what Holt said to the police, but they didn't stop digging.

I slipped my hand into Shannon's and was glad when he didn't pull away. "Your dad's going to get himself in trouble."

He shrugged. "Can't blame him. He has nothing to do with that man's disappearance."

"I know. But things might be more involved than we first thought."

His eyes narrowed as he stared at me. "What have you found out?"

His parents chose that moment to return. "Later," I told him. My imprint findings and Elliot's news would have to wait until we were alone. Raising my voice slightly, I said to Bonnie and Holt, "There's something I want to talk to you two about."

"And what would that be?" Holt was rubbing his back, his forehead creased.

"Maybe we should get some ice on that," Bonnie said.

Holt waved her away. "It's fine."

"That's what you said after you fixed those sprinklers at Magnolia Inn and had to stay in bed a whole week." Bonnie pressed her lips together and shook her head.

"Okay, I'll do the ice," Holt said. That resolved, they turned toward me, their faces expectant.

"I just came from Magnolia Inn." I chose my words carefully. "Lyndia doesn't seem to know anything about the arrangements for the land under Frontier Cabin. She's thinking about selling the inn, and she's worried about not getting a good price without that land."

Bonnie gasped. "What? But of course she knew about the arrangement! And she can't sell the inn. Old Welby would roll over in his grave."

"How can you be sure she knew?" I pressed.

"Well . . . I . . . uh," Bonnie spluttered. "I don't know. Anyway, she's a sweet, sweet girl. I'm sure all I have to do is talk to her."

"Right," Holt agreed. "She's probably feeling overwhelmed. We've known her since she was a child, and she's never been . . . um, really strong. I promised Welby I'd look after her, and I will."

"Okay." I was glad they didn't seem worried about Lyndia not backing them up. "There is an employee there—Deanna— and she says she knew about the agreement."

"See?" Holt said. "There's nothing to worry about."

Had eighteen years and blond hair really made it so Holt didn't recognize Deanna Lowe? I hadn't been able to identify her, but Holt would have had much more contact, not only now but at the time when Deanna's son had died.

"The thing is," I said. "I think Welby might have been poisoned. Maybe for as long as a year before he died."

Holt, Bonnie, and Shannon gaped at me for a long minute. Bonnie recovered first. "That makes total sense! I swear, if ever a man should have lived to be a hundred, it was him. And he was only eighty. His father and mother only died a few years back, well into their nineties."

"True," Holt said. "He went jogging on the beach every day. Maybe not as fast as the young kids, but he had more endurance than I did. I wonder if that no-good son of his was responsible. If he weren't missing, I'd have a thing or two to say to him."

"How did you figure it out?" Bonnie stared at me eagerly. "Was it your . . . you know, ability?"

I'd expected them to doubt me, so this immediate acceptance was crazy. Unless they'd been that puzzled at Welby's rapid decline.

"You thinking we need an exhumation?" Shannon said before I could respond. "Is your evidence that strong?"

I nodded. "It was only one imprint, and I know they can be misleading, but the intention was there."

"We'd need permission from next of kin to exhume." Shannon looked over at the still digging officers. "Because it's doubtful they'd believe you. But if we can prove Welby was poisoned, maybe they'd look in a different direction to find Nigel."

"Maybe it was Nigel, and someone found out and threatened him," Bonnie said. "Might have been why he took off."

Shannon frowned. "That doesn't explain his bloody hat."

I looked over my shoulder at the crowd that was still focused intently on the digging. "I can talk to the ex-wife. Looks like she's here."

"Maybe *she's* responsible." Bonnie sent a glare in the woman's direction. "Oh, what my guests must think about all this."

Holt chuckled. "Are you kidding? This is the most excitement they've had all week. It'll be fine." He put his arm around his wife, which was a little awkward given their difference in height.

"Why don't we go talk to Lyndia?" Shannon said to Bonnie.

"I should go say hi anyway. And if she agrees to have Welby tested, we can get the ball rolling. There's no reason why we can't do it fast and have him back in the ground the same day."

"You go," Holt said. "I'm sticking around until they're finished. And maybe I'll start letting our guests know it's a dog buried there. Poor Buster. He's more popular with the guests now than he was when he was alive. He liked to slobber a bit too much." Holt's expression wilted, and I guessed he'd loved the animal, slobber and all.

"There's no guarantee Lyndia will agree," I said. "She's pretty shaken up about her grandfather, and that makes it hard."

"Oh, but that's exactly why she'll want to know," Bonnie insisted. "She really cared about Welby. You should have seen how she worked so hard to get that outdoor firepit ready so he could sit out there and play his checkers." She paused. "I only wish it matched the existing décor better, but I have an idea to help her fix that."

"Well, if she needs more convincing, you'll have to tell her why I suspect poison," I said. "I might be able to find more, if she'd let me see his belongings."

Bonnie let out a frustrated sigh. "Ah, I actually helped her clear out most of Welby's things last week. It was a good thing since she'd been grieving so much. Now she doesn't constantly trip over reminders."

"I'm sure she's saved some things, and the common items they both used would also have imprints."

"If she's not too upset at the idea of exhumation, I'll definitely ask," Bonnie said.

Holt put a hand on his wife's shoulder. "If there's a chance, talk to her about the Frontier Cabin."

"Oh, sweetie." Her voice was all disapproval. "That can wait for another day."

"Okay, whatever." He lifted his hands in surrender, grimacing slightly at the sudden movement.

"And don't forget to ice your back," Bonnie said.

Shannon looked at me. "You coming?"

"I think I'll have a chat with Freddi first," I said. Maybe it was a little bit of wimping out on my part. I didn't want to see Lyndia's reaction about the exhumation. I remembered too well when they'd pulled my adoptive father from the Willamette River after a week of submersion and how he'd looked then. It wasn't something I wanted to think about. "If she agrees to let me look at their private quarters, I can go over later."

Shannon's gaze stayed on my face for several seconds, telling me he suspected my real reason, but like a good husband, he didn't push. "Okay." He leaned in to kiss me unexpectedly on the lips. "I'll meet you back at the cottage, and we'll talk about the rest."

"Right."

As he walked away, I wondered if I should have warned him about Deanna. If Holt had killed her boy, maybe her revenge wouldn't stop with Holt himself. But it was broad daylight, and with Bonnie, Lyndia, and all their guests there, it wasn't likely anything would happen. Besides, Shannon was a capable detective, and I trusted his gut almost as much as my own. He could handle himself, with or without his gun.

I turned back to watch the digging progress. "If I remember correctly, it's fairly deep," Holt said. "Did you know cadaver dogs can detect a body up to fifteen feet underground? But I'm surprised the dog could smell anything. I put stuff in there to absorb the smell just in case. Guess I didn't use enough for an animal that size."

"You mean like those little charcoal bags people use to get rid of the smell of a dead mouse caught in the wall?"

"Yeah." He smiled at me. "All the inns and motels use them. Only with us, it's for birds. They keep getting caught in the dryer exhaust that vents on the roof. If we hear them I can get to them in time, but if we don't they leave a smell."

"How many more would you need for a dog?" I said. *Or a man,* I thought.

"I don't know. I guess a lot. I only had the one, and I knew if I got down deep enough, no one would smell him, regardless."

Pondering this, I moved my toes in the grass, letting the feel of the area seep into my body. My gift always connected me to the ground and earth, even through cement, but it was different here than in Portland, like a new song I was trying to learn. I could feel a sense of permanence, though, a living presence that was hard to describe. There was no cold sensation and nothing to tell me a dog was buried only yards away.

We watched for another minute, and then Holt went to talk to his guests. A few of them began leaving as he personally spread the news about the dog, which was my cue to get working. I beelined toward Freddi, who was on the other side of the crowd, at the edge. Like yesterday, her flamboyant, short-sleeved, hot-pink pantsuit screamed for attention on her voluptuous figure, and if anything, today her blond hair was piled even higher.

I'd read the rest of the information Elliot had sent me about her this morning, and nothing had stood out. She was a forty-eight-year-old hairdresser from Palm Coast, who had a brother and sister-in-law in Orlando, a nephew in Palm Beach, and parents who lived in Miami. She had recently broken up with a boyfriend of several years. There were no red flags to point to her participation in her ex-husband's disappearance.

She glanced at me, and I smiled. "How are you?" I asked, moving closer.

She arched one of her perfect eyebrows. Her pink eye-shadow and heavy false eyelashes should have been garish, but somehow they weren't. "I'm good. You? Oh, you're the woman from yesterday who took my luggage upstairs."

"Yeah. How are you enjoying your stay?"

She smiled, revealing perfect white teeth against her hot-pink lipstick. "Well, it's certainly more exciting today, what with the police here and all."

"That's right," I said, lowering my voice, "of course you'd be interested. You're Nigel Carr's ex-wife." I pulled back slightly, hoping she'd follow so we wouldn't be overheard by the other guests.

She took a few steps with me. "How did you know?"

"I'm Holt and Bonnie's daughter-in-law. My husband is a homicide detective from Oregon, and we're here investigating Nigel's disappearance."

"Ah." She thumbed over her shoulder. "I'm hoping they find him there since those are the detectives on his case. It might be the only way I'll get my money. That man owes me fifty thousand dollars. If he's dead, at least I'll be able to make a claim on his estate."

"Wouldn't it be easier if he were alive?"

She snorted indelicately. "You'd think so, but I've been trying for five years. It's like getting blood from a turnip, or so my daddy always says. I tell you, I wasted ten years of my life on that man. Fifteen if you count the time since I gave him the boot, and I do because he was never truly gone. I deserve something for everything I've been through. Do you know that he borrowed my new car last year and crashed it? He ran my boyfriend off too. That was the end of my patience, I tell you." She half-turned to check on the shoveling.

"How'd you find out that Nigel's father died?" I asked.

She faced me again, folding her arms under her ample chest. "Nigel called me drunk one night a month or so ago. He was always doing that when he was between girlfriends. He said his daddy was sick and that he would be inheriting half an inn, which meant he was a millionaire with the current land prices here in Florida. He was bragging, of course, so I didn't think much of it until last week when the police called to see if I knew where he was. His niece had reported him missing. They also told me his daddy had died, and there wasn't a will. So that's why I'm here—to make sure that evil niece of his doesn't steal my money right out from under me. I also met with the police yesterday to give them a good description and a list of places Nigel might go. To light a fire under them, so to speak. Looks like I did the right thing, too. Calling every day wasn't getting me anywhere." The rush of words ceased, and her attention shifted eagerly back to the growing hole.

Holt was moving to chat with another set of guests, and beyond him I could see Tyrus in a serious grass fight with one of Micaela's twins—Dimas, I was almost sure, the rambunctious one.

I brought my gaze back to Freddi. "And where would Nigel go?"

"Ha!" she said. "That's just it. He had nowhere to go. It was work and to the bars for drinks and to pick up girls. That and to smoke himself to death."

Another two guests wandered off, the call of the beach a greater lure than the animal bones Holt promised them.

"So, about your ex-husband's niece," I asked. "I take it you don't know her very well?"

"I know her well enough," Freddi said without hesitation. "She's slime, plain and simple. And I do mean she's simple, meaning dumb. Do you know she wouldn't even let me stay there? I was lucky this place had a cancellation when I called last week, or I would have been stuck in some sleazy motel."

"She might have been full. These places book far in advance."

"Well, yes, but we're practically family, and I own a good chunk of that inn now. She could have found some corner for me so I didn't have to pay two hundred and fifty a night. Well, two can play that game. I'm not backing down just because Nigel's got himself into some trouble. Besides, like I said, I'm more likely to get the money now."

"That makes it seem you have a motive in his disappearance." The words slipped out before I could stop them. If Freddi left Haven Retreat in a huff, would Bonnie be relieved or angry?

But Freddi laughed. "Oh, that's a good one. Yes, I could have lured him to a pier or someplace while he was drunk and pushed him off. I only wish I'd had the courage to do that years ago, the cheating jerk." With one hand on her hip and the other examining her long, manicured fingernails, she looked like a brassy mother-in-law in a bad TV sitcom. "Anyway, if you ask me, it's that girl who has motive, what with all the money involved."

"You mean Lyndia?" At her nod, I added, "Well, she did grow up with her grandfather. Why shouldn't she inherit? He was like a father to her. Of course she would expect to keep running the inn."

"I guess so. But Nigel seemed sure she'd sell. He said she was as crazy about spending money as her mother."

"He knew her mother?"

"Well, yeah, who doesn't know their sister-in-law?" She heaved a sigh and turned back to the digging. "What if he really is down there?"

"It's Buster, the Martin's dog. He died a few months ago." I waved at the others. "That's why people are leaving."

"Hmm, you don't say."

"I heard Nigel has a child. Do you know anything about that?"

She waved her hand. "Not really. I think he said something about it when we first met, but it was an adoption situation, a closed adoption, so it didn't concern me. Although he could have a dozen more children I don't know about since then, especially since I couldn't get pregnant. He wasn't faithful." Her voice had grown hard with this explanation. "Maybe that's where all our money went when we lived together." She tossed her head, and her beehive hair drooped ever so slightly. "Anyway, that's all behind me now. I don't care if he's dead, I just want my money."

Her honesty had been refreshing up until that moment, and I'd felt sorry for her about not being able to have a child, but these last words came across as callous. "Witnesses say the inn was left to Lyndia, not Nigel," I told her.

"Well, they can't prove what they can't find, and I'm not giving up my claim." The calculation in her eyes was unmistakable. But was it because of her greed or my mentioning the will? Did she know anything about it? I couldn't begin to tell unless

I read more of her imprints. Maybe there were additional ones on her rings, the ones I'd glimpsed anger on yesterday.

I extended a hand. "Well, it was nice to meet you."

"Same here." She barely grabbed the tips of my fingers, shaking once before releasing me. No chance of touching her rings.

I eased away from her. Could she be responsible for Nigel's disappearance? Yes. Absolutely. I could imagine her pushing him off a ledge—and then going to get her long nails repaired afterward.

So did I go check out her room now or follow up on Tyrus? He seemed in no hurry to leave Micaela. Maybe they had plans all afternoon, and not only for dinnertime as I'd inferred at Lyndia's. And while Freddi was only a suspect, I knew Tyrus was not only hiding something from the police, but he had an agenda with Lyndia.

Tyrus first, I decided. With the way the Martins felt about Micaela, the sooner I figured him out, the better.

I was already at the edge of the few remaining onlookers, and no one looked my way as I retreated across the grass, except Lucio, the twin who wasn't trying to stuff grass down his mother's shirt. He waved and then walked over to Tyrus, who lifted him up on his shoulders for a better view of the growing pit.

I stopped first at Rose Petal Cottage for a stack of fresh towels—in case Tyrus happened to come back and catch me. It wasn't a solid reason to be inside his place, since I didn't work for Haven Retreat, but it was better than nothing.

Once I reached Frontier Cabin, I rechecked the antler door for additional imprints. But after reliving the three imprints from earlier, there were only impressions of sadness mixed with determination. Still, the initial imprints were important enough to reaffirm my need to see what else Tyrus Lockwood might be hiding. Glancing once over my shoulder, I unlocked the door and slipped inside.

Chapter 10

The interior of Frontier Cabin was about as large as Rose Petal Cottage, and there was even a loft for sleeping, but the similarities ended there. While Rose Petal Cottage looked like something from *Snow White and the Seven Dwarves,* Frontier Cabin came directly from *Little House on the Prairie.*

Near a stone fireplace sat a couch whose frame was made of rough-hewn logs, covered with quilted cushions I was sure Bonnie had made herself. The square table in the kitchenette area was made of logs cut lengthwise and pieced together while the chair bottoms were a crosscut of a log, complete with age rings that were fascinating to see. Rag rugs, an antler chandelier, a black cast-iron stove, and cast-iron pans hanging on the wall above the short counter added to the frontier feel. The place was perfectly neat except for the stacks of paper on the table. Unless someone had cleaned today, Tyrus must be naturally neat.

I started at the table, touching the loose pages, which were mostly handwritten except for a single neat stack that appeared to have come out of the printer on the nearby countertop. No imprints on the papers or the printer, except for one of frustration a year earlier when the machine had jammed.

The heavy-duty laptop on the table was closed, and I left it for last, touching the metal case with my fingertips. Imprints came immediately, all in a stream, but nothing about the missing man or Welby. That puzzled me, so I opened the laptop in order to touch the keyboard, thinking perhaps the keys had imprinted individually, as they often did.

The screensaver surprised me and sent a shock of unease through my belly. It was a picture of Micaela on the beach at sunset, her swimsuit coverup slipping down over one shoulder as she intently watched a handful of sand drip between her fingers. The waves covered her feet, and the wind whipped her curly dark hair from her face. Her Mozambican heritage was prominent in the bronzing of her beautiful skin. She was both exotic and unreachable. It was an amazing photograph.

But this Micaela was clearly much younger than the one I'd met yesterday. This Micaela was full of hope and excitement and maybe even love.

"Okay," I murmured, my mind racing. Tyrus must have taken this picture from one of his previous visits. But why didn't she recognize him? Was he stalking her?

I moved my fingers over the keys and the flat edges of the keyboard. As with the rest of the laptop, there were lots of imprints.

I have to find a way to get closer to her. I've been here six weeks already, and where am I? I stared at her face on the screen. "*I can't let you go again without trying,*" I said aloud.

I was seriously lame! I'd let this thing with Welby and Nigel overtake me. If I didn't act now, I had only myself to blame. With a decisive motion, I tapped a key, and Micaela's image vanished.

The imprint was from two days earlier, the desire in his emotions so intense that I started missing Shannon. The imprint was followed by brief, faded ones of his work.

But at five weeks ago, another vivid imprint captured me.

I stared at the screen in shock. This could be the poison. That's it, I had to act—and act now.

I waited for more imprints, but they weren't connected, so I drew my fingers away. But one thing was clear: Tyrus had known about the poison for at least a week before Welby's death. Did that mean he'd become suspicious, or that he'd been somehow involved? I needed more information.

I began searching for more imprints, but those I found belonged to others. The time Tyrus spent here was obviously at the table or outside. Where was his filming equipment? That would be important to him and thus riddled with imprints. I debated whether to check out the bathroom or the bedroom and decided to go upstairs first. Bathrooms were always easier to gain access to than a bedroom if my time here was cut short.

The bedroom in the overhead loft wasn't quite as immaculate as the downstairs. The covers on the bed were pulled up, but not neatly, and a few items of clothing were unfolded on a log shelf. No camera or filming equipment here, so he must have it in his car or with him, though I hadn't noticed it earlier. I began searching for imprints. But there was no phone, no personal knickknacks or books. I'd known that would be somewhat the case, as he was only visiting, but surely there was something here with imprints. The clothes were also a bust, as I suspected they would be. If he owned a belt, it wasn't here. His shoes held a few mild imprints, but none were important. Not surprising; very few people felt intensely about things at foot level.

Finally, I gave up. I'd have had better luck picking his pocket or asking to borrow his cell phone. Maybe the bathroom was a better choice.

I was going down the stairs when a key turned in the lock. I froze on the middle stair, which gave a loud creak. My heart pounded furiously. There was literally nowhere to hide up in the loft except maybe under the log bed—though the possibility wasn't a guarantee.

I scuttled back up the stairs and crouched near the bed, ready to dive underneath if I heard footsteps on the stairs. I'd probably fit. Maybe I'd get lucky, and he'd just forgotten some papers on the table or needed to grab drinks from the fridge.

Whistling met my ears, barely audible above the furious pounding of my heart. And it was coming up the stairs. A creaking told me when the person was halfway. It looked like under the bed was my only choice.

My body slid under easily enough, but not my head. I stifled a curse. What was I going to do now? I couldn't even use the excuse that I'd been interested in looking at the loft décor. Never mind that he might be a murderer. How could I defend myself in this position?

I was halfway out from under the bed when a soft exclamation came from the top of the stairs. I leapt to my feet, landing in a ready stance, my training taking over. I opened my mouth to say something—anything—when my eyes landed on Holt, his brow drawn in puzzlement.

I sighed with relief.

"Autumn, what are you doing here?" Since I'd seen him last, he'd changed out of his nice clothes and into worn jeans.

"Delivering towels?" I hadn't meant for it to end in a question.

His gaze narrowed. "You're investigating him, aren't you?"

"Yeah."

Holt shook his head. "Tyrus is a good guy. You've got it wrong."

"He's mixed up in this somehow. Come on. I'll show you."

"Okay, just a minute." Holt walked across the room and went to the bedside antler lamp. Bending over stiffly, he turned it on, and nothing happened. Setting down the small box he carried, he opened it to reveal a light bulb, which he traded for the one in the lamp. This time it worked.

He turned to me. "Next time you want to do reconnaissance in one of my guest's rooms, you should give me the heads up. I've always got work to do in the rooms."

"Yeah, the light would have been a better excuse. Then maybe you could be icing your back."

He touched the offending area. "I've got an ice pack belt on. I'm good."

Nodding, I headed for the stairs, and he followed. Back at the table, I flipped open the laptop and showed him the picture of Micaela. "This is from years ago, isn't it? Where would he get this? Did you ever meet Tyrus before he stayed here?"

Holt rubbed his jaw. "Can't say that I have."

"Lyndia says he's visited the inn every year for the past ten years. Just for a few days."

"Well, there you go. That must be how he has this picture. Lyndia used to follow Micaela around when they were teens. Lyndia is a lot younger, of course. Four years, I believe. Bonnie would know for sure."

"Tyrus never mentioned staying at Magnolia Inn?"

"Yeah, he did. He told me when I saw him playing checkers with Welby. I didn't know he'd been coming out so many years, but I don't get why that's important. I often recommend Welby's place and vice-versa."

"Is that what happened this time?"

Holt thought about it for a while. "Can't say for sure, but I know his reservation was made clear back in February. We actually had Frontier Cabin booked the first two weeks of the summer and a couple of other weeks, but we were able to shift them to the other two cottages."

"It doesn't make sense why he'd come here then," I mused. "Magnolia Inn would still have had rooms. So why did he come here instead?" I paced several steps. "I'm missing something."

"For such a long stay, he probably wanted more privacy than you get at an inn."

"Maybe. Look, does this cottage have a safe like ours?"

"Yep, sure does. Right there under that painting." He pointed to the wall next to the fireplace. "The painting comes open like a door." He frowned before adding, "But I don't know the code he's put in, and the keys and tools to get in are back in my big safe."

I snorted. "Everyone knows hotel safes are not secure." I could get in them even without my ability, though that's what I'd use first.

"I don't feel right about that," he said. "Besides, he'll be along soon. He was playing soccer with the boys, but I heard him mention a swim at the beach."

"I only want to check if there's something with imprints. Look out the window and tell me if he's coming. He knows you were going to replace the light, right?"

"Right." Holt didn't sound very happy about it, and I knew I was probably blowing any good impressions he'd had of me.

"So how did it go with the police?" I opened the painting

and began touching the keypad to see if Tyrus had left any imprints on it. They'd likely be faint, even if he concentrated. Unless he had left a boatload of money in here.

"They found old Buster, and the poor cadaver dog got a chewing out—not that it's his fault."

Finding the code was a lot easier than I expected. Not only had Tyrus left mini-imprints, one after the other, on the keys, but his heart had been pounding almost as much as mine had when Holt had come up those stairs.

I reversed the order of the numbers he'd imprinted, putting them in order of oldest to newest, and voilà, it opened.

"What the—" Holt muttered as his gaze landed on what was inside.

My thoughts exactly. A revolver with a shiny metal barrel and a wooden grip lay in the middle of the safe.

"Looks like a 38 special," Holt said, coming closer.

"The detective said the bullet they found was probably a nine mil or a 380, so . . ." I let the words dangle.

Holt shook his head. "All squished up, it's hard to tell if you don't weigh it. But if it's the same gun, ballistics might be able to tell."

I knew a better way. I reached out my knuckle and touched the grip. If this did end up on the police radar, I didn't want my fingerprints on it.

The old man shoved the gun into my hand. "Take it."

"Welby, I don't want it."

"If I'm right about this, whoever it is might come after you next."

"You should call the police if you think someone is poisoning you."

"I will." The old man looked frail in the doorway under his

shock of white hair, a shadow of his former self. It hurt to look at him. To know I was responsible.

"Okay, I'll keep it. Wait a minute for me to put it away. I'll walk you home." I wasn't all that sure he would make it on his own. *The safe. That's where I'd put it. For now.*

The frantic emotions broke off after he opened the safe and set the gun inside. A new imprint followed, which I assumed came from the old man as he dug the revolver from his safe at Magnolia Inn.

I might not be around, but the inn would. My legacy would. As long as Tyrus took care of Lyndia when I was gone.

The third imprint came from a decade earlier when someone—probably Welby—put the revolver into that same safe. *Couldn't have a gun around a teenager, especially when she'd just lost her parents. Still, it would be good to have a woman around again, even if she was a sullen teen. She'd come around when she realized I wasn't going to dump her.*

When nothing else of interest followed, I pulled back my hand.

"Welby gave it to him," I said.

"And I suppose you know that because of your . . ." Holt waved a hand in the air, his doubt clearly showing.

Yeah, I'd done a lot of damage to how he thought about me in the past ten minutes, but I wouldn't back down or excuse myself, not even for Shannon's dad.

I held his gaze. "I know it in the same way I know you don't want to tell Shannon the real reason you left the police bureau. But you have to know he's going to find out about Brysen Lowe. He's a good detective. And from my experience, it would be a lot better if you tell him yourself. He'll understand."

Holt's jaw dropped, and his stare was hard enough to make

me feel uncomfortable. It reminded me of how Shannon had seen me in the beginning—either as a psychic freak or a fraud bent on stealing money from the weak or the desperate.

Without waiting for a reply, I turned and headed for the bathroom, my thoughts racing. Welby had given Tyrus a gun, which told me he trusted him. Whether or not that trust was well-placed, Welby must have suspected Nigel or Deanna, though why Deanna would want him dead, I didn't know. To control the inn? Because she was in love with Nigel? Or maybe because she intended to take down everyone Holt cared about.

The first imprints I'd experienced on the gun had been barely a month ago, possibly the day before Welby's death—I'd have to check the date on that. Welby certainly didn't have enough time to tell his suspicions to the police.

In the bathroom, I began running my hands over the faucet and sink. If Tyrus had shot and disposed of a body, he would have needed to wash up. Only a cold-blooded killer wouldn't leave imprints after something like that.

I found nothing.

I move to the personal items on a shelf and in the drawers. Again, I found nothing important—until my hand touched his razor. It was one of those metal ones with real blades, lying next to a thick shaving brush and a flat tin of shaving cream.

"Nigel! But where—how did you get in here?" I demanded, staring at the wiry man standing outside the bathroom doorway. This close up, his shriveled face vaguely resembled Welby's. I hated that.

He laughed. "I left a little bit of gum in the door when you were out taking pictures of those flowers behind the cottage." No missing the disgust in his voice.

"I told you last year—I want nothing to do with you. And I'm not giving you more money. Why are you even here?"

"The old man asked, and like a dutiful son, I came," Nigel sneered. "And I don't need your money."

"Sure." My hand gripping the razor began to ache. "Look, we may share genes, but you are not my father in any way that counts. I already have a father, one who was there for me as a child, one who actually supports himself and my mother. Now get out of here before I call the police."

The imprint ended instantly as Tyrus threw the razor into the drawer.

I withdrew my hand, stunned at the revelation. Tyrus was Nigel Carr's biological son. That made a lot of sense, especially in light of Tyrus's interest in Magnolia Inn and his repeated visits, especially this long one that just happened to coincide with Welby's death and the battle for his inn. There was a lot more playing out here than I'd expected.

"Autumn, hurry!" Holt's voice came to me from the other room. "He's coming!"

I hurried out of the bathroom, letting the bits of imprints settle into my mind where they would become a part of me like all the others I'd read. Were they changing me? Sometimes I wondered.

I had almost reached Holt when the door opened, and Tyrus stood there staring at us.

"I got your light fixed," Holt said, lifting the box where he had put the spent bulb. "I hope you don't mind. Autumn hadn't seen this cottage yet, so I let her come in with me."

Tyrus smiled. "Not a problem, as long as my underwear wasn't lying around anywhere. Thanks for taking care of the light."

Holt chuckled. "Not a problem."

"I didn't see any underwear," I added, striving for a normal tone. Rather difficult when my brain kept repeating, *He's Nigel's son! He's the missing man's son. Maybe the grandson Welby tried to write the letter to.*

That had been Tyrus's lie by omission, but were there more? One thing I knew for sure, this put him at the very top of my suspect list, but I wanted more time to think about it before I confronted him. "This is a beautiful cottage."

Tyrus scanned the room. "Better yet, it's comfortable." He started for the stairs. "Well, if you'll excuse me, I'm going to change into my suit. Micaela and I are taking the boys on a picnic to the beach."

"Sounds fun. We'll let you get to it then." Holt started for the door.

We hurried outside, where Holt heaved a sigh the instant the door shut behind us. "That was close."

I barely registered the words. "I need to talk to Shannon." I started down the path toward Rose Petal Cottage, planning the text I'd send to have him meet me there.

"You're going to tell him?" Holt sounded wounded as he hurried to catch up with me.

I stopped and stared at him before I realized what he was asking. "You mean about why you left the force? If you don't tell him, I won't have a choice. Even if I tried to keep it from him, I'm a terrible liar. Besides, I don't keep secrets from Shannon." Not these kinds of secrets, anyway. I might not tell him every aspect of my investigations, but that wasn't the same thing.

"I didn't mean to hurt the boy." Holt's voice came out like gravel. "Even when I thought he had a gun."

"I know that, and so will your son. But he needs to know

what happened. And you should also be aware that the boy's mother is here in Florida and working at Magnolia Inn. That cannot be a coincidence."

"It's not." Holt flushed his discomfort, his eyes refusing to meet my gaze. "But how did you—never mind."

"You knew she was here?"

"Of course. We've been in contact, and when her husband got sick a few years back and needed a warmer climate, I got her the job."

My turn to gape. "You got the woman who publicly accused you of murdering her drug-dealing son a job?"

"Yes."

"Why?"

"Because I kept in contact with her, to help her out when she needed it. I felt I owed her that. Anyway, a few years after he died, she found out from his friends that he really was selling drugs that day. We'll never know for sure if he had a gun, but she decided she didn't want to live with the anger. She forgave me." His tone hinted that her forgiveness was more than he'd given himself.

I loved that he was willing to help her and to give her another chance. That was something my adoptive parents, Winter and Summer Rain, had believed in with all their hearts. Once, before imprints, I had been more like them.

"Or she's here to get revenge." I waited until that sank in to add, "She might be involved in all this."

"What about Tyrus and that gun?"

I hadn't forgotten that either. I thumbed back at Frontier Cabin. "Right. We'll have to look into that too. But there's something more you need to know, and I admit it puts Deanna a little lower on my suspect list."

"What?" His voice was full of dread.

I was glad to get the news out in the open where I could study it better. "Tyrus Lockwood is also Nigel Carr's biological son."

Holt's head bobbled back and forth from me to the cottage, his expression shocked. But slowly he began to nod. "I guess that would explain his connection to Welby. But I wonder why Welby never told me?" He paused before rushing on, "You think Tyrus might have been the one to get rid of Nigel? Or even Welby?"

I shrugged. "Maybe he got rid of both of them."

His face paled. "If that's the case, Lyndia might be next."

I drew out my phone. "Let's get Shannon over here. We need to make a plan."

nce inside Rose Petal Cottage, I texted Shannon to hurry back, and then I called Elliot on my laptop. His face appeared on my screen almost instantly, the advantage of having an agoraphobic partner.

"I'm here with Holt Martin, Shannon's dad," I said, so he would know not to say anything about Deanna and her son. To Holt, I added, "This is my partner, Elliot Stone."

"Right, the PI," Holt said. "We met at the wedding."

Elliot nodded. "Call me Eli."

I tried not to roll my eyes. "I have more news," I told Elliot. "I found Nigel's son—Tyrus Lockwood."

Elliot groaned. "You gotta be kidding. No wonder I couldn't find him. I was totally looking for someone under twenty, and more likely under ten." He looked away from the camera and started typing. "I've pulled up his website and video channels. Let me recrawl it with my programs for anything useful. Now that we know what we're looking for, I can use a few keywords." He stopped typing and added, "That's motive, you know."

"We thought so too." I hesitated. "Look, did you find any connection between Tyrus and Micaela? Because he had a picture of her on his laptop from an earlier visit here. It's a stunning picture. You'd probably remember it. She's at the beach at sunset, watching sand fall from her hand."

"Just a minute." He typed a few more strokes, and a picture came up on the screen instead of his face. "This one?"

"That's it."

"He put it in his first book, and there's this from the related video." The picture vanished, replaced by a video of that same moment. After the sand ran out of her hand, Micaela looked up as if hearing something, a smile breaking out on her face. She started running as if to meet someone, her hair streaming in the wind, but the clip ended before she reached her destination. "And I guess that's the connection between them you wanted to find because there is nothing else online."

"Send me a link to that clip, will you?" I wanted to show it to Micaela. Had she given her permission for its use, or was that not necessary because she was out in public?

"You think he's here stalking her?" Holt sat heavily in a chair at the table, out of view of my laptop camera.

"Well, none of you remember him before this summer, right?" I asked. "Besides Lyndia and Welby."

Holt sighed. "No. But so help me, if he hurts her, I'll kill him."

I faced him, leaning back in my chair. "One body at a time, please," I said. Or two, if you counted Welby, which I was for now.

"Body?" Elliot asked. "Are you leaving something out?"

I shook my head at him. "No. You already know I suspect Nigel is no longer with us. And hopefully only Micaela's heart is at risk. But Tyrus seems to be playing Lyndia as well. She told me she has a crush on him."

"You think Tyrus is trying to steal Magnolia Inn from her?" Worry deepened on Holt's face.

"Possibly." I had no way of knowing, but his parentage was likely what the imprint on his door meant regarding the secret he hadn't wanted the police to discover.

"Then why keep his connection secret?" Elliot answered. "Look, I'll do some more digging and see if I can—wait, I've got something already." He looked away, typing again on his keyboard. "Okay, it's a blog entry from ten years ago. It says Tyrus finally received the funds to buy his video equipment, thanks to the owner of Magnolia Inn in Jacksonville Beach." He paused a moment. "Hello. It also says he has met the girl of his dreams, but she's already taken. There's that same picture of the girl with the sand."

A growl sounded in Holt's throat. "That must have been when Micaela was dating her husband."

"So is Tyrus playing out those old fantasies now, or does he really like her?" I wanted to believe in romance, but we had proof that Tyrus was a liar.

No one offered an answer.

We said goodbye to Elliot after that, and I had only begun to worry about what was taking Shannon so long when he appeared at the cottage. "What's the rush?" he asked, striding over to the table where we sat.

"You first." I tapped my laptop with my fingertips. "How did Lyndia react to the idea of an exhumation?"

Shannon frowned. "Not well. She nearly fainted when we told her about the possibility of poisoning. I think it was the whole idea of having to live through all the emotions again. She broke down and cried."

"So it's a no go?"

"Oh, she'll agree. She wants to know. It was just a shock."

"I'll bet. Poor girl."

"Mom's still with her, giving her reassurances about how we are going to solve the case quickly." He glanced at his father. "Mom wants you to man the fort until she gets back—her words, not mine." To me, he added, "So why did you want me back?"

I glanced over at Holt, who studiously ignored me by examining his fingertips. That left me to give Shannon the rundown of what I'd learned about Tyrus.

"This changes things." Shannon settled into a chair opposite his father and kitty-corner from me. "That gun might be the one the police are looking for."

"If the imprint on the door handle to Frontier Cabin was any indicator," I said, "Tyrus was mad enough at someone to kill. But we've all felt that way before. Feelings aren't actions."

"I want to see everything Elliot digs up on this guy." Shannon laid his hand over mine on the table, and a flutter of excitement zipped through me despite the worry I felt. He was mine. It was still hard to believe. "And Paige might have more info for us by now. She didn't the last time I checked."

"If there is something on his record, wouldn't the detectives on the case already have found it?" I asked.

"Not if they weren't looking at him. But I'll pass on the information about Tyrus to Detective Wallace when I talk to her about the exhumation."

"She's not going to be happy," Holt muttered. "She wants to pin it on me."

Shannon's gaze shifted to his father. "Speaking of that, why did you confront Nigel? You had to know all the proof was in your corner. What really made you so angry? Come on, Dad.

I know Mom is the one behind us coming here—what are you hiding from me?"

That was my cue to step away from the table and give them a little space. I pulled my hand from Shannon's and went to the sink to begin brewing a bit of chamomile tea for everyone. Shannon would prefer coffee, but I was making inroads with herbal teas that were better for his sleep at night.

Stark silence met Shannon's question, but he didn't back down. I risked a peek as I set the water boiling and saw them glaring at each other. *Great.*

"Okay," Holt said finally. "A year before I left the force, I shot a kid. A seventeen-year-old, drug-dealing kid. I thought I saw him go for a gun, and I was protecting my partner, but when we got inside the house, there wasn't a gun. Just the kid, bleeding out on the ground." Holt's voice caught in his throat. "It's a moment I relive every day. And his mom, well, at the time, she was quite vocal about her innocent son being gunned down. Work wasn't the same after that. I couldn't stay on the force."

Shannon arose and came around the table. He put a hand on his father's shoulder, looking him in the eyes. "You were doing your job. You can't keep blaming yourself."

Holt covered his son's hand with his own, and for a long moment neither of them spoke. Then he said, "I didn't want you to know."

"Why? Of course I'd understand."

Holt shrugged. "I don't know. I was weak. I should have stayed on the force. I should have gotten both the guys. I should have shot a little lower."

"Lower?" Shannon's brow rose. "That tells me you would still do the same thing."

"I'd have to." Holt's voice was almost inaudible. "But the

uncertainty . . . it haunts me. Maybe I was wrong. Maybe the kid didn't need to die that day."

"You know you did the only thing you could." Shannon pulled his father up from the chair into a hug. "I love you, Dad. You protected your partner and stopped a drug dealer. That saved lives."

"I appreciate that."

With a little awkward back pounding, they appeared to be finished. Meanwhile, I still had enough questions about the shooting and Holt's reasons for hiding it to fill up several hours, but I'd stow most of them for now.

"The problem is," I said, "the boy's mother is here in town. Your dad got her a job two years ago at Magnolia Inn."

Holt shot me an aggrieved stare. "And I don't know what Welby would have done this past year without her. I told you she forgave me, and she needed help."

"I realize that, but we don't know if someone is trying to frame you. It could be her. What about the anonymous tip to the police about you meeting with Nigel?" I couldn't believe he hadn't made the connection.

"Autumn's right." Shannon returned to his seat. "And the bloody hat doesn't seem like something you'd overlook in your yard maintenance."

That was when I remembered what Elliot had said about Holt's possible motives for wanting to get rid of Nigel. "Nigel didn't by chance know about you and Deanna's son, did he?" I asked Holt.

Still standing where Shannon had left him, Holt nodded. "Yeah, he did try to use it for leverage so I wouldn't dispute Magnolia Inn's claim to Frontier Cabin. But I told him where to go."

Shannon groaned. "Oh, I see. So that's what got you angry enough to confront him."

"Well, I knew you were coming. Plus, he was going to tell everyone around here. Except for the tourists, we're a tight community, and I didn't want to deal with all that."

Shannon jumped to his feet. "And how did Nigel find out? It had to be from the boy's mother. Unfortunately, that means your motive for getting rid of Nigel just doubled. Or it will if the police find out about it."

Holt rolled his eyes. "Which is exactly why I didn't tell them."

"For an innocent man, you're sure hiding a lot," Shannon ground out. "If I were the detective on the case, and we weren't related, I'd suspect you too. Who else knew about the shooting? Welby? Lyndia?"

"Welby, yes. Not Lyndia. We didn't want her treating Deanna poorly because of the past. Or me, I guess."

Shannon shook his head. "We'll talk more about *that* later. Right now, I'm going to the police to see if I can get them onboard with the exhumation."

"I can go with you." Holt started around the table.

Shannon pointed at his father. "Nope. You have to stay to man the fort."

Holt sighed. "Right."

The water was finally hot, so I dropped in an infuser containing my loose tea. "I do have another worry," I said. Both men looked at me. "Tyrus is going on a picnic to the beach with Micaela and the twins. Should we worry about that? At what point do we warn her about him?"

Holt's shoulders slumped. "Shoot. And just this morning she was saying how much the boys liked him. Anyway, they always go right down by the pier. As soon as Bonnie gets back from helping Lyndia, I'll go down there and keep an eye out."

"Or I can go." I moved the infuser around in the water. "I might be less conspicuous since I'm supposed to be on my honeymoon after all."

Shannon stood and moved around the table toward me, slipping his arms around my body. "Good. I'll meet you there."

"Only if you bring me food."

He laughed. "You never change."

"Not about food."

Holt brightened at that. "Bonnie has a picnic lunch planned for you guys. It was supposed to be a surprise."

"After the police, I'll stop by the house first for the food then," Shannon said. "Shouldn't take me more than an hour." With a nibble on my neck, he released me and started for the door. "See you soon."

"Wait! Take Nigel's cards. Maybe the detectives will want them." I tossed Shannon the sack with the cards.

Holt turned to me as the door shut behind Shannon. "I'm sorry. This is all such lousy timing."

"It's okay. You're family." I meant it. Besides Tawnia's family and my biological father, they were all the family I had.

He started to leave but hesitated halfway to the door. "I'm sorry I didn't believe about your . . . you know."

"Oh, you're not done doubting," I said with a grin. "And that's okay. I'll win you over yet." Just like I had Shannon.

He laughed. "Well, Bonnie left a beach umbrella over there by the door. Better take it. It gets hot out there around this time of day."

"Okay. I will."

I was the only one left to drink the tea, which I had with

a huge slice of lightly toasted whole wheat bread from the gift basket, slathered with organic peanut butter that I'd turned upside down last night so the oil would go to the bottom. The combination reminded me of Summer, who had taught me to make bread the year I was nine, before the breast cancer had taken her from us. We'd always eaten the hot bread with peanut butter or with honey butter, and the taste was pure love.

Thus fortified, I changed into a swimsuit, pulled my shorts back on, and packed a bag with water, sunscreen, and a towel. At the door, I reached for the umbrella in its carrying case next to the metal detector Shannon had taken from his father's garage. We'd have to remember to return it, but maybe it would be fun to give it a try on the beach later in the week.

I received a text from Shannon's mother that made me smile. *I'm in my kitchen here packing a lunch for you two. Do you like turkey in your sandwiches? It's organic.*

Absolutely. I texted back. *Thank you so much.*

Minutes later as I passed Magnolia Inn, I thought about going inside to ask Lyndia if she was aware of Tyrus and Micaela meeting ten years earlier, but now probably wasn't the time. She might have recovered from her shock, but she'd had enough worry this morning.

I retraced the same steps to the pier that we'd taken the day before and found the beach packed as it hadn't been last night. I walked out onto the pier and gazed off the side, much like the woman in the blue raincoat had been doing the night before. There, I spotted Micaela and Tyrus, but only because of the boys digging in the sand near the receding tideline. They'd set up three umbrellas next to each other, creating a small tent of shade, none of which they were using at the moment as they were building a sandcastle.

As I watched, Micaela grabbed a handful of dry sand and sprinkled it over the courtyard, much as she had let the sand seep from her fingers on Tyrus's video. In her shorts and bikini top, Micaela looked like a model with her slim figure and smooth, dark skin. Tyrus threw his head back and laughed. He was shirtless and his tanned muscles well defined, tapering to a narrow waist. They appeared to be a perfect match.

I went down to the sand, weaving through the crowd until I found a tiny open spot that was far enough away that it wouldn't be weird if they noticed me at some point. It was unlikely that anything sinister would happen here in front of all these people, but when they left, I'd have to follow.

What is your game? I mentally asked Tyrus as I removed my camouflage shorts. I needed to touch his phone or something.

The beach was incredibly beautiful, but after an hour and a half of dozing under the umbrella, I grew bored. Where was Shannon? Leaving my bag under my umbrella, I walked down to the beach for a swim. The water was deliciously cool against my legs, instead of shockingly so like I'd expected. The rush of the waves as they closed over my head made the crowded beach seem far away. I floated in the water for long, delicious minutes, occasionally glancing at my belongings and Micaela's umbrellas.

On my way back to my towel, a voice called out to me. "Autumn! Hi!"

I looked to see one of Micaela's boys near his sandcastle, his mother and brother nowhere to be seen. "Hey, Lucio," I said. "Are you having fun?"

"That's Dimas," said a still-shirtless Tyrus with a chuckle, approaching from my other side. "Not Lucio."

I looked at the boy, but the name didn't fit the vibes radiating from him. "No, it's Lucio, right?"

Lucio nodded. "Sorry," he said, squinting up at Tyrus. "Dimas likes to fool people."

Tyrus laughed. "Okay, he got me. So you're the one in the blue swim trunks."

"It's my favorite color. Dimas likes red. Mom says that's because he's bossy." With a grin, Lucio ran to dig into his mother's beach bag for a granola bar before throwing himself down on a towel.

"Cute kid," I said with a smile.

"Yeah." Tyrus gave a forced laugh, his grin fading. "Everywhere I go lately, I keep running into you. Are you following me?"

"Why? Do you have something to hide?" I countered, slightly adjusting my stance. Water sluiced from my swim bottoms and down my legs with the motion. If he wasn't into martial arts, he probably wouldn't notice the change, but I had to be ready for anything.

"No, of course not."

Another lie. "Actually, you do," I said, keeping my voice steady. "I know who you are, and if you have anything to do with your biological father's disappearance, you should tell me now."

"I don't know what you're talking about."

I arched a brow. "And I suppose you don't know anything about poison either? You should know they're going to exhume Welby's body for tests."

The shock on his face couldn't be more apparent. "Lyndia agreed to that?"

"She was upset when Bonnie asked, of course, but she agreed."

He nodded. "Good."

Good? I'd expected him to make excuses and run away, but what did *good* mean in this context? Good that Bonnie had been with Lyndia or good that Lyndia had agreed to the exhumation?

"You should know that my husband is meeting with Detective Wallace right now. They'll have questions for you about your biological connection to Nigel."

His face paled, turning him a sickly color under his nice bronze tan. He looked around at Lucio, as if making sure the child hadn't overheard. "I had nothing to do with Nigel's disappearance. I have no relationship with that man except a little cell he implanted at my conception. That wasn't my fault."

"Tell me about the money you gave him last year."

"What money?" he demanded. "And who are you really?" He looked around pointedly. "Are you even married to the Martin's son?"

"Yes, and I'm here to make sure my father-in-law doesn't take the blame for something he didn't do. And if you want to give me a sob story about your birth and adoption, I have a worse one. My biological father was drugged up when he raped my teenage mother, who later died in childbirth. My twin and I were given to different foster families to fulfill both her contract with an adoptive family *and* her last wishes to have the couple she was staying with raise her child. I lost my mother and my sister for thirty-two years because of that man, so I doubt whatever Nigel did to you is worse than that. But I'm willing to be disproved."

He stared at me for a long, silent moment. "Okay, it wasn't like that at all. My parents were great, and I never cared that I was adopted. I don't know how Nigel found me, but he somehow did, and he showed up at my apartment in Tampa.

Tried to pretend he wanted a relationship, but he'd seen my online stuff and wanted money. I refused to give him cash, but I paid back rent that he owed and told him never to contact me again. He didn't—until I showed up here this summer. He's a loser, through and through. Lyndia should have made him leave right after the funeral. Better yet, Welby shouldn't have asked him to come in the first place. Nigel hasn't changed from the day Welby kicked him out."

Something was off about the statement. "I thought Lyndia found Nigel and invited him."

His feet shifted in the sand. "Welby asked her to. He was hoping for a reconciliation."

"And how did Welby and Nigel get along?"

He snorted. "Nigel was only interested in an inheritance. He didn't care about Welby."

"What about you?"

"Me?" He appeared genuinely shocked.

"You're Welby's grandson, every bit as much as Lyndia is his granddaughter." Or if we were to split hairs, he was even more Welby's grandson, biologically speaking, since Lyndia had been adopted into the Carr family. "That means you and Lyndia both stood to gain."

"That's ridiculous!" he spat, flushing with anger. Several sunbathers glanced our way, and he quickly lowered his voice. "Welby was my friend."

"Then why did you stay at Haven Retreat instead of the inn, and for so long instead of your usual visit?"

His jaw worked, and his eyes radiated a silent fury. He obviously didn't want to tell me anything. Finally, he said, "Welby didn't think it was safe."

"What?" My mind turned over the unexpected words,

making the connection at once. "Because he thought someone was poisoning him."

"Something like that. He wrote and asked me to come, so I made plans and came for the summer." Tyrus hesitated. "At first I thought it was just him getting old, or maybe he needed help with renovations, but when I saw how changed he was from last year, I began to think he was right."

So Welby had at some point finished the letter I'd seen him begin—and sent it. "Why didn't he go to his doctor?"

"He did, but he didn't talk about his suspicions as far as I know, and I guess his doctor thought he was one more retiree dying of old age."

"Why wouldn't he say something? It doesn't make sense."

Tyrus's jaw jutted forward—his very good-looking jaw that had once again been shaved—probably in honor of his day with Micaela. "I don't know."

"But you do." I avoided the temptation to fold my arms as a measure of my assurance, instead keeping my hands loose and ready at my sides.

He glanced again at Lucio and then further up the beach behind me. I followed his gaze to see Micaela and Dimas heading back toward the wooden path leading down to the sand. Our private chat was about to end.

"Well?" I prompted.

"Welby was worried it was Lyndia." His voice dripped with reluctance. "He didn't want to get her in trouble. He loved her."

"And what do you think?"

"It had to be Nigel. Or someone else. Or maybe Nigel's ex-wife has something to do with it. She was screaming at Lyndia at the inn yesterday."

"Did the ex-wife have access?"

"How do I know?" The irritation in his voice was clear.

"It could have been you. You've been here seven or eight weeks, right?"

"Or it could have been Holt." His glare was clearly unfriendly now, though that was probably my fault for pushing. "But something else has to be going on. Especially if Lyndia has finally agreed to the exhumation. I've been asking her to do it."

Asking her to do it? Could that be what he'd meant by convincing her? I had read two imprints from him to that effect, but I didn't know whether to believe him.

"Okay, one more thing. Does Micaela know you included a video of her in your first travel video? And a picture in the book?"

His gaze went past me. "I have a signed permission form if that's what you're asking," he said. "But no, she doesn't remember the video or me at all. It was a long time ago. The book wasn't even published until four years later."

And Micaela didn't have a screensaver of him on her computer to remind her of their encounter.

"How'd you meet her?"

He shrugged. "She came to the inn a few times to invite Lyndia to the beach when I was here to meet my grandfather for the first time. Lyndia was in therapy because of her parents' deaths, and Micaela mentioned to me that Bonnie asked her to help Lyndia adjust. But Micaela had met her husband right before that, so she didn't have a lot of time for Lyndia. Or me." His tone held a touch of bitterness. "I guess you might say I met her a month too late."

Because she was already in love. "You didn't tell her how you felt?"

A rush of breath escaped him. "I was fresh out of college,

scrawny, pimple-faced, and awkward—and finding out about my biological family for the first time. The guy she ended up marrying had a lot more going for him back then, and since he was from Brazil, he spoke Portuguese like she did. So no, I didn't tell her." He shrugged. "It doesn't matter now."

Except it did to him; I could tell. But until I knew the full truth of his connection with the case, I wasn't going to encourage him to start a relationship with Micaela.

"I'm guessing Micaela is why you wrote a travel guide about Portugal?"

His nod was sharp. "For all I knew, she was happily married. I thought it would get her out of my system."

From his tone, I was sure it hadn't worked. "So Lyndia and Micaela are friends."

"Not exactly. There was a big difference in age back then, so I don't think they were ever really close. At least, I never saw Micaela again on my trips here until this summer."

"When you ran into her at Haven Retreat."

"There and when Micaela would go to sit with Welby or help at the inn."

A high-pitched squeal cut through our conversation, and we turned to see Lucio striking out at Dimas, who struggled to save his ice cream cone from falling into the sand. By the big white mark on Lucio's back, Dimas had obviously run ahead of his mother to press his freezing ice cream into his brother's sunbaked flesh.

"Stop it," Dimas shouted. "You stupid dummy. You almost made me drop it."

"Dimas Eduardo da Silva de Carvalho de Santos Ribeiro," Micaela said, handing one of three wrapped ice cream cones in her hand to Lucio. "Apologize this instant."

"Sorry, stupid," Dimas muttered.

Micaela reached over and snatched his cone from his hand and dropped it into the sand. "Too bad, too sad," she said. "I've told you before that's not the way you treat people."

Dimas looked ready to cry, but in the next second, he was blinking away the tears and shrugging. "Okay, I'm really sorry." He looked hopefully at the remaining ice creams, but his mother ignored him, handing one to Tyrus.

"Hey, Autumn," she said with a smile. "Do you want one? It was our price for using their bathroom."

"No, thanks," I said.

She started unwrapping the last cone. "It's a beautiful day."

"Yes, I'm waiting for Shannon. We're going to have a picnic."

"He's late," she said with a laugh. "It's almost one-thirty. Definitely time for ice cream." To Dimas's devastation, she bit into the chocolate swirls that topped her vanilla cone. "Mmm," she said. "These remind me of Portugal. I have a soft spot for them." She glanced at her son before taking another bite. "Now you're really feeling sorry, right?"

"Mom," he whined.

She looked back at me without responding. "If you get tired of waiting for Shannon, we have plenty of leftovers." Her gaze drifted to Tyrus, who was scooping the fallen cone into a trash bag. Her smile at him was dazzling.

"Thank you," I told Micaela. "But I had a snack before I came."

I watched as Lucio sidled up to his brother and put an arm around his brother's waist before offering him a bite of his ice cream cone. Dimas bit into the chocolate, then hugged his brother. Both smiled, their squabble apparently forgotten. A tiny gap opened somewhere inside me. This was what I'd missed growing up without Tawnia. This is what we'd both missed—the closeness of us against the world. And even though we loved our respective parents and wouldn't undo knowing them, this would always be something we'd missed.

"Well, I'd better get back and check my stuff," I said. "Nice to see you." Swallowing the sudden lump in my throat, I nodded at Micaela and walked away.

Back at my towel, everything was intact. But I had four missed messages and two calls—all from Shannon.

Change of plans, said the first only ten minutes ago. *I finally got back to the house to pick up the lunch when an employee called from Magnolia Inn. They said Lyndia collapsed, and they took her by ambulance to the hospital. Heading there now.*

The next text was the address, and the third was my name and a question mark. The fourth read: *Just let me know you're okay.*

A fifth message came in as I read the others. *The thing is, the EMT's suspect some kind of substance. I'm thinking it's poison.*

There was another option, of course. Lyndia might have crumpled under the pressure and ingested sleeping pills or something to that nature in the two-plus hours since Bonnie had left her. The idea contrasted with the determination I'd witnessed that morning. But if it was poison, who was responsible?

I looked over to where Micaela was still standing near her umbrellas next to Tyrus. If he was responsible, I couldn't leave her alone with him, could I? Especially now that I'd told him what I knew.

I hit the button to call Shannon, who picked up immediately. "I was in the water," I said. "How bad is it?"

"I don't know yet. Mom and I are barely in the car now. I think you should come. Maybe you can find an imprint."

"I told Tyrus we know who he is." With my free hand, I shoved my towel into my bag, not caring about the particles of sand I'd take with it.

"So you don't want to leave him with Micaela. Tell her my mom wants my dad with her and ask if can she watch the inn. That will buy us time."

"Okay."

I finished packing, pulled on my shorts, and hurried over to Micaela. "I'm sorry to bother you, but Lyndia has been rushed to the hospital. Bonnie is on her way with Shannon, but she'd like Holt with her. Can you go to Haven Retreat and cover in case the guests need something?"

She gasped, eyes widening in shock. "Of course, but what's wrong with Lyndia?"

I glanced at Tyrus to see his reaction to what I'd say next. "They think it might be poison."

He shook his head. "No. That's impossible. Who'd want to hurt Lyndia?" He hesitated and added, "Unless Nigel is back."

From the dead? I wondered.

I started to turn, but he reached out and touched my arm. "Wait, I'm going with you." He looked with concern at Micaela. "If I take the cooler and one umbrella, can you take care of the rest?"

"Of course. Go." She shoved her nearly untouched ice cream at a startled Dimas and started taking down an umbrella. "Please let me know if she's okay."

Chapter 12

$\mathcal{I}$ hurried back to Haven Retreat with Tyrus keeping pace even while carrying a full cooler.

"When I said I'm going with you," he said, sounding a little winded, "I meant only so you can give me the address of the hospital. I have my own car."

But I didn't have a car, and I'd have to wait until Micaela returned to the B&B if I wanted to hitch a ride with Holt.

"Good," I said. "I'll ride with you then. I just need to stop for a shirt." I'd also pull on a pair of barefoot sandals because hospitals were sometimes funny about wearing shoes, and the beaded loops that went from my middle toe to my ankle mimicked sandals at least enough to pass casual inspection.

Tyrus glanced down at the bright orange shirt he'd pulled on before picking up the cooler. The front of the tee featured a large drawing of the Jacksonville pier. "Me too. I'll meet you in the parking lot."

That was how, a few minutes later, I found myself in a sleek gray car heading to Baptist Medical Center with a man who might or might not be responsible for at least one poisoning. I consoled myself that the hospital was only six minutes away,

Shannon knew where I was through my phone's location, and Micaela had seen us leave together. Besides, there had been nothing in Elliot's information about Tyrus knowing martial arts.

I tested the door handle and as much of the interior of the car as I could for imprints, but all I picked up on was a three-month-old imprint from a woman Tyrus had asked out on a first date. We barely spoke on the drive, and when we entered the emergency waiting room together, Shannon's brow rose.

I shrugged in response. "How is she?"

"We don't know yet," Bonnie said, wringing her plump hands. "They said they'd let us know when they had something to say." She glanced at the reception desk. "But it looks like the woman I was talking to isn't there anymore. Maybe we need to ask again." She smiled at Tyrus. "I guess she's your cousin, isn't she?" I was glad Shannon had filled her in.

Tyrus's answering smile looked more like a grimace. "I guess so."

"Does *she* know that?" I asked. She hadn't hinted at that when I'd talked to her.

He shook his head. "Or at least I didn't tell her."

"You should," Bonnie said, patting his arm. "The poor girl would probably feel better knowing she's not alone in the world. I mean, she has us, but it's not the same thing as related family."

I didn't point out that they didn't share blood, and with Tyrus's adoption, they were in different families, because it didn't really matter. Family wasn't always about blood, and whatever his motives, Tyrus was in this thing clear up to his neck.

More people entered the emergency room, and I was a little

surprised to see Detectives Wallace and Burke, Wallace's bulky figure imposing and official next to her scrawny partner.

"Look who's here." Bonnie pointed, even though we were already staring.

"I texted them," Shannon said. "They weren't willing to give much thought to our idea of exhumation, but maybe this will change things."

The detectives strode to the reception desk without looking in our direction. After a brief discussion with one of the two women at the desk, they were allowed through a set of double doors behind them.

"If they're letting them back, they must know something." Bonnie started toward the counter to talk with the remaining receptionist, a woman who looked like she could match Detective Wallace in an arm wrestle.

As we neared the desk, a sudden cold enveloped me. That had happened at a hospital before, but I didn't know if it was connected to the case. I paused, but the coldness receded. Whatever—whoever—had caused it didn't seem related to us.

"I'm sorry," the woman at the desk said when she'd listened to Bonnie's request. Her face was impassive. "Are you relatives?"

"We're close friends," Bonnie said. "She doesn't have immediate family. That's why her employee called us after the ambulance came." She gave a frustrated sigh. "I told all this to the woman who was here before. She said she'd let us know how Lyndia's doing."

"I can't release information without the patient's permission, except to next of kin."

"I'm her cousin," Tyrus said. "Does that make me next of kin? I can give you my ID."

"Cousin?" The receptionist folded her arms over her white

uniform, her pale face doubtful. "Right. You'd better wait right here until I have approval."

Shannon flashed his badge. "Look, this is all part of an investigation, and I can vouch that this is her cousin."

She squinted at the badge, losing the attitude. "Okay, the news is she's awake, but not lucid. I'm not sure when that will change."

"But she is going to be okay, right?" Tyrus asked.

"Looks that way, but that's really all I can tell you. I'll let the doctor know you're her cousin."

"Thank you," Shannon and Tyrus said together. We all nodded at the woman and retreated from the desk.

"What a relief," Bonnie said, sinking into a waiting room seat. "But who would have done such a thing?"

"It might be an accident," Shannon said, sitting beside her.

I chose a chair across from them, making sure not to touch anything that might have imprints—emotions always lurked in hospitals. Tyrus remained standing, glaring down at us as if we'd been the ones to poison Lyndia. I stared back until he looked away and began pacing up and down the aisle.

"When she called from Magnolia Inn, Deanna said something about Lyndia drinking her grandpa's elderberry wine—do you think it was a bad batch?" Bonnie said. "Maybe he didn't cook the berries enough."

I pulled a foot up on my chair, draping my arms around my knee. "If that's the case, she should be okay. Even if a buildup of cyanide in the wine made her sick, as long as she's here, it shouldn't be enough to be fatal. I've heard of elderberry poisonings where people get really sick or animals die, but no human fatalities."

"That's good, at least." Bonnie leaned back in her chair,

interlacing her arms over her rounded stomach inside the church dress she still wore. "Maybe it's all a mistake."

"I don't believe in coincidence," Shannon said, right on cue.

I couldn't help smiling. "If Lyndia is out of it, that will delay Welby's exhumation."

Shannon shut his eyes momentarily and groaned. "Oh, you're right. We won't get anywhere without next of kin."

"What about me?" Tyrus stopped his pacing. "I could sign, couldn't I? Especially with the letter Welby sent me saying he thought someone was poisoning him."

"You have the letter?" I asked. "With you?"

He shook his head. "I could get it."

"And you'd be willing to sign." Shannon sounded doubtful.

"Of course. Ever since Nigel disappeared, I've been encouraging Lyndia to do just that—to have Welby tested. Even told her I'd pay for it."

I exchanged a glance with Shannon, and I knew he was contemplating whether Tyrus was telling the truth or if he was trying to situate himself to inherit.

"Maybe the detectives learned something." Bonnie gestured to where the police were emerging from the double doors leading into the emergency rooms. Shannon popped to his feet and waved.

Wallace shook her head but started toward us. "Well, it looks like we've got an interesting spin on this case," she said without preamble. "The doctor found a high trace of arsenic in Miss Carr's blood. We don't know the delivery method yet, and she's not lucid enough to answer questions."

"Arsenic and not cyanide?" I asked. "Because she might have been drinking homemade elderberry wine."

She met my gaze. "That's interesting. We'll go over to the inn and look around."

"How much arsenic?" Shannon said, playing his favorite role of devil's advocate. "Could have been an accidental ingestion. There might be an old well on the property. They could have made the wine using that."

"There isn't a well—we looked." Wallace gave him a hint of a grin. "Believe it or not, that's one of the places missing people tend to end up. And yes, it could have been accidental, but given everything that's happened, it's suspicious. As for how much arsenic, the doctor doesn't know if it was enough to be fatal, but it was certainly enough to make her very sick. Not likely an accident. Still possible, but not likely."

"So I take it you'll now be wanting to exhume Welby's body," Shannon said. "To see if he had any of the same signs."

"Well, I haven't drawn that conclusion yet since we know so little about what happened to Miss Carr. Unfortunately, even if we agreed to exhume her grandfather, she is in no condition to give approval, so we'd need a court order."

"What about me?" Tyrus asked.

Detective Wallace looked him up and down. "You must be the long-lost grandson Detective Martin told me about. Unfortunately, you have no rights in the matter because you are not legally related, blood or no. Leastwise, not while Miss Carr, his heir, is alive."

"But what if I—" Whatever Tyrus was going to say, he changed his mind and fell silent.

"A court order then," Shannon said. "How long?"

Wallace shrugged. "Depends on what else is on the docket. A day or two at least." Her eyes went back to Tyrus. "Since you're here, we'd like to have a word with you."

"I also have a question for him," I said. He turned in my direction as I asked, "What were you searching for in Lyndia's office this morning?"

Tyrus's nostrils flared, and he appeared ready to lash out. Instead, he said tightly, "Something Welby told me about."

"What?"

"I'd like to know too." Wallace folded her arms and stared down at him.

Tyrus shifted his body toward her, as if shutting me out. "It was a new will. He wrote it by hand after I arrived. I didn't see it myself, but he told me about it."

A new will, I thought. Definitely not the one I'd seen burning in the imprint from the office. That one had been two years old. Maybe it was the same will the cold presence had referred to in the chair imprint at Lyndia's outdoor firepit.

"And what did it say?" Detective Burke spoke for the first time. It was easy to forget his presence when his partner was so imposing.

Tyrus's face flushed. "That he was leaving the inn to me. That's what I was searching for in his office."

"You?" Bonnie gasped. "And not Lyndia? But he loved that girl."

"I guess he thought she needed help to run the inn. He trusted that I would take care of her."

I noticed Tryus didn't mention Welby's suspicion about Lyndia being the one poisoning him. Either he was completely against it being a possibility, or he was protecting her.

"And why you?" Wallace asked.

Tyrus shrugged. "I think because of the money I gave him."

"What money?" Shannon and I said together.

"Well . . ." Tyrus looked decidedly uncomfortable now.

"My understanding is that there have been some problems at the inn in the past few years. I've had to give Welby quite a bit of money. Don't get me wrong. I'm not complaining. He bought my first real camera equipment that got me started when my parents were still urging me to go into retail management like my father, which I hated. I owed Welby a lot for the faith he put in me, someone he didn't even know. Anyway, I looked through his books, and things don't match up, but I don't know enough about it to understand why." He met Bonnie's eyes. "That might be why Lyndia wants to sell."

Bonnie's face wrinkled with concern. "She should have come to us."

"So was Welby bad at managing money?" I wanted to know.

"No." Bonnie's answer was immediate. "Welby is one of the few people I know who refuses to live beyond his means." She sighed. "I mean, refused. It still feels like we could run next door and ask to borrow some eggs." She held a hand up to her right eye, blotting a sudden rush of tears.

I placed a comforting hand on her shoulder. "Maybe someone's stealing money."

"Possibly." Tyrus dipped his head in acknowledgment. "Maybe it was Nigel."

"Who is conveniently missing," Wallace said, frowning. "Do you have proof of any of this, or do we have only your word?"

Tyrus's shoulders slumped. "I don't have proof. I mean, I can prove I gave Welby money, but for the rest, I only know what he told me."

"We need to talk to Lyndia," Shannon said.

Wallace pulled back her head and looked down her nose at him. "Not today, you won't. She was conscious when I went back, but she wasn't making any sense. The doctor said maybe in a day or two." The detective's stare returned to Tyrus. "If you're not busy, we can have that discussion now."

"Okay."

They moved off together, Tyrus the picture of submission.

"You believe him?" Shannon asked.

"I'd feel better if I could touch more of his things. He's still our most likely suspect."

"And to think that I—" Bonnie put a hand over her mouth, as if to stifle her emotion. "That I set Micaela up with him."

"We don't know he's guilty. We need proof." I glanced over at the detectives, now deep in conversation with Tyrus. "You tell them about his gun?"

"Yeah, and I told them we also suspect it was Welby's." Shannon paused in apparent frustration. "But if Welby gave it to him, and there are no other imprints, he didn't use it to shoot Nigel."

"Unless he wore gloves," I said.

Before we could decide what to do, Deanna Lowe hurried into the waiting room. More of her hair had escaped her ponytail, and the wrinkles around her eyes were more apparent. She'd traded her pink Magnolia Inn uniform for cropped jeans and a frilly white blouse that was tight enough to show the mushroom of fat around her waist. She was almost too thin everywhere else.

Spying us, she hurried over. "How is she? They won't tell me anything over the phone. I thought I'd check here on my way home."

"She's going to be okay—we think," Bonnie said. "They haven't let us see her, though."

Deanna didn't show any reaction except to nod and say, "I guess I called the ambulance in time."

"Thanks for letting us know too," Bonnie added.

"I couldn't leave at the time, but I didn't want her to die alone." She paused. "I mean, if that was what was happening."

"What exactly did happen?" I asked, moving so I could see her while keeping an eye on the detectives and Tyrus, who were closer to the desk.

"I'm not sure." Deanna rubbed her temple as if fighting a headache. "After you"—she nodded at Bonnie—"went with Lyndia to her room, I thought she'd be there the rest of the day. She's been in there a lot since Welby . . . you know. But right after you left, I heard some banging around, and then I heard a blow dryer or maybe a vacuum. I clean too when I'm upset, so that's what I figured she was doing. When she finally came out, I asked her if she wanted lunch, but she said she wasn't hungry. Anyway, she was outside by the pool when she had another visitor."

"Who?" Bonnie asked.

"A woman. Blond hair piled up to here." Deanna put her hands a foot above her head. "And lots of makeup. I hadn't seen her before, but Lyndia knew her."

That sounded like Freddi, Nigel's ex-wife.

"You hear what they talked about?" Shannon asked.

Deanna glanced over at the detectives, whom she obviously recognized, and her voice lowered. "Not the details. It was about money, though. It sounded like the woman thought Lyndia owed some to her." She snorted. "Wouldn't be surprised, actually."

"No," Bonnie said firmly. "Freddi used to be married to that horrible Nigel. He's the one who owes her money, not Lyndia."

"Well, I was trying not to eavesdrop. That's probably it."

"You said you wouldn't be surprised," Shannon prompted.

"What do you know about the money situation at Magnolia Inn?"

"Just that the staff hasn't been paid since Welby died. What with the probate and everything since Nigel went missing, there haven't been funds."

"We'll see about getting that fixed." Bonnie reached out and touched her arm.

Did Bonnie also know this was the woman who made her husband's life difficult after the shooting? If she did, she didn't seem to hold a grudge.

"About what time was this?" Shannon asked.

"Sometime after one, I'd guess. I still hadn't eaten lunch." Deanna shrugged. "You can ask Lyndia, or have her look up the camera feed. She can get to the live feed and the backups on her phone. There's no sound, but it will have the time."

"You can't access it?" I asked. "We have no idea when we'll be able to get in to see Lyndia."

"Back at the inn, I suppose. There's a laptop we use for scheduling that links to it, but I've never needed to access the feed, so I'm not sure about it."

"The police will want all the footage, I'm sure," Shannon said.

"What happened after Freddi left?" I asked.

"Well, she stomped out actually. Lyndia went into the pantry for a bottle of her grandfather's elderberry wine and disappeared. I was cleaning windows a short time later when she came stumbling into the lobby, clutching her stomach and carrying the bottle. She fainted, and the bottle shattered on the floor. I tried to wake her up and get her out of there before anyone saw her, but she wouldn't move. That's when I started getting worried and called the ambulance."

"You didn't think it was poison?" I asked.

"Not then. There was hardly any wine left, so I thought maybe she was drunk—though I didn't think you could get drunk that fast. The ambulance workers did a few checks, I guess, and I heard them say it looked like poison or an overdose or something. Did she take too many sleeping pills?"

"It was arsenic," Bonnie said.

Deanna gaped. "That's crazy."

"So what did you do with the broken bottle?" The tautness of Shannon's body told me he felt his question was important. And maybe it was. If someone had put the poison in the wine, I might be able to find an imprint that would lead us directly to the person.

"I cleaned it up and threw it away, of course," Deanna said. "Last thing we need is for guests to cut themselves or slip and fall."

Another angle occurred to me. "Were you around when Welby made his elderberry wine? Do you know what water he used?" Wine making from berries always involved sugar and water of some sort, and water could be tainted with arsenic.

"Yeah. Just tap water, I think."

"Well, thank you." Bonnie smiled at her. "I appreciate you coming here."

"There's one more thing," Deanna said. "I can't be there tonight, and the employee we have there now goes home at eight. Usually Lyndia does the graveyard shift on Sunday nights because it's so slow. She locks the doors and puts out a sign for guests to call her if they want to come in after midnight or if they need something else. I'd stay, but I have something important to do. A previous engagement."

"We'll figure something out, even if I have to send Holt over there to sleep on a couch in the lobby." Bonnie smiled. "Thanks again."

Deanna nodded, and with another glance toward the detectives, she hurried away.

"I'm not liking the idea of Dad hanging out there," Shannon said in an undertone.

"Me either," I agreed.

Bonnie stared at us as if we'd gone insane. "Why ever not?"

"Because dad shot and killed that woman's son," Shannon retorted. "Do I need another reason?"

Bonnie moved her hand in a dismissive motion. "Oh, Deanna's forgiven him."

"Or she poisoned Welby and Lyndia, and Dad's next."

Bonnie put her hands on her hips and said, "My money is on the ex-wife or on Tyrus. Autumn, we should go home and get you into Freddi's room."

I'd opened my mouth to agree when we were interrupted by a young Hispanic nurse who came up behind Bonnie.

"Um, excuse me?" she said, her smile wide and her eyes kind. "Are one of you Bonnie?"

Bonnie whirled to face her. "That's me."

"Lyndia Carr is asking for you."

Chapter 13

onnie's face split in a wide smile. "She's awake?"

"She's still in and out, but we told her you were here." The nurse looked between Bonnie, Shannon, and me. "Only two back right now, okay? Until we get her in a room, which we are working on now. We need to keep her overnight for observation. I have to warn you that she's not making much sense because she was in a lot of pain when she came in and we had to sedate her, but we know patients are much happier when they see someone is here for them."

"Thank you," Bonnie said.

"You go with Mom," Shannon told me. "That way you can check on Lyndia while I go talk to the detectives." By check on Lyndia, he meant read imprints. "I want to find the broken bottle, and any others that may be around." He leaned over and kissed me. "I'll text you if I have to leave with them, okay?"

"Okay." I tried not to feel torn at being separated from him once more on what should have been our honeymoon. But the more details we learned, the closer we were to solving this thing and getting back to our new life together.

The nurse led us through the emergency room doors to a

curtained partition and left us with Lyndia, who appeared to
have drifted off to sleep again. Her face was pale, and her figure
in the hospital gown seemed far too thin under the partially
drawn-up sheet. An IV connected her to a bag of liquid, and
monitors showed her oxygen level and heart rate. Bonnie and
I stared awkwardly at the pitiful figure for a moment before I
began touching things.

"What do you hope to find?" Bonnie asked.

"Probably nothing," I admitted, gliding my finger along
the edge of the bed railing. "But you never know."

Bonnie combed her fingers through Lyndia's spikey hair.
"Poor dear. Who would do this?"

I didn't know, but likely it was for money, love, or revenge.
Shannon always bet on money, but love also drove people to
do crazy things.

I touched the controls on the bed and gasped as a vivid
imprint of someone in pain overtook me. It was all I could do
to tell my hand to break contact. I breathed a sigh of relief.

"That bad?" Bonnie said.

I nodded and continued my search of the bed. There were
imprints from frustrated or enamored hospital personnel,
more imprints from people in various amounts of pain, and
even an imprint from a boy faking illness to get the attention
of his parents. I found nothing from Lyndia in a moment of
lucidity.

"Do you see her belongings anywhere?" I asked, opening a
cupboard. "Too bad she's not wearing jewelry. I could relive the
experience for myself, to see if the poisoning was accidental or
if maybe she noticed something important."

"She has a ring from her mother that she sometimes wears,"
Bonnie said, stroking Lyndia's hand. "I wonder if they took it

off. She should have clothes somewhere, at least. They've got her in this gown now."

The next cupboard was locked. I sighed and checked three more, finding only bandaids, sheets, and pillows.

"Bonnie?" Lyndia's eyes fluttered lightly. "Is that you?"

"Yes, sweetie. I'm here. And so is my daughter-in-law, Autumn. Shannon's out in the lobby, and Holt is on his way. Even Deanna was here to check up on you. You are not alone. I promise. We'll get you through this."

"Tyrus?" Lyndia asked.

"Well, um," Bonnie began.

"I think he likes me," Lyndia whispered.

"Of course he does, but you really should be . . . Lyndia? Are you okay?"

At Bonnie's panicked voice, I experienced a momentary rush of fear that Lyndia had stopped breathing, but a quick peek at the monitor showed she was stable.

"She's okay," I said, coming over to stand by Bonnie. "She's probably still recovering from the poison and whatever they did to counteract that."

"Should I tell her?" Bonnie asked.

"You mean about the new will, or the fact that Tyrus searched her office for it—or whatever else he was really looking for if it doesn't exist?"

"I mean about him being her cousin and that maybe she shouldn't trust him." Her voice stumbled on the last words.

"Given where she's at right now, it might be a good idea for her to be careful."

Bonnie leaned close to Lyndia. "Sweetie?" she said. "Look, you need to be careful around Tyrus, and your uncle's ex-wife, and just about everyone. Can you hear me?"

Again the flutter with the eyes. With apparent effort, they finally stayed open. "Bonnie? Is that you?"

"Yes, we're all here for you."

"Thank you." Lyndia's voice was so faint, I also leaned over to hear. "Is Deanna staying at the inn tonight? I-I . . . the guests . . ." Her eyelids closed again.

"Don't you worry about a thing, sweetie." Bonnie patted her hand. "We'll take care of it. If it comes to it, Holt can go over there and sleep on one of your lobby couches."

A strangled laugh burbled up from Lyndia's throat. Her eyes opened halfway, her gaze in the general direction of Bonnie's face but obviously not focusing well. "Poor Holt and his back."

Bonnie chuckled. "Yeah, but don't let him hear us saying that." To me, she added, "I told Lyndia this morning about the police digging up Buster, and Holt pulling another muscle. And his back was still weak from the last time. It's a good sign that she remembers our conversation." She turned back to Lyndia. "Thanks for thinking of him, dear. But we'll figure it out."

"Maybe Micaela?" Lyndia said, a bit breathlessly. "She knows where . . . the cot in Grandpa's . . . office."

"That's right, she does. I'm sure she wouldn't mind, and the boys love to sleep over with me. How does that sound?"

But Lyndia was out again, as if she already knew Bonnie would take care of everything.

"I'd like to stay here with her," Bonnie said. "At least until I know Tyrus is gone. Will you go ask Shannon if they can make sure he doesn't come in here? Or anyone else we don't approve? What if whoever did this tries again?" She sat on one of the two chairs in the room and folded her arms over her chest. "I'll stay right here until I make sure they know what to watch out for."

My mouth twitched slightly at that. As far as I knew, this

was Bonnie's first poisoning case, but maybe being a police officer's wife was something you never forgot. "Well, okay, but it's not likely anyone will hurt her here in the hospital," I said, though it had happened in at least one of my cases. "All those cameras, you know."

"Right. That's good because I can't stay long. I have to get back and work things out for her at the inn anyway."

I was tempted to volunteer to go to Magnolia Inn myself, but I knew nothing about running an inn or where anything was. "Okay. I'll tell Shannon. Call me if you need anything."

As I turned, the Hispanic nurse opened the curtain with a jerk, startling me. "Um, I'm really sorry, but I'm going to have to ask you both to leave. I'll be taking her up to her room now, and apparently, the police have decided to put her on a watch list. No unapproved visitors until they decide if she's at risk, or until she is able to consent."

"You mean in case one of us tries to finish the job," Bonnie retorted.

I held back a laugh. "It's a good idea," I told her. "Now you won't have to worry."

"Yeah, but blocking *me?*" Bonnie shook her head.

"As long as Holt's a suspect in Nigel's disappearance, it makes sense. But at least it means no one else can come in, including Tyrus and Deanna."

"And Freddi," Bonnie muttered.

"Tyrus?" This from Lyndia, whose eyes opened the merest slit. "Is he here?"

Bonnie patted her. "It's okay, sweetie. You sleep, and we'll figure all this out." After Lyndia settled, Bonnie fixed her eyes on the nurse. "We can call once she's properly awake, right? Do you have paper? I want to leave her a note."

While Bonnie wrote in beautiful cursive on a notepad, I asked the nurse about Lyndia's belongings.

"Oh, she was worried about her phone when she came in," the nurse said, "so one of the other nurses locked her bag away. We'll stop and get it on the way to the room, so she has it handy. She'll be awake soon enough to want it."

Just my luck. "Well, thanks."

With a little help from a different nurse, we found our way back to the emergency room where Tyrus and Holt were standing together looking out of place and upset. The detectives and Shannon were nowhere in sight.

"They won't even let me see her now," Tyrus agonized, sending me an unfriendly stare. "Thanks to your husband. He convinced the police to put her on a watch."

Holt clapped him on the back. "Well, he has a point, and it's for Lyndia's protection. They can't call it attempted homicide until there's more evidence, but it's enough to require the hospital to limit visitors. It's a good thing, seeing as Nigel might still be out there somewhere, gunshot or no."

"But now that they know about my adoption," Tyrus said, "they think I'm responsible."

"Actually, it's probably me they want to keep out." Holt stretched slightly to the side, rubbing his lower back and grimacing slightly. I'd have to remember to stop by an herb shop in town to see if they carried the ointment I always used for strained muscles.

"Where'd Shannon go?" I asked.

"To show the police where Welby keeps his elderberry wine. Or kept." Holt sighed. "With Deanna and Lyndia not there, we wanted to make sure they wouldn't tear the place apart looking for it. Of course I had to tell him where it was."

"Good idea." I looked at Bonnie. "Can I get a ride back with you?"

"Of course, dear."

We parted ways with the men and walked out to her car. The heat of the sidewalk was searing, and I was grateful for the calluses on my feet. I could sense the heartbeat of the city now, and it was beginning to feel familiar.

I hadn't checked in with Elliot for a while, and he hadn't contacted me, so I shot him off a text with a quick update. *Do any of our suspects have a history with arsenic?* There was no immediate response, which didn't surprise me. Until he knew one way or the other, he wouldn't commit to an opinion. Then I looked up arsenic and wine on my phone's browser.

"Listen to this," I said to Bonnie. "On average, there is a hundred and fifty times the arsenic in wines, especially cheap wines, as the safe level allowed in water in the US."

"Wow, really? Maybe this *was* all an accident. Especially with the wine being something Welby made at home. Even if the detectives don't think so."

I shook my head. "The highest of the wines tested were seventy-two parts per billion, and Canada's safe level is one hundred parts per billion. And only one person out of a hundred who drinks wine with arsenic for a lifetime will die from the arsenic—actually, of cancer caused by the arsenic. Not anything like what happened to Lyndia."

"Oh." Bonnie slowed the car and turned into Haven Retreat. "I guess that means we're right back to where we started. What are you going to do now?"

"I'll go meet Shannon at Magnolia Inn. I need to find more imprints to read."

She smiled. "I was hoping you'd say that."

If I had told her what I was really thinking, she might not have smiled at all. She might have called me crazy and wished her son had never married me.

What I really meant was that I was going to try to talk to the dead.

Chapter 14

As I approached the front of Magnolia Inn, I caught a glimpse in their side parking lot of a police car, a forensic van, and the same unmarked police car the detectives had been driving. I couldn't see the covered parking area from the front, so for all I knew, there were more official vehicles. A few bystanders stood on the walk, talking excitedly. It didn't take me long to see that the police weren't allowing anyone except employees or guests to enter. So much for my plan of reading imprints from Lyndia or from the cold presence.

Shannon was outside the main entrance talking with Detective Wallace, who had a bored expression on her face. I wondered if this was her day off or if she always had the weekend beat. But the bored expression became calculating as she spied me.

Shannon broke away and sauntered in my direction. "They found traces of cyanide and a high amount of arsenic in three of the unopened elderberry wine bottles they've tested out of the six remaining bottles," he said in an undertone, his eyes going behind me to the people on the sidewalk, who looked more thrilled than upset at the police presence. "Which means they're taking all of the bottles for more testing."

"Yeah, but how much arsenic?" I asked.

"Enough that one glass might cause a stomachache, but an entire bottle? Definitely enough to kill."

That was sobering. "She was lucky then," I said, my mouth abruptly dry. "Can you get me access to her rooms?"

He shook his head. "No, not even the police are going in right now to the private areas. They're locked up tight. The employees don't have a key or permission to let them in anyway. Detective Wallace could get a warrant now that they've found the poison, but they're in no hurry since they have the bottles, including the broken one she was drinking from, and it's unlikely whoever did this has access to her private rooms. And before you ask, no, they won't let you touch the bottles, though I finally decided to tell Wallace about your ability."

Which explained the reason Detective Wallace was still staring at me from across the front yard. "I guess now she thinks I'm a flake."

"Oh, she's more into it than you might think."

"So no burning at the stake?"

He laughed. "Maybe from Detective Burke when he gets back from wherever he went—if she tells him. But I did manage to get you something." Turning so his back was to Wallace, he let go of my hand and pulled a tissue from his pocket, unwrapping it to reveal a dark chunk of broken glass as he held it out to me. "Be careful. The edges are a bit sharp."

"Nice," I said, not touching it. If what I suspected was on that piece of glass, I'd be reliving Lyndia's poisoning—not something I wanted to do with the detective watching me. "Will they let us go around the back? I'd rather be sitting."

I also wanted to check for more imprints from the cold presence, or talk to the dead as I was now thinking of it.

"I believe so."

The pool area was being used by a couple who had left the door open just as Lyndia had that morning. Or maybe they always left it open during the day. We went inside and sat near the fireplace. I chose the white lounge chair Lyndia had been reclining on and touched the surface gingerly before sitting on it. There were plenty of imprints, but none earlier than a week and mostly faded.

"Weird," I said.

"What's weird?"

"Lyndia was sitting here when she told me she was crushing on Tyrus. I'd think she'd have imprinted at least something. Especially when she teared up when we were talking about her grandfather." Though her hands had been over her face at the time, so maybe not. Still, I'd have thought there would be some remnant left through her bare feet or legs.

"How do you know it was this particular lounge chair?" he said, waving first at where I sat and then at the dozen others around the pool.

"Well, it was the only one here by the fireplace this morning, just like now." My stomach took the opportunity to growl noisily, and we both laughed.

"Our lunch," Shannon said, "is still at Mom's. And it's almost four already."

"Let's get this over with then." I held out my hand and waited for him to move his chair closer and hold out the glass. My finger touched the surface, warm from his pocket.

I'm going to die! I need help. I stumbled to the door of my suite, clutching the bottle. The pain in my stomach was excruciating.

Had Grandpa felt this way on that last day? It was a horrible thought, one I couldn't bear. I had no idea my stomach could hurt so much. Why had I drunk the wine? This was Nigel's fault . . .

The doorknob stuck under my hand. Terror shot through me. I tried to drop the bottle, but I couldn't control my fingers. Why had I even picked it up? If I didn't get help soon, I would suffer here all alone. Maybe I would die.

Panic filled me.

Blinding terror.

The door gave way. I stumbled down the hall into the lobby. "Deanna! Help! I—" I began to vomit. The bottle finally slipped from my fingers.

"Oh," I gasped, glad when the pain vanished.

Shannon said something, but another imprint was following the first. A brief sensation of satisfaction as someone— Welby?—put the bottle on the top shelf in the pantry nearly a year ago. This was followed by another one from a day earlier.

I leaned over the table out on the patio, looking up into an old man's face. The part of me who was still Autumn recognized him as Welby. The other part of me felt a rush of affection for the old man.

"Hold it steady," he told me.

I did. The glass felt cool against my fingers, though it warmed as he filled it with the fermented elderberry wine. "Are you sure it's worth it?" I asked. "It's been a lot of work from what I've seen."

"It'll be worth it. You'll see," he said with a laugh. "Just wait for a few months. And thanks for helping me, Deanna. Lyndia hates making it." He laughed. "Though she seems to like drinking it enough."

"I'll bet." His granddaughter was a horrid, spoiled little brat, but I wasn't going to be the one to tell him. He'd never see it anyway.

"You can let go now," he said. "I'll be right back. I forgot the corks in the office."

When no more imprints surfaced, I pulled my hand away.

Shannon closed his hand over the glass and folded it up in the tissue. "Well?"

"Lyndia's collapse happened exactly the way Deanna described. But she didn't imprint before that, so I don't know what she was thinking when she started drinking. But she does seem to believe her grandfather was poisoned now, maybe because of what you and your mom said to her this morning."

"Possibly."

"She blames it on Nigel. But there was more." I described the last imprint.

"So Deanna Lowe helped Welby bottle his wine. And left her alone with it."

"Yes, but she wasn't thinking about poison. I got the feeling she liked him."

"That doesn't mean she didn't put in some elderberry leaves while they were doing the brewing."

"That would have been days earlier, then. Because you let it sit for weeks before bottling. And it would explain the cyanide, but not the arsenic."

He sat back in his chair. "Maybe the cyanide didn't work fast enough. And maybe she was hoping Welby would give some to my parents."

"Maybe he did."

Shannon stared at me for several seconds before whipping out his phone and texting. A response came back almost as if the person on the other end had been waiting. "Mom says he gave them two bottles, and she still has them. They aren't big wine drinkers." Shannon jumped to his feet. "I'm going to get them and have the police test them too." He grinned at me. "Come on. I'll let you touch them first."

"Thanks." I pushed to my feet, feeling dizzy.

"You have that hungry look," Shannon said, his arms going around me. "We'd better fix that." He nuzzled my ear with his lips.

Nice as that felt, I had something more to do. "Wait a minute." Moving away from him, I touched the firepit top, feeling all around the faux stones. The stones were lovely colors, some a deep brown marbled with differing amounts of orange and off-white while others were tan marbled with brown and orange. But there were no imprints. Likely the heat from the gas fire was great enough to obliterate them.

Then I went for the chair Shannon had been sitting in earlier, hoping to find at least the imprints I'd felt there from the cold presence, but they were gone. Had I imagined it? The other two chairs also showed nothing except vague, old imprints from people who'd probably been guests. There was certainly no cold presence here now.

Shannon and I discussed options as we walked back to Haven Retreat to get the elderberry wine and our lunch. "So you felt this cold outside Frontier Cabin and around the firepit," he said. "If it is someone who is no longer with us— and I'm not saying it isn't—it could be either Nigel or Welby. We know Welby liked to play checkers outside near the pool even before Lyndia put in the firepit table for him. And we know both he and Nigel went to Frontier Cabin at least once to talk to Tyrus."

"Twice for Nigel," I said. "He was shot there." This I added with a trace of self-justification because it hadn't been all that long ago that Shannon had doubted me.

"Right. The blood on the bullet is his. But was it a killing blow? We still don't know if he's dead for sure."

"Well, if I feel the presence again, I'm going to talk to it. Whoever it is cares about what's happening here, and if he can imprint, even if temporarily, we should learn something."

Shannon considered that. "The strange thing is that imprints have been almost impossible to remove. Unless you apply extreme heat. So why would that one vanish?"

I shook my head. "I don't know. Except maybe because they don't have flesh to touch it? But then why did I feel it in the first place?"

"I don't know. I always thought your gift was more mental than physical. Makes sense to me that their energy could still imprint."

I considered that for a moment. "I guess we can make up the rules as we go along since Cody is the only other person we know who has felt anything like it."

"Of course that would make you more of a psychic." His deep chuckle filled the space between us.

I scowled at him. "Let's go eat before I become crabbier than that statement just made me."

"Okay." His grin didn't fade. "I should know better than to tease you while you're hungry."

Back at Haven Retreat, Bonnie was manning the kitchen. She'd already put a bottle of Elderberry wine on the counter, and also a small cooler. "I could only find one bottle," she said, "so we must have opened the other. You know, you two should still go on your picnic."

"Where's Micaela?" Shannon asked. "Not with Tyrus, I hope."

"She took the boys home so she can nap while they watch

TV or something. They'll be back at eight because the boys are sleeping here tonight while Micaela camps out at Magnolia Inn."

"Hopefully the police will be gone by then." Shannon frowned at the bottle of wine before pulling it closer to us. "Where's Dad?"

"Lying down and alternating heat and ice on his back. He'll need to help me with breakfast in the morning if Micaela will be holding down the fort at Magnolia Inn."

"I can help," I said.

She shook her head. "We can handle it. You two need some time alone together." Her gaze dropped to the wine, and that was my cue to start reading its imprints.

Ignoring my rumbling stomach, I reached out and placed a knuckle on the middle of the bottle where someone might carry it. The imprints were similar to the last ones on the piece of glass in Shannon's pocket. "Deanna helped with the bottling. It's from the same year as the other one."

"Then I'd better get it to the police," Shannon said.

I was already pulling the cooler toward me. "They looked like they're going to be awhile. Should we eat first?" I'd gone past hungry and was now feeling shaky inside.

He grinned at me. "We could take it to the beach."

"That might not be such a good idea," a voice said from behind us, stopping my protest before I could voice it. We all turned to see Holt standing in the doorway to the kitchen. His hands were dirty and so were his jeans.

"What on earth?" Bonnie put her hands on her hips. "I thought you were lying down."

"I was going to, but then I remembered I hadn't put water on the spot the police dug up, and seriously, they did a terrible job putting it back together, so I had to fix it. I don't want to be dealing with an uneven yard there. The last thing we need is people tripping and bringing lawsuits."

"What about your back?"

"I took some painkillers." He moved slowly to the sink and began to wash his hands.

"Well, they've found poison in some of Welby's elderberry wine, and the kids are going to give this bottle to the police who are still at Magnolia Inn—and then they're going on a long-overdue picnic to the beach."

Holt turned with a frown, his hands still in the water. "You might want to rethink that, or at least don't stay too long. I heard on the radio a few minutes ago that there's a thunderstorm warning for today and tomorrow."

"They'll be fine. Long as it's not a hurricane," Bonnie said with a shiver.

Holt finished washing and eyed the cooler with interest. "I'm a little hungry too."

Bonnie sighed and moved toward the refrigerator. "You go change, and I'll make you something."

"Okay, but I think I'll go as far as Magnolia Inn with them first." Holt came around the counter and sat on a stool. "I need to tell them what we did with the other bottle, and I want to make sure they're not scaring off Lyndia's guests."

"It might be better if you stay here," Shannon said. "Out of sight, out of mind, so to speak."

Holt snorted. "They've got to know by now that this doesn't involve me. Welby was my best friend besides your mother, and I want to help find out who did this to him."

Once a cop, always a cop, I thought but didn't say aloud. I was too busy watching Shannon open the top of the cooler.

He extracted a sandwich and handed it to me. "In that case, I think we'll eat here before we go for a walk on the beach," he said. "We never know how long it will take, and Autumn needs to eat now."

Bonnie looked at me with interest, but Shannon shook his head. "It's the imprints, Mom, not a baby. Reading imprints for her is like running miles."

"Oh, of course." Bonnie plastered a large smile on her face that was only a little forced.

Sliding onto a stool, I pulled off the wrapper from the sandwich and bit down in a single motion. It tasted heavenly, even if the bread was fake whole wheat and obviously contained more refined sugar than anything called bread should ever have.

Shannon grinned at my sigh and pulled out one for himself and another for Holt. The last one he handed to his mother, who laughed. "Glad I made enough, but let me find a little more to supplement."

We made short work of sandwiches, sliced fruit, leftover cheesy rigatoni, and chocolate cake, washed down by cans of pop for Bonnie and Holt, coffee for Shannon, and sparkling apple cider for me. The shaky, shivery feeling inside me was gone, and even though it wasn't romantic, being there with his family gave me a sense of belonging that I'd missed since Winter had died.

The doorbell rang as we finished, and Bonnie hurried to the front door ahead of everyone. Two men waited on the porch, dressed in dark suits and dress shirts even in this muggy heat. They looked vaguely familiar to me.

"May I help you?" Bonnie asked in a clipped tone.

"We're here to talk with Holt and Bonnie Martin," said the taller of the two. Sweat beaded his forehead.

Holt stepped closer to Bonnie. "We're Holt and Bonnie."

"Good." The man handed over a gold-embossed business card. "We're real estate investment attorneys, and we are in discussion with Lyndia Carr about purchasing Magnolia Inn on behalf of a group of developers."

Right, they were the men I'd seen at Lyndia's after breakfast this morning. So much had happened since then—the dog exhumation, the imprints at the inn and Frontier Cabin, and Lyndia's poisoning—that my glimpse of them seemed far in the past.

"So?" Holt asked, taking the card. "What does that have to do with us?"

"Well, it's come to our attention that there is a section of disputed land between the inn and your property that is important to the project our investors wish to build. We would like to make you an offer of two hundred thousand dollars for the land."

Holt snorted. "Right, not a chance. With the landscaping and the cottage, it's worth more than that, even if I did want to sell. This is prime real estate, and you know it."

The man smiled as if at a simple child, emphasizing his slight double chin. "That's true, but we would also have to pay Miss Carr's interest as well, which is why we really can't go any higher than two hundred and fifty thousand."

"I don't care how high you go." Holt's face flushed. "We are not selling our land. Period."

"I'm sorry you feel that way," said the second man. "If we do end up purchasing Magnolia Inn, it will be with the understanding that we will fight your claim in court. Our backers have rather deep pockets."

"You can take your deep pockets and get off my property!"

Holt growled, taking a menacing step toward them. Both men backed up before stumbling down the porch stairs.

"We will be in touch," the tall one said, squaring his shoulders and tugging the sides of his jacket straight as if to emphasize his point.

"I'm sure you will." Holt took another threatening step, and the men turned and headed for a black sedan parked in front of the house.

"Stupid vultures," Holt muttered.

Bonnie rubbed his arm. "They're just doing their job. I'll talk to Lyndia as soon as she's home. We'll present a united front, and they'll have no choice but to back down. It'll be okay."

"Right. Of course we will." Holt looked at Shannon and me. "Well, come on. Let's get this show on the road."

We walked back to Magnolia Inn, moving more slowly now because Holt was obviously favoring his back, despite his show for the attorneys. I could see no sign of his promised storm, except for some faint dark clouds far off in the distance.

Outside the inn, we found Freddi Dottson arguing with Detective Wallace. She'd changed from the hot-pink pantsuit to a lightweight, brilliant blue and green, paisley cover-up with long, sheer sleeves. I could see the strap of a blue swimsuit underneath. Her eye shadow was now also a bright blue.

"Ridiculous," she was saying. "This is partly my property now, with Nigel missing, and I should be able to go inside and get my papers."

"Sorry, Ma'am," Detective Wallace said. "We'll be finished here within the hour, but we didn't find any blue folder in the office, and if Miss Carr took the papers you gave her back into her personal quarters, those will remain locked until she's out of the hospital."

Freddi scowled. "Hospital? And when is that?"

"Tomorrow . . . possibly. Or the next day."

"Humph!" Freddi obviously wasn't pleased with the answer. "If you ask me, this is all a smokescreen. Lyndia wants to make sure my husband and I get nothing."

"Don't you mean ex-husband?" Holt said, coming to a stop next to her and flashing a charming grin. "But I can tell you, I talked to Welby myself, and he never intended to leave anything to Nigel."

"Oh." Freddi looked taken aback. "Well, I'm not sure about that. And if you ask me, this is all suspicious timing."

"I'll agree with you on that." Holt tipped his head agreeably, his smile widening. "Some even say there might be another will."

Freddi smiled back, her anger receding. Shannon had done the same thing to me when we'd been at odds. His smile had made me want to forgive him anything.

Detective Wallace looked happy to have Freddi's attention directed elsewhere. "Hey," she said to Shannon, "do you know where Tyrus Lockwood is? He's not answering his phone. My chief has decided to give the go-ahead for the exhumation after all. With the poisoning, we can get a court order, of course, but they're careful about granting those, so we'd have to finish our testing first, and the chief always likes to avoid the possibility of a lawsuit."

"I thought you said Tyrus couldn't give the okay," Shannon said.

She shrugged. "Apparently, since there is no will and he could be considered an heir just as much as Miss Carr, and they are technically both grandchildren, my chief thinks he can. It helps that your mother said Miss Carr agreed to the exhumation before her poisoning. But we don't want to wait until tomorrow to start the paperwork."

I guessed they wanted to bypass a court order and cover their bases at least enough to prevent a lawsuit in case Lyndia changed her mind.

"I haven't seen Tyrus since the hospital." Shannon paused and then lifted the reusable grocery bag where Bonnie had tucked the bottle of elderberry wine. "Look, this is from the same batch that you found the poison in. He gave my parents two, but only this one is left."

Wallace took the bag without looking into its depths. "Okay, we'll take it to the lab. But did anyone get sick from the other bottle?"

"Nope." It was Holt who answered. "We popped it at the open house here after the funeral. Only the neighbors came, and there were other drinks, of course, but everyone had at least a small glass of the elderberry wine for the toast."

"I see." Wallace motioned to a man in a uniform and gave him the bag, talking with him briefly for a moment before turning back to Holt and Shannon. "It would really help if you could track down Lockwood. I'd like to have things in place for the morning. We'd also like to test the gun you say he has."

Holt looked at Shannon. "We can find him, right?"

Shannon glanced at me. "Go ahead," I urged. "I'll wander around the area next to the beach. I want to find a health food store anyway." For Holt's back ointment, but I would save that for a surprise. I also wanted to take advantage of running into Freddi to ask about her confrontation with Lyndia.

"Native Sun Natural Foods Market is probably the closest on foot," Wallace said to me. "But they'll be closed on a Sunday."

"That's okay. It'll be fun to explore the town anyway."

"Did you say health food store?" Freddi turned to face me. "I'd like to know where it's at too. I got a little burned this afternoon on my shoulders, and a little aloe always helps it heal faster."

"Well, I'd love the company." I smiled at her, thinking it couldn't have worked out better if I'd thought about inviting her along.

"You two have fun." Shannon barely held back a knowing smile at the false brightness in my voice. "I'll call after we find Tyrus so we can meet up."

"Okay."

Freddi and I walked companionably together down the sidewalk toward the beach. The day was still bright and hot, but maybe a little less blazing than it had been earlier. Whether because of the approaching storm or because it was nearly five o'clock, I didn't know.

It wasn't until Magnolia Inn was out of sight that I got the text from Elliot. I strained to see it in the bright light. *One of Freddi Dottson's ex-boyfriends went to the hospital once for arsenic poisoning last year,* he wrote. *And another died of suspicious circumstances before she married Nigel. But there's more. I can't find an official divorce decree. I believe she is still officially married to Nigel Carr.*

I gave the woman a sidelong glance. Her face was serene at the moment, and though her hair bordered on ridiculous, she didn't look sinister. But with a suspicious death and an arsenic poisoning in her past, appearance didn't matter. In a single instant, she had jumped to the top of my suspect list.

Chapter 15

"That Holt Martin is one handsome man," Freddi said as we paused at a crossroad so I could search for the health food store's address on my phone. "That curly blond hair—it's not something you see a lot in men these days. I gotta hand it to Bonnie for snagging him." She paused before adding, "She's such a gracious host. It's obvious what he sees in her."

I started walking again, having plotted our path on my phone. "I agree, though I haven't known either of them long myself. I've only been married to their son for a week. And I met them in person a day before my wedding. We're visiting from Oregon."

Her gaze snapped to me. "Oh, I didn't realize. Your husband is the blond guy who was with Holt just now? I thought they might be related when I saw them together earlier. Congratulations. It looks like he comes from a good family. Though I guess that's not always a guarantee."

"No, it isn't."

We walked together in silence until we hit the cobbled pathway near the beach. It was slightly longer to the health food store this way, but when the options had come up, I had chosen this path next to the beach rather than the sidewalk along one of the cross streets.

"So," I said. "How long have you been interested in alternate health remedies? My parents owned an herb shop—that's my excuse."

"Oh, everyone here in Florida tries every remedy at least once. We're a pretty hip bunch. Or hippy bunch." She laughed. "So many are retired, you know, and finally have money to spend. Not me, yet. I'm only forty-eight. But I'm old enough to know that doctors don't always know everything."

She and my parents would have gotten along great. "So, I couldn't help overhearing your discussion with the police. Did you leave something with Lyndia?"

"Oh, it was copies of papers with the amounts Nigel owes me. I was hoping she would agree to pay me so I could go home."

"But with Nigel not here, and witnesses saying he wasn't in the will, do you think she'll agree?"

"If she doesn't, I'll cause problems." If anything, her determination had increased over the hours since we'd talked near Buster's graveside.

"You hate Lyndia that much?"

Freddi shook her head, her piled hair barely moving with the motion. "This has nothing to do with her. Nigel told me half the inn was his, and if something's happened to him, I at least need what he owes me. Like I told Lyndia, I'd go away, and I wouldn't try to get more. I'm trying to be fair. Nigel was Welby's only living son, after all. He deserves an inheritance every bit as much as she does."

"How could you get more?" I asked. "I mean, you have a

claim on your ex, but not the inn itself, right?" I waited to see if she'd tell me she was still married, but she didn't admit to anything, and she didn't look my way. Time to shake her up a bit. "Maybe it doesn't matter now that Nigel's son has been found."

She stopped walking and faced me, her eyes wide. "He has?"

"Yeah, apparently he's been in touch with Welby for ten years, only no one knew his identity. He's staying in one of the cottages right now at Haven Retreat. Nigel visited him there. I hope he doesn't counter any claims you might have."

"Oooh, that stinking, no-good, two-faced rat of a man," she exclaimed, clenching her fists. "That's just like Nigel to screw things up for me. Well, it doesn't matter, I'm not giving up. I need to pay for my car, and I'm three months behind on my rent." She glared at me as if it were all my fault. "Take my advice—never trust a man. If Nigel wasn't already dead, I'd kill him myself!" She started walking again.

Goose bumps ran across my flesh as I hurried to catch up. "How do you know he's dead? When we talked earlier today, you said it would be easier to collect now that he was dead."

"Because he's a greedy son of a gun. He'd never walk away from this." Tears glimmered in her brown eyes. The brown surprised me, because with the bright blue eye shadow, I'd registered them being blue only seconds ago. Her false eyelashes looked impossibly long under the bright afternoon sun.

"This is Lyndia's fault," she continued. "I bet she had one of her developers get rid of him."

"Lyndia's the one in the hospital," I reminded her.

She stopped walking again. "The police mentioned that. Is that why they're at the inn? What happened?

"She was poisoned. Arsenic. And maybe Welby was too."

Her already pale face lost any hint of color save for two bright spots of rouge. "Arsenic?"

"They found it in some wine bottles. Lyndia was having pretty severe stomach cramps and someone called an ambulance. She'll be okay."

She nodded, relaxing slightly. "I knew someone who ingested arsenic once. I was with him when he had the reaction. The doctor said he was lucky the dose wasn't a little stronger, or he would have died." She gave a little groan. "Oh, they're going to think it's me—the police, I mean." Her eyes looked huge in her pallid face. "Especially because I was trying to get inside her office."

"You were trying to get inside?"

"Well, yes. I had heard that something was going on, and Lyndia wasn't there, and I didn't want the police to find my papers." She paused for a moment before rushing on. "Have you heard anything about suspects? Didn't you say your husband's a detective? Do you know if I'm under suspicion?"

"They have several suspects," I said, watching her closely. "Holt and Tyrus among them."

"You mean the travel guide author? Nice man. I met him this morning when the police were digging up the dog."

"Yes. He's Nigel's son. He was put up for adoption thirty-two years ago."

She heaved a sigh. "Well, at least that was before I met Nigel, so he wasn't cheating on me." She looked around. "Is this store much further? I'm suddenly not feeling well."

"The store is a bit further, but there's really no reason to go there while it's closed." I pointed to a bench a little further down the path. "Why don't we sit down? Or we can find a restaurant and get you a drink of water or something. The ones we've passed seem to be open."

"Here's fine," she said.

The clouds I'd seen earlier in the distance were coming closer now, and I considered how long we might have before the storm hit. I needed to find a way to touch something personal of Freddi's before then.

"So how'd you meet Nigel?" I asked.

She thought a moment. "At a friend's party." A faint smile curled her lips. "He was so charming. I thought he was the one." She shrugged. "Guess I was wrong."

I wondered if that was why she hadn't divorced him for real, or if she had known about the inn and that was her reason.

"Did you know Welby?"

"I met him only once. He didn't come to our wedding, but he stopped by a week after. He said he and Nigel didn't see eye-to-eye, but that if I ever needed anything, he'd try to help me."

"That was nice."

"It was." She hesitated. "I mean, I think so now. At the time, I thought he was condescending, and I believed everything Nigel said about their falling out."

"And what was that?"

"That Nigel was misunderstood, and his dad expected too much. Stuff like that. Later, I realized that was always his excuse." She crossed and uncrossed her legs, then shook her sandaled foot as if to remove sand. "We'd been married only two years before his brother died. Nigel believed his brother's death wasn't an accident."

"I thought Lyndia's parents died in a car crash."

She lifted both shoulders in a dramatic shrug. "That was

the official story. From what Nigel said, I assumed it had something to do with his dad, but I never really knew. Nigel did go see Lyndia a few times, I know that much. I went with him once or twice."

The wind was picking up now. Freddi shivered, though the air was hot and muggy, not cold. "I think I'll go back to the B&B," she said.

I looked down at my phone. "Why don't you let me plug the store address into your phone so you can have it tomorrow when it opens?"

"No, that's fine." Freddi stood. "I'll remember. I'd better get back. It was nice to chat with you."

"Wait, there is something more." I looked up at her, hoping she'd sit back down, but she didn't. "I told you my husband and I were investigating Nigel's disappearance. You had to know we'd find out you and he aren't divorced."

The words were a gamble because Elliot could be wrong. But her shocked expression told me everything I needed to know. "We separated five years ago," she said. "We're not really married, even if we didn't get around to divorcing. No one knows. Not even the police have dug that deep yet."

"I'm sure they will. But that's what you told Lyndia today, wasn't it? That if she didn't pay, you'd go after all of Nigel's share—as his wife."

She stared down at me. "Yes. I guess a fourth now that Nigel's son has shown up."

"Right. So did you mean it?"

She lifted her chin. "I don't know, but she told me no way. That the inn was hers, and Nigel knew that, wherever he is. Now please excuse me—I'm going to take a cold shower and try to nap. It's been a long day."

I watched her go, kicking myself for getting nowhere. I'd have to go into her room as soon as I could to see what I could uncover. Meanwhile, three suspects topped my list for both the poisoning and Nigel's disappearance: Tyrus, Deanna, and Freddi. That didn't mean any of them were ultimately responsible. For one thing, even though I thought he was dead, Nigel might still be alive and pulling strings from some hiding place.

At least I could have Shannon pass Elliot's information about Freddi Dottson on to Detective Wallace. They couldn't help but find both her marital status and her connection with arsenic poisoning interesting. I typed out a quick text, adding that I was no longer with Freddi in case Shannon decided to come running to my rescue.

I continued along the path, finding the health food store that was closed as predicted. Buttoning my phone away in the leg pocket of my shorts, I headed east toward the beach with the idea of returning to Haven Retreat on the same pathway I'd come on, but when I reached the first wooden walkway leading to the beach, I went down to the sand instead. The wind blew around me, still muggy but cooler than even ten minutes before. People streamed past with beach paraphernalia tucked under their arms or slung over their shoulders, their hair and clothes whipping around in the increasing wind. By the time I'd reached the water's edge, the last few beachgoers were packing to leave.

I wasn't ready to leave yet, so I turned north, away from the pier that I was too far away yet to see, and walked along the agitated water, ankle deep, feeling a connection with the city here even more strongly than before. The clouds overhead had blotted out the sun, and the sea was raw and tense and alive. I was grateful to still be wearing my suit under my clothes, and

I removed my T-shirt, stringing it through a belt loop on my camo shorts. I lifted my face to the wind, loving the feel. It was a perfect moment.

Until my thoughts crowded in.

I was missing something in this case—I could feel it. Maybe even something in plain sight that would make the case clear. But what? I needed more information—more imprints. Or to figure out how to talk to the cold presence, which seemed to be attached to either people or places. Welby had loved both Lyndia and Tyrus, so he might be holding onto them. Nigel had been shot outside Frontier Cabin. Could I be dealing with two people who'd passed on or just one? Were they trying to protect or out for revenge?

Or I could be going crazy. My biological grandmother had been shut up in an institution for the visions she'd seen. My sister and I thought it was because she didn't understand them or have support. If she'd lived, our lives might have been different. Our biological father might not have tried to silence his gift of reading imprints with alcohol and drugs, which meant I might not exist. Or maybe Tawnia and I would have been raised together. I shivered at the thoughts, pushing them aside and wanting nothing more than to go back to Rose Petal Cottage and find comfort in Shannon's arms.

The wind picked up even more, and the sky had turned almost black. A few drops of rain landed on my face. Time to head back. I checked my phone in my pocket, amazed to see it was already after six. Sand now stung my legs as I ran through the shallows. It was almost enough to drive me back up to the cobbled walkway next to the beach, but I decided that without the water, it would be worse there.

The water now skidded across the sand, pushed by the

wind. The drier sand further up the beach also skimmed across the more packed sand beneath it. I'd never seen anything so strange and thrilling during the times I'd visited the beach in Oregon.

At that moment I glanced up at the Jacksonville Beach Pier, now back in sight. It was completely deserted except for a solitary shape leaning on the railing. Thunder cracked and lightning illuminated the sky far in the distance. Definitely time to wrap this up. I started jogging. As I approached the pier, a glimpse of bright blue made me look up at the figure again.

A blue raincoat, I thought.

Cold enveloped me, far icier than the cool wind swirling around me. I felt compelled to run to the wooden walkway leading off the beach. Sand stung my feet and arms as I ran. I reached the walkway, and the stinging was less here near the beach vegetation. I considered pulling back on my shirt, but it was soggy and damp.

I put my hand on the railing. Immediately, an urgent imprint took me: *Finally, the red-haired woman was on the walkway. You have to duck! I screamed. But she couldn't hear me.*

The imprint was from right now, and it wasn't mine.

I lurched forward, tripping inelegantly on the last step, which marked the beginning of the bridge over the vegetation. My face planted on the hardwood as something slammed into the opposite railing, passing through where I'd just been standing. The rail splintered. Was someone shooting at me? Whatever it was seemed to have come from the pier. But no one was there now, not even the figure in blue.

Keeping low, I army-crawled over the wooden path, fearing at any moment to hear another splintering sound.

Nothing.

I reached the cobbled path and heard a car door slam. I rose high enough to see two teens driving away in a tiny car from the parking lot opposite the beach.

What now? I thought. I was shivering, though from cold or terror, I couldn't say.

Or was it from something else?

"I read imprints," I said aloud, sounding strange to my own ears. "I felt you say duck. Is it safe to go now? Touch the railing and think hard about it." I felt stupid. What if the cold presence was gone or couldn't hear me?

I touched the railing myself, but there were only old imprints. Nothing new.

And then a rough and furiously angry imprint appeared: *Run.*

I did. I ran over the cobbled path and through the parking lot, finding a swath of palm trees and grass. I ducked between the trees and panted for a minute before running to a car parked on the side of the road. If anyone was watching, they'd think I was crazy.

The sky began dumping rain then, like buckets of water, uneven because of the wind. In a single moment, the rest of me that was only damp was suddenly soaking. My next dash was toward a coffee shop. I ran through the uneven rain, relieved when I touched the doorknob, but cringing as a furious imprint from days earlier assaulted me. Where were my gloves when I needed them?

The coffee shop brimmed with people taking refuge from the storm, and no one seemed to notice me as I stood by the door, pretending to be waiting for someone. I debated whether or not to call Shannon or go back and see if it really had been a bullet crashing into the railing. I also thought of my insane grandmother. What if the bullet wasn't there?

Instead, I texted Shannon: *Call me when you get this.*

People were finally beginning to stare at me. Maybe because of the gash on my knee and the wet trickle I could feel on my cheek. Or perhaps it was my lack of shoes. Whatever their interest, the wind outside was only getting worse. I needed to move. Pulling my scattered nerves together, I took a deep breath and went outside, hurrying down the sidewalk until it crossed the main street and led to the sidewalk that would take me back past Magnolia Inn. Goose bumps raised on my arms and neck. I told myself that was due to the storm, not because someone was following me.

When I reached Magnolia Inn, the police cars were gone, and the wind was growing worse. Lightning cracked nearly overhead, sounding like a gunshot. My heart pounded furiously. I thought about going inside the inn but rejected the idea immediately. I wanted to be back at the cottage, locked safely inside.

I passed the boulder marking Haven Retreat, expecting to feel relief, but the wind made the trees wave wildly, loosening their blossoms and creating a mini snowstorm. Dark shadows danced ominously. Hurrying past a very dark Frontier Cabin, I finally reached Rose Petal Cottage with a sigh. I looked around as I opened the door, seeing no one behind me, and slipped inside. Comforting light bathed the room when I flipped on a switch.

I could feel that Shannon wasn't here, but I hadn't expected him to be. Starting for the couch, I ran into the metal detector, which we still hadn't returned to Holt's garage. I reached to straighten it. The same fleeting imprints I'd read before rushed over me, speeding backward over the years. I was about to pull my hand away when an imprint captured me.

I watched the two beautiful people laughing together as they played with the volleyball—Tyrus and Micaela.

She was prettier than me. I knew that, but she was taken. Sure, I hadn't been at all happy when she'd started going everywhere with Gencio Ribeiro, that delicious Brazilian. I'd met him first, after all, when I'd saved his soccer ball from going into the ocean on one of Micaela's charity outings with me. That day I'd cursed Grandpa for talking to Bonnie about finding me a fake friend.

But now I was glad she was in love with Gencio because Tyrus was much more my type. Older but young enough to still be around when I finally stopped being a teen and got out from under Grandpa's thumb. No more therapists and talking about my relationship with Mother. Three years I'd been doing that already, and it couldn't be over fast enough. Mom had made her choices; they had nothing to do with me. And maybe when I was old enough, I'd be beautiful too. Like Mom. Like Micaela.

"Come on, Lyndia," Micaela called to me with a smile. "We need you." I hated the way her black hair was so curly and framed her beautiful bronze face like some exotic model while mine hung limp and lifeless. But if she hadn't pushed, I wouldn't have dared ask Tyrus to come to the beach with me today. I only wished he didn't look at her like some lost puppy.

"Are you afraid?" Tyrus called with a wink. "If you are, I don't blame you. I am pretty good."

"I'm not afraid." But I was a little. Afraid that if he knew my feelings, he'd laugh. I'd have to wait until I had something important to offer him.

The imprint ended, and there was nothing after that except more transitory imprints that meant nothing. Lyndia's imprint had been from that summer ten years ago when Tyrus had come to meet his grandfather. She hadn't been joking about her long-time crush on him. Knowing that only made me feel more sorry for her—and more concerned about Tyrus's motives now.

I balanced the machine against the wall and went to the couch, grabbing the throw-blanket there and sinking onto it with a sigh.

Who had been at the beach? Freddi would have had plenty of time to come back to her room to get a gun. Maybe she had shot her husband and then had somehow taken him to the pier and pushed him off and was now thinking to stop my questions in the same way.

Or maybe it was Tyrus. He might have learned about the imprints and wanted to keep me from finding some that detailed his true intentions.

And what did Deanna have to do that was so important she couldn't stay one night for Lyndia at the inn?

I looked down at myself, shivering. I was soaked, my shorts were ripped and filthy, and my knee was bloody. Nothing a few bandaids wouldn't fix, though.

One thing for sure: someone was getting nervous about what I might find.

Or I was going crazy.

My phone buzzed with a text from Shannon. *On my way back to Haven Retreat. Where are you? Still want me to call?*

An hour had passed since my text to him from the coffee shop, which seemed impossible. *No.* I wrote. *Come to the cottage.*

I was sitting on a chair in the kitchenette and cleaning my knee wound when he arrived. He barely caught the door to prevent the wind from slamming the door open as he came inside.

He hurried toward me. "What happened?"

"Can you help me with this?" I waved tweezers from my suitcase at him. "I have a sliver."

He knelt on the ground and took it out as I told him about the shot and the figure on the pier. "You're sure it was a gunshot?" he asked.

I was too tired to bristle at the doubt in his voice. "No. There was a lot of noise and wind and sand. For all I know, the railing split because of the wind."

"But you felt the imprint."

I sighed. "Yes."

He stood and pulled a chair close to me, taking my hands in his. They felt hot against my flesh. "That's pretty dangerous," he said, "shooting into the wind like that. And impossible to be accurate."

"Maybe they were only trying to scare me away."

"We'll have to check out the railing tomorrow."

"Did you find Tyrus?"

"Yes, finally. He was at Ocean Front Park, taking pictures of the storm. I think the guy must be a little nuts. Sorry I missed your text. The storm was so loud."

"Where is the park?"

"A few minutes south of the pier. It's not much to look at, but we can go one of these days."

That wasn't what I was angling for. "What time did you find him?" I asked, thinking of how long it had taken me to get back on foot.

"At least half an hour before I texted you."

So plenty of time for Tyrus to drive there after shooting at me. It wasn't a happy thought—I was actually hoping it would have been impossible—for both Micaela and Lyndia's sakes.

"That reminds me. Paige finished the background check on Tyrus. He has a record."

A sudden chill made me shiver again. "For what?"

"Something about defacing a historic building in Orlando. I don't see how it ties in with this case, but it could indicate a disrespect of authority. A lot of times the arrests you see are only the tip of the iceberg."

"Could be a connection."

"The police are getting his gun from him now. With how willing he was to hand it over, I doubt it will be a match to the bullet."

I had to agree. "Any news about Lyndia?"

"She called Mom a little while ago, and Mom says she seemed alert. She will probably come home tomorrow. Mom's relieved, naturally."

"Good. I need to ask your mom if Freddi was in her room the past few hours, and I want to find out what Deanna Lowe had to do tonight that was so important she couldn't help Lyndia out at the inn."

Shannon chuckled. "You can do all that tomorrow. We'll know more then. Thanks to your information, the detectives are contacting the Palm Coast Police to see about exhuming Freddi's ex-boyfriend's remains. If they find arsenic, it could be a pattern."

"A black widow, you mean."

He nodded. "I know—she doesn't seem the type."

"Is there a type for murder?"

"Not that you can always see." He rubbed my hands. "We'll be exhuming Welby tomorrow morning, so that's another step closer to the end of this mess. I want to be there since Lyndia can't. If I don't go, I'm afraid my dad will insist on going himself, and the police don't want him there."

"I'll go too, then." If the cold presence I kept running into was Welby, maybe he'd make an appearance.

"You don't have to." Shannon trailed his fingers down my bare arm. "I think you should take it easy tomorrow. No beach, no imprints, just rest."

"Maybe." What I meant by that was no way, and Shannon's frown told me he'd received the message loud and clear.

He reached over and touched my face. "You're all scraped up." His finger came away with a bit of blood. "And your skin is like ice."

"I have an idea." I leaned forward and kissed him. "You can warm me up."

His low, sexy chuckle made me forget my pain. "Good idea. There's no way we can go anywhere for at least a few hours anyway, and by then it will be too late for more investigation." He returned my kiss for a long moment before coming to his feet and pulling me up. "We can try out that bath right now if you're up to it."

"Oh, yeah," I said, putting my arms around his neck. "I'm definitely up to it."

I was ensconced chin deep in hot, bubbly water when a thought occurred to me. If I actually had been reading an imprint from the dead at the pier, I didn't think it was Nigel. From everything I'd learned about him, Nigel had been a self-centered, greedy man. He wouldn't be interested in saving me from anything. And maybe he wouldn't even care enough about anyone he'd left behind to stick around.

But if Welby wasn't resting in peace, there had to be a reason, something happening with someone he loved. If Lyndia was safe at the hospital, did that mean Tyrus, Holt, Bonnie, or Deanna might be in danger?

Chapter 16

The next day shortly before noon, Shannon and I watched as graveyard employees exhumed Welby Carr's coffin. Someone from the media had gotten wind of the event, but they were kept back by crime tape, their view partially hidden by a hastily-erected tent. Tyrus was here also, standing apart from us, looking like a man who hadn't slept. The exhumation was to have taken place hours earlier, but a delay with the disinterment permit and heavy rains had kept us waiting in our cars for hours. The wind and rain had finally died down, but the sky was still dark and angry as if at any moment it might unleash another storm.

"You feeling anything?" Shannon said to me.

I shook my head. "Nothing."

Detective Wallace left her partner and came over. "Look," she said as the small crane pulled the casket from the hole made by a backhoe, "you can touch the casket if you'd like. I'll even open it and let you touch his clothes or whatever. After that, we're taking him to the medical examiner's lab. The autopsy will only take a few hours, and he'll be back in the ground before nightfall. We'll have initial tests then, but the rest won't come in for months unless we figure out what else we might be looking for. We'll take enough samples to do additional tests."

"We're good with that. Thanks," Shannon said.

The coffin, having been in the ground only a month, was new-looking under the dirt, and the only imprints I felt were those of sadness that must have been left by the pallbearers. I bit my lip when they opened the grave, preparing myself for the worst, but besides some swelling, the old man looked peacefully asleep. He wore no jewelry and his suit looked new. I found faint imprints on the suit, but nothing important.

"Your mother bought this suit," I told Shannon. "Lyndia was with her."

Detective Burke rolled his eyes. "She probably told you that."

Tyrus moved closer. "Are you about done?" he demanded of the detectives, his good looks marred by irritation. "I have an appointment. Why are you opening the coffin here? And why is she touching him?" He thumbed at me without looking in my direction.

"Just making sure it's Mr. Carr," Detective Wallace said smoothly. She gestured for the graveyard personnel to close the coffin.

Tyrus glanced inside as the lid lowered, his face paling. He looked squeamish. Was his conscience catching up to him? "It's him," he growled.

"You look exhausted," Shannon said. "Were you out partying all night? In that terrible storm?"

I could tell he meant it as a joke, but Tyrus didn't find it amusing. "I'm fine." He kept his voice terse.

Shannon threw me a look before adding, "Well, we're about ready to head out for lunch. Would you like to come?

Our treat." It was a good idea, especially if I could find a way to touch the phone Tyrus was holding in his hand.

"Can't." Tyrus lifted his phone. "I'm going to the hospital. Lyndia texted me a few minutes ago. She's getting out of the hospital and wants me to pick her up."

I wasn't surprised Lyndia had texted him, given her feelings for the man. "That's great," I said. "How is she?"

He shrugged and stifled a yawn. "Good enough to come home. But I don't like the idea of her staying at the inn now." Either he was serious about protecting his cousin, or this was the next step in his plan to steal her inheritance.

"I bet my parents would let her stay with us," Shannon said.

Tyrus nodded grudgingly. "I'll ask her."

"I'm sure we'll find out who's responsible soon." Detective Wallace smiled a thanks at the graveyard workers who had finished lifting the casket onto a truck.

"I hope so." Tyrus stalked off without another word, leaving us all staring after him.

"I'm not sure he should be alone with Miss Carr," Detective Wallace said.

"I'll let my parents know she's coming home. They'll look after her."

Detective Burke snorted. "As if that's any better."

"You can't possibly still believe my dad is a suspect," Shannon shot back. "Not after all this."

"We'll see." Burke turned his back and walked away.

"Don't mind him," Detective Wallace said. "Our chief is under pressure to solve this thing, and we bear the brunt of that. Burke's suspicious nature actually makes him a good detective, but for some reason, your dad rubs him the wrong way.

We did find out something interesting this morning. There was no arsenic in the bottle of wine given to your father, which might mean the arsenic was added later, though the corks don't seem to have been removed. We're examining them for needle holes now."

"Which makes this exhumation that much more important," Shannon said.

Wallace nodded. "Exactly. I'll be in touch about what we find with the autopsy."

"I really appreciate that." Shannon nodded at her and put his arm around me.

We'd started to turn when the detective asked me, "What happened to your face?"

I glanced at Shannon, his expression telling me it was my call whether or not to say anything. "I got caught on the beach last night in the storm," I said, wiping a damp hand on my jeans. "I fell." Until we checked out the railing, I wasn't going to talk about what I thought had happened with this detective.

Wallace glanced up at the still-cloudy sky. "Yeah, that was something last night. Looks like we're in for another storm tonight as well, but it's supposed to clear by tomorrow morning."

"Good," Shannon said. "Hopefully, we'll have time to get suntans before we leave." We were supposed to fly back to Portland on Saturday morning, but until this was solved, we'd have to extend our stay. Shannon had another week off from work, but we'd been hoping to use that to make headway on setting up my new shop.

I drove the rental car to a fancy health food diner we'd chosen while Shannon texted his parents about Lyndia being released from the hospital. We had reached our destination and ordered our lunch before the reply came. Shannon read the text once, then a second time before holding it out to me to see.

Have you talked to Micaela? Bonnie wrote. *We can't seem to find her. And she's not answering her phone.*

"She was at Magnolia Inn last night," I told Shannon. "She's probably asleep in the office there or something."

Shannon exchanged several more texts with Bonnie while I carried our food to a table. His face was tight with worry. "She already called the inn, and Deanna says Micaela wasn't there when she got in this morning. She thought it was weird and was put out about no one being at the front desk. She made it barely in time for a guest checkout."

I pushed back my chair as I stood. "I'll get a takeout bag."

I ate my lunch on the way back to Haven Retreat, but Shannon had lost his appetite. "She probably went home to sleep," he reasoned.

"Probably."

When we arrived at Haven Retreat, Bonnie was in the kitchen with the boys, looking frazzled. "Thank heaven you're here," she said. "We're about to call the police."

"You check her apartment?" Shannon asked.

"Yes, of course. Your dad's leaving there now. We have a key." Bonnie wrung her hands. "Oh, I don't know how much more of this I can take."

"Is Mommy gone like our daddy?" Lucio asked, his voice matter-of-fact, though his chin wobbled slightly. He was holding it together better than his more rowdy twin, Dimas, whose face was slick with tears.

"No," Bonnie said. "She's just gone to the store, or she had an appointment or something she forgot to tell me about."

"What if she got in a car accident?" Dimas asked, hiccupping with his sobs.

"Her car is still at your house, honey." Bonnie wrapped her arms around both boys. "Remember how she was afraid to drive in the storm last night?"

That made me wonder how Micaela had brought the boys over, but before I could ask, Shannon said. "I'll call the detectives. And we'll go over to the inn. Someone has to know where she is."

"Of course. You have to be right." Bonnie's reddened eyes met mine. "You'll find an imprint, won't you?"

"I'll try."

Leaving our rental car in the Haven Retreat parking lot, we hurried to Magnolia Inn. As we walked, Shannon talked with Detective Wallace's answering machine. Once at the inn, we found Deanna sitting on a stool behind the reception counter, staring at a small, brown, hard-backed book. She put it under the counter and regarded us warily as we approached.

"Have you searched the inn?" Shannon said without preamble. "Do you have any empty rooms?"

"Only one, and I checked it already. You're welcome to do that again. A new guest doesn't arrive until tomorrow."

"Have you asked the guests if anyone has seen her?"

"Not yet." Deanna reached under the desk and pulled out a sheet of paper on a clipboard. "But the log says she let someone in the building at two in the morning—one of the guests was caught out in the storm and sheltered in a bar somewhere. We keep track of that sort of thing in case we need the information later. We include a reason only if the guest gives one, which you can see he did in this case."

We stared at the clipboard, seeing Micaela's signature, a

man's name, and a comment about the storm. "Did you talk to the guy she let in?" Shannon asked.

Deanna shook her head. "He's the guy who checked out this morning."

"And Micaela hasn't been seen since?" Shannon's face was drawn.

"I guess," Deanna said. "I don't really know."

"I'm going to need his contact information." Shannon snapped a picture of the log with his phone.

"Um, I don't know if I'm able to do that," Deanna said.

"Then I'll get it from Lyndia." Shannon snapped another picture. "And where were you during that time?"

She blinked "Me? Well, I wasn't here. I had nothing to do with it."

"Or maybe you know Micaela is like a daughter to my parents." Shannon glared at her.

"Of course I know that. Why does that matter?"

"Because I know who you are, and what happened with your son."

Deanna drew herself up straight. "This has nothing to do with my son or what happened to him." Her voice was as hard and cold as ice. "And I *like* Micaela. She's always been willing to help here—without pay, I might add—since Welby got sick."

"Shannon," I said, placing one restraining hand on his arm. I understood why he was caught up in emotion, but he'd forgotten about my ability. With my free hand, I reached to place a finger on the clipboard.

"I don't blame you for keeping out of the storm," I said, writing down the name the young red-haired man had given me. He smelled like alcohol but was walking steadily enough. "I had to ask someone to drive me here myself."

"Well, like I said, I'm sorry. I know it can't be fun being pulled out of bed this late."

"Oh, I wasn't in bed." I glanced over at the set of couches in the lobby where Tyrus sat with a grin on his handsome face. It was strange and wonderful how strongly I already felt about him in such a short time. The boys were both crazy about him too, despite their initial reluctance, if their asking for him constantly was any indication.

And now that he'd told me everything, I couldn't believe I hadn't recognized him as the boy I'd briefly met that summer when I was nineteen. I also couldn't help but wonder how my life might have been different if I'd met him a few months earlier. I'd loved Gencio—desperately—but the devastation of losing him and raising two children alone had been the hardest thing I'd ever done. I hadn't expected—or wanted—to ever feel this way again about a man. But here I was.

"That's good." The guest left toward the stairs, whistling under his breath.

Tyrus came up behind me as I finished writing, kissing my neck. "Where were we?" he murmured, his breath hot against my skin.

Laughter bubbled up inside me. "We had just finished with the last movie, and you were leaving. I really do have to take a nap tonight if I'm going to be any use to the boys tomorrow."

"Okay, okay. But give me one more for the road." His lips came down on mine, soft at first and then with more passion. Could he be the one to heal my broken heart? I wanted to believe it.

His kiss said it was possible.

The imprint vanished as Micaela must have lost contact with the clipboard.

"She wasn't here alone," I said. "Tyrus Lockwood was with her."

To my surprise, Deanna laughed. "How do you know that?" When I didn't answer, she added, "Well, I hope you're right. I've been worried he was falling for Lyndia." She rolled her eyes. "That would ruin his life, I tell you."

"Why's that?" I asked.

Deanna pursed her lips. "It doesn't matter. But if Tyrus was with Micaela, he might know where she is."

"Where who is?"

The male voice came from behind us, and we turned to see Tyrus helping a fragile-looking Lyndia across the lobby floor. Her shorts and V-neck shirt were rumpled, but her hair looked freshly washed—no spikes today. A plastic sack with a hospital logo swung on her arm.

"Micaela is missing," Shannon told him. "When Deanna came in, she wasn't here. She hasn't been back for the boys, either, and she's not at her apartment, though her car is there."

Tyrus stopped walking abruptly, and Lyndia jerked to a halt next to him, wavering off-balance. He cast an apologetic look at her before starting forward again.

"How'd she get here without her car?" I asked.

"She called me," Tyrus said. "The storm was abating a bit, but she was nervous, and I . . . had to go sign a document for the police anyway, so I gave them a ride. After we took the boys to Haven Retreat, I walked her over here. The wind was picking up again, and I didn't want her walking alone in the dark."

But he'd done a lot more than walk her over. "You mean you came and stayed." I moved around the reception desk in search of the pen Micaela had used. She might have continued holding it for a while after releasing the edge of the clipboard.

He shrugged. "Yeah, so what? We talked and watched movies."

And kissed. But I didn't add that aloud because I didn't want to hurt Lyndia, who was staring at him intently. Her face looked more pinched than ever—thanks, I thought, to the poison and her illness.

"When did you leave?" Shannon asked.

Tyrus shrugged. "I don't know. A little before three maybe. By then the wind was almost gone."

"It was still dark?" Shannon pressed. At Tyrus's nod, he asked, "And where were you watching these movies?"

"On the couch over there. I'd brought my laptop."

I wondered if Micaela had seen his screensaver. Maybe that was part of the "everything" he had explained.

"She's got to be somewhere." There was no missing the concern in Tyrus's voice.

Lyndia smiled up at him. "We should start a search. She's probably not far. We'll go door-to-door."

"Yeah. That's a good idea, but you should be in bed." He looked past the office where her rooms must be located.

"Well, then I can stay here in case she comes back," Lyndia said. "I can send out information to everyone on any sightings."

He patted her arm. "You're a good friend."

"Micaela was always so good to my grandpa. Of course we need to do everything to make sure she's safe." Lyndia shifted her two-handed grip on his arm, freeing one hand to wave at the couches. "Do you think you can help me over there? And bring the clipboard? I'll sit there with my phone and write any notes on the back of the log."

"Sure." Tyrus grabbed the clipboard. "But promise me if it's too much, you'll have Deanna help you back to your room."

"I feel great," Lyndia said. "Just a little weak. And that's probably from the anesthesia they gave me when they pumped my stomach."

I'd found a couple pens and touched them. Micaela had indeed continued to hold one while she kissed Tyrus. But besides experiencing her rush of excitement, I didn't learn anything more. I released the pen and pointed to the camera on the wall above the desk. Shannon nodded and started off after Tyrus and Lyndia.

"It would help if we could see the camera footage from last night," he said. "Can you give me access? That may tell us what time she left and if she was with anyone."

"That's a great idea." Lyndia fumbled in her pocket for her phone. "It will take a minute to bring up the feed."

Still behind the counter, I looked at the book Deanna had been reading. It appeared to be a battered leather journal. Deanna caught my stare and picked it up, tucking it under her arm. We stared at each other for a few seconds before she said, "How did you know Tyrus was here with her?" She glanced down at where the clipboard had been.

"Because she imprinted an emotion on the clipboard." Not because she cared about it, but because of her strong feelings about being here with Tyrus. I was showing my cards, but it wasn't likely she'd believe me anyway.

Her expression turned to one of doubt. "So you're one of those psychics. Is that the real reason you wanted access to the office?"

I nodded and pointed at the book. "I can show you. Or I can try."

She shook her head and edged away from me, but not before I caught a sheen of tears in her eyes. We both walked over to the couches where Lyndia had finally settled and was now on her phone.

That was when Detective Wallace walked through the door, this time without her partner. We all looked in her direction. "Well, did you find her?" she asked. "Please tell me you have because after the very long weekend I put in, I wanted to get off early today."

"We're looking at the surveillance footage now," Shannon said in answer. "No one has seen her since about three in the morning."

"Normally, we wouldn't be worried this soon when it's an adult," Wallace said, using her long strides to come to the couch where Lyndia sat, "but this makes two missing people and two poisonings."

"Two?" Shannon barked.

"The autopsy is still in progress, but the initial condition of Mr. Carr's organs do seem to indicate long-term poisoning of some kind."

Lyndia let out a little cry. "Oh, no!"

We all turned to her. "You knew poison was a possibility," Tyrus said as if talking to a young child.

"Not that. The footage." Her eyes looked impossibly wide as she stared at Tyrus. "The server went down last night. It must have been because of the storm. I don't have anything beyond midnight last night because I didn't get the alert, and I wasn't here to reboot the machine. I don't know what's wrong with it, but it won't start by itself anymore until the error is cleared."

"The lights did go out last night," Tyrus said. "But they were only out a minute or so before your generator kicked on. The regular lights came back on five minutes later."

Lyndia tore her gaze away and focused on Deanna. "Can you go get the scheduling laptop? We'll have to check the settings there. Maybe it's just my connection that didn't reboot." She tucked her phone under her leg. "I can't believe this is happening."

Shannon and I exchanged a look, and a tremor of fear for Micaela ran through me for the first time. Sure, the storm might have knocked out the server, but it also could have been tampered with.

By the time Deanna returned with the laptop, Lyndia was clinging to Tyrus, who sat next to her. "Will you do it?" she asked him. "You know more about computers than I do. It doesn't have a password."

He blinked. "Since when?"

"I took it off after Grandpa died. I kept forgetting it."

Which might mean anyone with access could have stopped the cameras.

Tyrus typed away on the keys. After a while, he said, "It's true. The cameras went offline at eleven forty-five. There's nothing for me to retrieve after that because nothing was recorded. The automatic reboot is turned off."

"Was there anyone near the desk or this laptop when it happened?" I asked, leaning over to let my hand rest near the keys as I stared at the screen intently. Only hazy imprints came to me, which was odd. Even computers used only for work often contained occasional vibrant imprints of excitement or frustration. But though some of the imprints seemed to be recent, they weren't vivid enough for me to identify anything more than vague impressions of sadness, anger, or happiness. None of them came from yesterday.

"No one was here except us," Tyrus said.

Shannon took my hand and drew me aside. "I don't like this."

"I know." I glanced back at the others. "But we're all here except Nigel and Freddi." I wasn't sure what I meant by this, but as Wallace had said, this had to be connected with our case.

"We need to get into Freddi's room," Shannon said.

"I need to," I countered. "And I'll do it as soon as we finish here. After I help Bonnie contact all Micaela's friends. Meanwhile, you do what you can to help Wallace search." The stint he'd worked in missing persons made him invaluable, even if Wallace didn't know that yet. She would know, like we did, that the first hours after a disappearance were the most vital to a safe recovery. Time was ticking too fast.

Shannon went back to the others, and I followed, stopping to straighten the magazines on the coffee table and to brush imaginary lint off the vacant couch opposite the one where everyone sat. All I got for my efforts was another vivid glimpse of a makeout session between Tyrus and Micaela, this time from his point-of-view.

She tasted and smelled so good. It was right, telling her everything.

She pulled away. "It's getting late. We should start the movie."

"It can wait," I said with a chuckle. I'd been waiting ten years to hold her like this.

Her smile widened. "Good thing Lyndia isn't here. I think she has a crush on you. I'm not sure how she's going to take the idea of us dating."

I wanted more from her than dating, but I wouldn't scare her off by saying that so soon. "She's just a kid—and my cousin to boot."

"Not by blood." Micaela shrugged, and the movement fascinated me. I needed to kiss her again more than I needed to breathe.

She leaned forward and pushed play on my laptop screen. I wanted to groan in protest, but when she cuddled up to me and pulled my arms around her, it was almost as good as tasting her lips.

Okay, so the imprint wasn't helpful, except to tell us that at eleven o'clock last night, Tyrus was here with Micaela—and not planning to hurt her. Had something changed between them after these happy imprints? It was possible that his wanting more than dating didn't refer to a future together.

I became aware of Deanna staring at me, and I pulled my hand from the vacant couch and straightened, returning my attention to the others. Detective Wallace was on the phone, arguing with someone, and Shannon was asking Lyndia, "Can you think of anyone she's been seeing lately?"

Lyndia started to shake her head but paused, her hands clutched tightly on her lap, her back becoming rigid. "No, not really."

"Why did you hesitate?" Shannon pushed, sinking onto the couch next to her. "Anything you can think of might help."

Lyndia sighed, her gaze drifting briefly to Tyrus on her other side. "It's just . . . one time I saw her and my uncle talking together. It seemed . . . well, intimate." She waved the words away with a hand. "It was probably my imagination."

"No," Deanna said. "He definitely had a thing for her. I know because every time she was over, he quit hitting on me."

Tyrus's face flushed a bright red. "Nigel was an old

lecher—way too old for her. And Micaela wouldn't want him anywhere near her children."

"But I saw him playing cards with them when she was here working," Lyndia said. "And when I talked to his ex-wife yesterday, she told me he was seeing someone here. She didn't know or wouldn't say who."

"It wasn't Micaela." Tyrus's voice was firm as he looked across Lyndia at Shannon. "But what if Nigel's behind this? No one ever found a body, and Nigel knows the inn. That means he could have been watching us all evening. He could have been waiting for me to leave."

"And do what?" Lyndia asked. "If she didn't open the door, he couldn't get in. We changed all the key cards after he disappeared. And those don't even work between midnight and five in the morning. Besides, Nigel wanted half the inn. He wouldn't just leave."

"There's another possibility," Detective Wallace said, folding her big arms across her abdomen. "If Micaela was seeing your uncle, maybe she didn't take it so well when she learned he wasn't really divorced. Maybe she had something to do with his disappearance and your poisoning."

That shocked us all. I'd never considered Micaela as a possible suspect, and with her little boys waiting at home, the idea was ludicrous.

Wasn't it?

Chapter 17

"That's absurd." Shannon's eyes glowed with barely concealed rage. If I'd had any doubt about his cousinly feelings for Micaela, they were swept away in that moment.

"It's unlikely," Wallace agreed, "but we have to consider all the angles."

"No, we don't." Tyrus jumped to his feet. "We just have to find her!" His eyes scanned us, stopping at Shannon. "What can I do?"

"Well, if you were listening, you heard Detective Wallace convince her precinct to put out an all-points bulletin," Shannon said, coming to his own feet. "While they start their investigation, you and I can talk to the neighbors. Even in a storm, people would have seen something."

"I can't authorize that," Wallace said.

"You don't have to." Shannon smirked at her. "The last I checked, it's a free country and talking to people is still legal."

Wallace considered him. We all knew she could make sure he didn't use his badge in an official capacity where he had no authority, or she could look the other way. Finally, she said,

"Okay. Let me know what you find. We'll see if we can ping her phone and check records. I've got two more officers coming to dust the doors for fingerprints. But I don't know what good it will do with all the people coming and going." She looked at Lyndia. "I'll need a list of all the guests. Are you going to make me get a search warrant?"

"No, of course not." Lyndia blinked in surprise. "Deanna will print you out a list right now."

"Good. In the meantime, I'd like you to look around with me here to see if anything is out of place."

"She should probably rest," Deanna said. "I'll look with you, but I've already been everywhere today, and there isn't anything different—except no one did breakfast prep before I arrived."

"What about the media?" Tyrus said. "They were at the cemetery this morning. Maybe they can get the word out and urge people to start looking for her. I have a few media contacts as well."

"We can try that. Reporters who follow the police beat will see the bulletin, but it never hurts to have someone close to the victim give an interview." When no one responded or made further suggestions, Wallace clapped her hands. "Come on, people, let's get moving."

"One more thing," Shannon said to Tyrus. "You were arrested before—what was that all about?"

Tyrus snorted. "Really? That's what you want to know?"

"If we're working together, yes. I need to know."

Tyrus's jaw worked, and for a moment, I thought he'd refuse to answer, but he finally did. "I was taking pictures to preserve an old church before they let it crumble to the ground from neglect. Maybe I shouldn't have climbed the outside, but it was the only way to get to the top to see a good view of everything. I almost fell for my efforts, if you must know. I was young and stupid, but I'm still glad I did it because I got amazing pictures and videos that will preserve it forever."

A giggle came from Lyndia. "That's just like you." To Shannon, she added, "Surely you're not afraid he's involved with all this craziness. I'd trust him with my life."

Tyrus nodded at her gratefully before turning a hardened stare at Shannon. "Satisfied?"

"Sure." Shannon gave me a wave and started for the door.

Tyrus touched Lyndia's shoulder. "Will you be okay?"

She nodded. "Just be safe, okay? I couldn't bear to lose you too."

"I'll be fine." With a final pat, he hurried after Shannon.

Wallace and Deanna were already walking toward the kitchen together, so Lyndia and I were alone. I took the opportunity to sit in Shannon's vacated place next to Lyndia to test that couch for imprints, but nothing interesting met my touch.

Lyndia gave me a grateful smile. "Did you come to the hospital with Bonnie, or was that a dream?"

"I was there."

"Well, thank you. It made me feel better, especially having Bonnie close. She and Holt have been such a support."

I nodded, though my mind had already rushed on. I needed to get back to Bonnie's to help her contact Micaela's friends. I also wanted to read the imprints on Freddi's personal belongings. Until Wallace could clear it for me to examine Nigel's things, that was my best lead. That and Lyndia's personal quarters where Nigel had stayed, though with her gone last night, her suite wouldn't likely hold clues to Micaela's whereabouts—and Micaela had to take precedence.

"Could you help at the desk?" Lyndia broke through my thoughts. "Looks like one of the guests needs something."

"Sure." I went over to the desk, where a young woman with hair bleached as blond as Lyndia's asked me to leave a note for her grandmother, who was coming to join her later.

"Just in case I don't get back in time," she said. "I want to buy her favorite treat as a surprise, and she doesn't do texts."

Looking around for a moment, I retrieved a notepad and pen from under the counter—no imprints on either—and pushed them over to her. "You didn't happen to see a pretty, black-haired woman here last night, did you?"

"Oh, yes, when I came in last night during the lull in the storm. About ten, maybe?" She pointed to the couches. "They were over there. Not the couch where that woman is sitting. The other one."

"And you saw nothing out of place last night?"

She laughed. "Oh, yes. That storm. Made it seem like shadows were trying to get in the windows. I swear I heard a huge crash somewhere, but it was probably some branch banging into the inn."

"Yeah. Probably."

She finished her note, folded it, and wrote her grand-mother's name on the outside. "Thank you so much." She turned and strode across the lobby. I touched the note and pen, hoping to relive the noise she'd heard, but the woman hadn't felt strongly enough about what she was talking about or writing to imprint.

Leaving the note on the counter, I returned to Lyndia. "I'll take off now to see if I can help Bonnie track down Micaela's friends. But before I go, I talked to Freddi Dottson yesterday, and she claimed you have a file of hers—she was here trying to get it back. If you like, I could take it to her." If I could get my hands on the file, I might be able to relive their entire confrontation.

Lyndia's eyes widened. "File? She didn't give me any file. She did come yesterday, waving some papers around and yelling about me giving her money because of Nigel. It made me mad because Grandpa always said this place would be mine." She let out a long sigh. "I guess I should just pay her to get her off my back. She used to be nice to me, you know. I mean, when I met her years ago. Maybe living with Nigel changed her."

"I don't think you should give in to pressure," I said. "But did she leave the papers?"

"No. She took them with her."

No file or papers? If Freddi was lying about that, why had she wanted to get inside Magnolia Inn yesterday? To cover her tracks? Or for some other purpose? If her motive was important, she might have come back when Micaela was here all alone.

"Anyway, I don't have any money." Lyndia blinked rapidly to stave off tears. "Oh, I wish my grandpa was here. He'd send her packing like he did Nigel all those years ago. You know what? I should never have looked for Nigel or let him come. I think he probably killed my grandpa, and that makes it my fault." She choked on the last words.

Pity rose up inside me. "I know it's hard. I lost my own father not too long ago, and I never stop wishing he were still here. But we'll find out what happened—to your grandfather, Nigel, and Micaela. I promise you that."

Lyndia sniffed. "I know. But I've already made up my mind. I don't want to stay here anymore. I'm selling to the investors, and I'm going to travel the world with Tyrus. I'll help him with his business."

Unless she thought the money from her inheritance would be enough to conquer all, she obviously had no inkling of the powerful attraction between Tyrus and Micaela.

"I don't know if Tyrus told you yet," I said carefully. "But it turns out he's Nigel's birth son."

She stared up at me for a long moment, the surprise obvious in her wide, beautiful eyes. "Oh," she breathed, a tiny sound of despair. "I guess that explains why Grandpa never made him pay when he came." Her pinched expression became firm. "Well, it's not like we're actual cousins. I'm adopted, you know."

"Right. And did you ever consider that there might be another will? Tyrus told the police he believes there's a new one." Better for Lyndia to understand that now than when it was too late.

"There's not! Grandpa loved me. He wanted me to have Magnolia Inn. But if Tyrus and I . . . well, we might both still benefit, even though Grandpa only left the inn to me."

I couldn't help but feel sorry for her blindness. "I thought you should know. There's plenty of time to decide things later."

"I guess."

"There is." I turned my body toward the door. "Before I go, are you hungry? I can have Bonnie bring something over."

"No, thanks. Tyrus and I stopped to eat on the way home." Her smile was faint and sad. "I was famished, and he's always buying me stuff. He's sweet that way. Anyway, I think I need a nap. And I want to have Detective Wallace check inside my suite before I go in. After yesterday, I'm a little nervous."

I hesitated, wondering if staying meant I could get inside those rooms too. But the memory of Dimas's tears and Lucio's solemnity was more pressing.

"You could come back to Bonnie's with me."

She shook her head. "Grandpa always taught me to face my fears. I'm going to do that for him."

"Okay. You still have my card, right? Please call if you need anything." I bid Lyndia farewell and hurried out of the inn.

Back at Haven Retreat, Bonnie was on a stool at the kitchen counter with a laptop. "It's Micaela's," she said. "The boys knew the password. I already called everyone from church, so now I'm trying to figure out how to email all her friends. And she should have phone contacts somewhere, right? I use a Mac, and this is so different."

"I can look at it." I pulled up a stool next to hers. I was late to the game of computers, but in the past year, I'd come far enough to find an email program on a laptop. "By the way, do you know if Freddi Dottson has gone out?"

"I think she's in her room. At least, I haven't seen her leave, and I changed my settings to make sure I get a notice every time the camera is activated. I've been watching carefully in case Micaela comes home."

"After we're finished here, maybe you can invite her down for a cup of tea or something."

Bonnie's plump face set in uncharacteristically hard lines. "I can do that."

The computer wasn't as new as mine, but it was nearly the same setup. "Here's the email," I said, bringing up the Windows button. "It has an address book with her contacts' email addresses. And I bet she saves her phone contacts online. If she's logged in already, we should be able to access them." It took me a few minutes of poking around to find them, but it was easy enough. "She's probably logged onto Facebook too, even if she usually uses her phone to access it. We should post on her feed. Someone might have seen her."

"But what would we say?"

"The bare minimum, but something that gets people looking."

Micaela's browser was logged onto Facebook, and we spent the next ten minutes putting together a post with the words HAVE YOU SEEN MICAELA? in capital letters, followed by a recent picture of her with the boys and two sentences saying we were concerned about her not checking in and asking for information from the past twenty-four hours. Three responses came in immediately, but no one had seen her.

Next, Bonnie sent a little more information in an email to all Micaela's contacts before printing a list of phone numbers. As we sent texts, I asked, "Where are the boys?"

"Holt has them in our sitting room watching TV. Poor Dimas cried himself sick." Bonnie shook her head. "He might be a big stinker, but deep down his heart is tender. He's really attached to his mother." She gave a little moan. "I hope this will be something we'll laugh about tomorrow—and something she'll get mad at me for. But I swear this isn't an overreaction. Micaela is very careful with the boys. There's no way she would leave like this."

"Tyrus was with her last night."

Bonnie's fingers stopped moving over her phone. "What?"

"At the inn. They were watching movies, and the surveillance cameras just happened to go down. Presumably when they lost power because of the storm. But we can't know that for sure. We didn't lose power here last night, did we?" I'd slept like a log after my misadventure on the beach.

"No, but we're on a different circuit than Magnolia Inn. Ours seems to be less trouble. That's why Welby got a generator. But where is Tyrus now?"

"Canvassing the area with Shannon. He'll keep an eye on him, but if Tyrus did something to her, he's not going to say."

"It doesn't have to be him." Bonnie sounded despairing.

"I know. Anyway, the police will try to track her phone."

"I swear, I will never play matchmaker again."

"This isn't your fault. Something else is going on here, and we'll figure it out." I only hoped we did so fast enough to help Micaela.

We were still working on sending the texts when Freddi Dottson appeared in the kitchen, her piled hair only inches away from the top of the doorway. Today she was wearing vibrant teal culottes and a matching three-quarter-sleeved open jacket atop a cream blouse. It was perfect timing.

I glanced at Bonnie, who stared at me blankly for a few seconds before nodding. "Oh, Freddi, how lovely to see you. We were about to have a cup of herbal tea. Would you like some?"

Freddi peeked at her phone. "Well, I guess I do have time, but I wanted to let you know I'm checking out."

A cold shiver ran over me. "Checking out? But what about your husband? Have the police found him?"

She shook her head. "No, but I don't have to stay here anymore. I got a text from Lyndia, and she's promised to give me forty thousand dollars if I sign a paper saying I won't ask for more. I think it's as good as I'm going to get without a fight, and I'm tired of fighting." She laughed. "If I'm careful, it'll be enough to pay my back rent and other bills so I can finally break even. I'm supposed to be there in fifteen or twenty minutes. I thought I'd make a detour to the health food store before I have to be there, but I can do that after." She met Bonnie's gaze. "I know I didn't give you any notice, but do you think you can give me a discount for tonight?"

"I think we can work something out," Bonnie said.

Freddi's red mouth stretched in a smile. "Thank you so much. Now, what's the tea? Do you have chamomile?"

I finished the text I was sending and checked it off the list while Bonnie started the water boiling. "If you'll excuse me for a minute," I said. "I need to do something. Be right back."

I hurried into the hallway, but my steps faltered in the entryway when I caught sight of Freddi's wine-colored suitcase, the sides looking more bulged than I remembered. A strong-looking lock secured the contents.

"She already packed," I grumbled under my breath. I touched the suitcase, feeling all over it. Just the same imprints as before. Nothing that would tell me if she was in league with someone, or if she'd killed her husband and gone after Micaela for some imagined jealousy.

I touched the lock, hoping to see the combination, which might have worked if she'd cared about it more, or if she'd been locking away something important. As it was, I found nothing. I went upstairs next to check out the vacated room, but the only recent imprint I found was one of momentary fear the night before when she'd turned on the bedside lamp during the storm after hearing something banging outside.

Maybe I should go downstairs and cut through the side of the leather suitcase. Wasn't getting in trouble worth possibly finding a motive for Micaela's disappearance? But by the time I reached the top of the stairs, Bonnie and Freddi were already in the entryway.

"Thank you so much," Freddi was saying. "That will go a long way to calming my nerves. I'm so thankful this is all over."

Bonnie inclined her strawberry-blond head. "I'm glad too.

But please let me know if you hear from your husband. I'm really worried about Micaela."

Bonnie had told her? Then again, at this point, we didn't have much to lose.

"Of course. But I'm sure it's not connected. That pretty girl would want nothing to do with that mean, shriveled, old man. She's probably gone to help a friend."

"I hope you're right," Bonnie said.

I watched helplessly as Freddi hefted her suitcase and left the house. I hadn't even found the time to check her little car for imprints.

Bonnie's sad eyes watched me as I hurried down the stairs. "It's not her," she said. "It can't be. She's so nice."

I hugged her. "It's going to be okay." The words sounded hollow even to me because I couldn't know that.

"I'm so glad you're here." She drew away, straightening her shoulders. "Okay, I'm going to finish those texts and then send Holt over to help Shannon. He can take another painkiller for his back if he has to. We have to find her."

"I'll help you with the numbers."

Holt met us before we reached the kitchen. "Come quick," he said. "You have to see this."

We hurried after him as he went back to their private sitting room. Both boys were asleep on the couch, lying snuggled together like little puppies. The television was low, but I could clearly hear the female reporter. And even more clear was Tyrus Lockwood's face.

"There you have it," the reporter was saying, "breaking news straight from travel book author Tyrus Lockwood, who is a close friend of twenty-nine-year-old Micaela Ribeiro, mother of twin boys, who went missing last night. With last night's storm picking up steam again, threatening to be as bad as it was yesterday, we need your help. Please call the police hotline below if you have any information or have seen Micaela Ribeiro in the past thirteen hours."

The breaking news flash at the bottom of the screen vanished as the regular show returned. "Tyrus said he had contacts," I said.

Holt nodded. "Yeah, but I noticed the plug for his books."

"There is that. But maybe the reporter knows him." I looked at the sleeping boys, apparently exhausted from worry. Both had tear-streaked faces. I needed to do something for them.

I sent off a text to Shannon: *We saw Tyrus on TV. It looked good.* Shannon hadn't been in the camera's view, but he would be somewhere nearby.

He answered almost immediately. *Tyrus is giving another interview now. It should help.*

I hoped so.

Freddi checked out, I told him. *No chance to read her things. We've about finished contacting friends, and after that I have one idea left that I don't think will work, but you know how I am. After that I'm going to the police station to camp out there until Wallace lets me touch all of the evidence she took from Magnolia Inn. Will you let her know?* I'd leave it to him to phrase it any way he wanted, but I was going there.

Okay, he texted. *I'll warn her.* I could imagine him smirking at the idea.

"Look," I said to Bonnie. "Let's hurry with the phone numbers. Then I'm going to the police station to touch some evidence."

"Of course." She looked at her husband. "You should go

help Shannon. I'll leave this door open and keep an eye on the boys."

We took another twenty-five minutes to finish all the texts and answer Facebook questions. No leads so far. The boys were still sleeping when I left a tearful Bonnie making chocolate chip cookies for them to eat when they awoke.

The heavy humidity outside felt like walking into a sauna. The wind was nowhere as bad as it had been last night, but it was picking up from that morning, and a new set of clouds was coming in from the east. I ran down the walk, through the parking lot, and over the grass that was still wet from the storm and the lack of sun today. I didn't stop running until I was standing outside Frontier Cabin where I'd first felt the cold presence. I touched the grass, walked around the flowerbed, and even felt the log side of the cottage.

Nothing.

"Welby?" I called. "Nigel?" The wind ripped my voice away.

I regarded the cottage, feeling a little stupid yelling into the wind at no one. Well, I hadn't thought it would work because the cold presence only seemed to appear when it wanted to, not when I was ready for a discussion.

So when had I felt it? Was it attached to the people it wanted to protect or to the people it thought responsible? I'd felt it here outside Frontier Cabin, near the pier, both in front and in the back of Magnolia, and in the presence of Tyrus and Lyndia and whoever had shot at me on the beach.

I was still trying to work it out in my mind, and getting nowhere, when my phone buzzed. *Shannon!* I thought. Maybe Wallace had agreed to my request. Or maybe there was news about Micaela. I dragged my phone from my pocket, fearing the worst yet hoping for the best.

It wasn't from Shannon but from Lyndia.

I found something of Uncle Nigel's. A pocketknife he always cleaned his fingernails with. Yuck! If you still want to see it, that is. I don't know how it would help, though. Lyndia had ended the text with a sick emoji, as if she knew I'd never want to see it.

But I did.

Be right there, I texted back.

Still no sign of lightning or rain, though the sky was growing dark and it wasn't yet five. I was feeling lighter now, despite the increasing howl of the wind through the trees. Magnolia Inn was probably the best place for me to be anyway. Micaela might have left important imprints on something there—a doorknob, the floor, a light switch. While I was there, I'd check the entire place, even if that meant telling Lyndia about my ability.

No one was at the desk when I entered, and I had begun to look around and touch things when Lyndia appeared from the hallway, dressed now in skinny blue jeans and a yellow top. She'd also styled her short hair since I'd seen her last, and it spiked up playfully on top.

"Oh, it's you," she said, holding a hand up to her heart. "I turned on the signal in my rooms to hear when the door opens. I'm a little jumpy—even after the detective checked out every room in the inn. Do you know four sets of guests left early because they were so upset at what's happened?" She sighed. "It's a good thing I'm selling because they're certainly not coming back. I can't do this anymore, and now that I know I don't have to, I'm anxious to get out."

It was a tough situation for her, though I could understand why having an employee go missing wasn't exactly reassuring for her guests. "I'm really sorry."

She peered past me at the double doors leading outside. "There's going to be another bad storm tonight, isn't there? I'm beginning to regret not asking Deanna to stay later."

"Speaking of Deanna, do you know where she went last night? And does she have any personal belongings here that I might look at?"

Lyndia tilted her head to one side, considering my question. "Someone came in from out of town to see her, I think. Someone who knew her son. He had something for her."

"Do you know what?"

"No. But we have employee cubbies in our breakroom I can show you when you're finished with the knife." Lyndia felt the pockets of her jeans. "I must have left it back in my room. I'll go get it. It's not like anyone needs me right now." Again, she looked past me. "Half my remaining guests are probably already up in their rooms, and the others will wait out the storm elsewhere."

I needed to go with her, and the best way was to keep her talking. "So I ran into Freddi a little while ago at Haven Retreat, and she said you decided to pay her?"

Lyndia shrugged. "Not yet, but I will—after I sell the inn. But she signed a paper saying she won't ask for more, so it's one less thing to worry about. Besides, we're still kind of family. Having to deal with Nigel for so long makes me feel sorry for her." She grinned at me. "I also realized I won't miss that much in five million dollars."

I stared at her. "They're paying you that much?"

Her grin widened. "I know, right? It's the location. We can barely make ends meet, and here we are sitting on a gold mine. I kept telling Grandpa that he should retire and sell out, but he loved it here too much. He wanted this future for me. Now that he's gone, selling is my future. Anyway, they're buying up some of the retirement homes across the street as well and are going to build a huge hotel."

A huge hotel didn't sound good for Bonnie and Holt—or for their straight access to the beach—but maybe that was my skepticism talking.

"I'm glad for you," I said, thinking of the imprint I'd found last night on the metal detector.

But if the inn was worth that much, why had Welby accepted money from Tyrus? Or was that another lie?

She grinned at me. "Why don't you come back with me? Freddi and I are about to have a snack, and I could use the support."

"She's still here? I didn't see her car." She must have left it in the covered parking that I couldn't see from the front. With no love lost between them, I didn't understand why they would prolong their negotiations, but at least I had another stab at reading Freddi's imprints.

"I let her use my garage," Lyndia said. "There's room without Grandpa's old truck, and that way flying branches won't damage it during the night. She was going to drive home, but she was worried about the storm, and since I have vacant rooms now, I offered her one. She's not as bad as I thought, now that we've really talked."

I didn't know if I should applaud Freddi's frugalness for getting a free night from Lyndia and a discount from Bonnie or be upset that Bonnie was the loser in the deal.

I pasted on a smile. "I'd love to join you two."

We'd reached Lyndia's suite, which seemed to take up a significant portion of the area behind the office. Excitement raced through me. I knew the police had searched it when Nigel disappeared, and again today, but they couldn't read imprints, so there was a good chance the rooms contained answers.

The door led to a spacious living room, complete with leather couches, a large screen television, a bar, throw rugs, and décor that rivalled Bonnie's. "This is really nice," I said, noting that Freddi was nowhere in sight.

Lyndia gestured to an adjoining doorway. "Wait until you see the kitchen. I remodeled it last year. I have this cute marble rolling pin and cutting board set I ordered from Europe." She laughed. "Not that I cook. It's a little sad that it's going to be torn down, but it made life worth living in a place that was never truly mine—not with so many people around all the time." A hint of wistfulness entered her voice. "Oh, there's the knife." She pointed to a rich, mahogany coffee table.

I leaned forward and touched it with a fingertip, picking it up only when I realized there weren't any imprints. It also looked brand new. I was about to ask when I became aware of coldness filling the space beside me. It pressed up against my body, as if urging me to move. The howling wind outside seemed to be growing stronger.

At that moment, a crash came from the direction of Lyndia's kitchen.

Lyndia started across the living room. "I hope I didn't leave the shutters unlatched. They're real shutters, you know. Grandpa never wanted to replace them with fakes down here like we did upstairs when we put in the stronger glass."

"Wait." I hurried toward her, dread growing in my chest.

"But—" Lyndia began.

"Let me look. You were almost poisoned, remember?"

Her eyes widened. "Okay. But I don't hear any more banging now. Maybe Freddi has already closed the shutters."

"Maybe." But something was off. The spookiness of the wind and the silence of the kitchen screamed warnings at me. I brought my fists up and made my body ready as I edged slowly into the kitchen.

Almost immediately, I saw Freddi sitting with her back toward me at a small, round table. Her blond hair was still piled high, though leaning slightly to the right like the rest of her teal-covered body. On the table, I could see a single delicate, white teacup trimmed with pink flowers. Cookies and biscuits filled two matching plates.

My steps faltered as I came far enough into the kitchen to see another teacup on the floor, broken into bits. "Freddi?" I said. "What happened?"

Freddi began to turn. Slowly. Then she moved with more speed, her body twisting out of her chair and landing with a dull *thump!* as she crumpled to the ground.

"Freddi!" I rushed to her, feeling for a pulse, my fingers frozen and clumsy. It was there but faint. I reached for my phone to call an ambulance.

It was that moment when I spotted another exit to the kitchen, through which I glimpsed a row of outdoor clothing near a door. A bright blue raincoat hung there.

A blue raincoat like the one worn by the figure on the pier.

A movement behind me caught my attention. I turned to see Lyndia with a black rolling pin, an instant before it slammed into my head.

Chapter 18

I pushed myself back, dropping to mitigate the blow. I swiped my feet out after banging into the ground, hoping to knock Lyndia off balance. She jumped over them and jabbed the cold barrel of a gun against the side of my neck.

"Sweet little new wife to the rescue," Lyndia mocked. "Bet you're rethinking everything now, aren't you? Guess I don't have to tell you that little Lyndia isn't as helpless as everyone thinks. And I'm a lot smarter than any of you." Her laugh sounded crazed.

"What did you do to Freddi?" My gaze went to the motionless woman now behind her. Was she dying even now? "More arsenic?"

"No. I'm fresh out of that, I'm afraid. But the doctors at the hospital were kind enough to give me a prescription of heavy-duty sleeping pills when I checked myself out last night. Once I mixed them with my old anxiety meds, they worked wonders." Her eyes dipped to her gun. "Turns out Freddi would rather take pills than be shot."

"Last night," I said, fixing on the words. "You checked out last night?"

"Late afternoon, really. I made a miraculous recovery after you and Bonnie left me in the emergency room. It still took me two hours to get released, and a lot of threatening to make sure they wouldn't notify anyone, but it was doable."

Things were beginning to click into place. "You poisoned yourself."

Lyndia laughed. "Ding, ding, ding. You win. With Bonnie and Shannon jumping on Tyrus's bandwagon to have my grandfather exhumed, I knew it was only a matter of time until I became a suspect. So after they left yesterday morning, I injected the rest of the arsenic through the corks in the bottles of elderberry wine as insurance. Of course, that wouldn't take me completely off the suspect list, but no one is stupid enough to poison themselves, are they?"

"So you drank the poison and faked being sicker than you really were." For the first time, I noticed she was wearing gloves. She must have pulled them on when I was entering the kitchen.

"Why not? If you calculate the right amount and get help in time, all it does is make you sick. I made sure not to put in too much. Not like I did with the other bottles."

Yet her imprints on the broken glass had shown that she'd worried about dying at some point, so maybe she wasn't as good at calculations as she thought. The idea made me more worried about the unconscious Freddi.

"You all made it so easy. Everyone rushed to help me. Even you. You should have seen yourself, so careful to warn me about big, bad Tyrus. Puh-lease. That man barely knows when he's being played. Of course I knew all along that he's my cousin. I've had a baby monitor in my grandpa's office for years. He didn't have any secrets. I even know how Tyrus feels responsible for me—all I have to do is bat my eyelashes, and he comes running." Her face twisted. "Or he did before he started mooning over Micaela."

Before I could ask about Micaela, she tossed me a pair of metal handcuffs that bounced off my chest and onto the floor next to me. "Put these on."

I contemplated how fast I'd have to move to take the gun away from her. As if reading my thoughts, she stepped backward over Freddi's body and shifted the gun to Freddi's head. "Do it, or I'll shoot her. No one will notice the sound in the storm."

My feet would still be free, but losing my hands would cut my chances of escape drastically. I needed to buy time. "You planned this all along?"

She snorted. "Just Grandpa. I was getting tired of being here, working all day and never having fun. It didn't used to be so bad, but he took away my credit cards. I've been putting elderberry leaves in his wine for years, but it never worked. Then Nigel came to see me last year, and he told me how much the inn was worth. He also told me he gave my mother arsenic, and that he could get me some."

"Your mother?" This line of thought confused me. "I thought your parents died in a car accident."

She shrugged. "They did, but there was more to it. At least according to Nigel, and I think he's right. That last day, Mom told me it was going to be over, and she wouldn't even have to go through a divorce. Guess she messed up."

"So where is Nigel now?"

She frowned, her eyes dodging my gaze. "It's his fault he

ended up where he did. He guessed I'd used the poison he'd sent me, and even before Grandpa died, he said I had to give him half the inn or he'd tell the police. That was his plan all along. He used me. He even burned Grandpa's will that named me as his heir and threatened to show the police the new one."

"The new one naming Tyrus, you mean." That meant the clear imprint I'd read on Nigel's cards had come from Lyndia and not Nigel. No wonder it had been so different from the other vague, alcoholic imprints I'd felt.

"Right. I was mad at first, but it didn't really matter about Nigel burning the will because everyone knew I was Grandpa's heir, and without the will, I could sell my claim to the disputed land between here and Haven Retreat for another half million."

"Half a million?" The real estate attorneys had offered Holt and Bonnie only half that amount.

"Pretty sweet, right? Now put on the cuffs."

"But Bonnie and Holt are your friends." I reached for the cuffs very slowly.

She shrugged. "They don't need the land. Besides, they think I should stay and waste my life here. I'm not going to do that."

"When Nigel threatened to give it all to Tyrus . . . you couldn't let that happen." The cuffs had an imprint from Lyndia from a few minutes earlier: anticipation and excitement. She was enjoying this immensely.

"I don't care if I love him—I'm never going to let a man control my life again. But I'd already known Nigel was going to be a problem, and I'd already figured out how to handle him. Unfortunately, I didn't plan on her." Lyndia kicked Freddi's curvaceous hip. "Nigel gave her Grandpa's new will to hold for him. She brought me a copy yesterday and threatened to go public if I didn't pay her. I decided to make sure she wouldn't be a problem—all while using an alibi no one might think to check."

So it hadn't been Freddi's threat about suing for Nigel's share that had provoked this attack, but about taking all of the inn from Lyndia. "That's why you checked yourself out of the hospital?" *And what about Micaela?* I barely held back the question—one thing at a time.

"I had to make sure she wouldn't be a problem. After I left the hospital, I called her from a payphone and told her that if the police found the copy of the will she'd given me, they'd suspect her of killing Nigel because she hadn't turned it in. Of course, I'd already gotten rid of it, so there was no chance of that, but there was still the original that I needed to get from her. I waited across the street from the inn and watched as she tried to get in, and then I followed her. And you."

"To the beach."

"I waited on the pier, but you came back alone."

"You shot at me!"

She chuckled. "Just a warning—which you deserved. I meant to follow Freddi and make her give me the will and use the storm to help me dispose of her, but you showed up and drew her away from me, so my perfect alibi was ruined." She moved the gun closer to Freddi's head. "Now are you going to put those cuffs on, or do I need to pull this trigger? I didn't want to do this here, but I have plenty of bleach for clean up."

I sat up and snapped the cuffs on loosely. If she planned to move us, I still had a chance.

"Tighter," she demanded.

I tightened one a bit. "Then what?" I asked. She'd obviously gone back to the hospital at some point to wait for Tyrus, but where had she been in the meantime?

"I checked myself back in the hospital—after I finished a little more business. I'm good at improv."

Goose bumps ran up my spine. "You mean Micaela. What did you do to her? I know you were watching her and Tyrus on the beach Saturday night." She'd been on the pier in her blue raincoat, which I now realized was why Lyndia had mentioned beach soccer on Sunday morning at our first meeting when neither Tyrus nor I had brought it up. It hadn't been a guess as I'd assumed, but an observation. "You thought she was stealing Tyrus from you like she did the boys' father. So you suggested to Bonnie that Micaela come here last night."

Her mouth twisted in a sneer. "This isn't because of a stupid soccer game. My only plan was to keep them apart while I established my alibi for Grandpa's poisoning and took care of Freddi. I was supposed to check right back into the hospital after that was done. Like I'd never left. But you ruined that. When I finally got back to the hospital, I checked my phone and saw her and Tyrus at the inn together, acting like starstruck teenagers. I sat there in the waiting room, watching them, and I realized my plan had backfired. I was too late." Her upper lip curled in disgust. "Then I thought, what if I simply didn't check in for a few more hours? Or even until the early morning? No one was going to visit me in the middle of the night, especially during the storm. I'd failed with Freddi, but I could grab the opportunity to make sure Micaela would never be a problem ever again. I gave her one man. She's not taking this one. No one is until I'm done with him."

The way she said it made me think Tyrus might not survive after she was finished with him. The present tense reference to Micaela also made me hopeful that she was still alive.

"Anyway," Lyndia said with a smile, "that's over now, isn't it?"

"What did you do to her?" I repeated, thinking of the seemingly innocent jealous imprint on the metal detector. As with so many imprints, it had ended up being important, and I should have paid more attention.

Again the crazed laugh. "Me? Nothing. Just as I'm not going to do anything to you or Freddi. It was Freddi who was jealous of Micaela and Nigel, so Freddi made Micaela swallow too many sleeping pills. And Freddi's going to shoot you because you discovered she was the one to kill Nigel after touching the pocketknife I gave you. I'll be the witness to that. Then she'll shoot herself."

"I suppose she'll use the same gun that shot Nigel outside Frontier Cabin." It all made a sick kind of sense. But if Micaela had been dosed with sleeping pills, where was she now?

"I'll be the only survivor," Lyndia continued, as if I hadn't interrupted. "By the time anyone finds Micaela or thinks to check the hospital records for my alibi, I'll be in Mexico with the money from the sale of the inn. I signed the contract this morning at the hospital, and they're wiring the money in two days."

I fought a wave of despair. Two days. The police had been working on this far longer, and with her poisoning, Lyndia wouldn't be a suspect right away, even if her setup of Freddi failed—which it might not with the arsenic in her past and with money as a motive for Nigel's murder.

"Okay, I understand about your grandpa and Nigel, and even Freddi and Micaela. But why me?"

A line appeared between her eyes. I'd thought them beautiful before, but now they looked mad and unfocused. "When Bonnie told me about your gift yesterday morning, I asked her a lot of questions. She's such a simple, helpful person. And my security footage verified her claims about you. I saw you checking out the place after we talked." Lyndia's smirk was pure malice. "So I moved the chairs from the firepit into the garage, and I ran a hot blowdryer over everything I thought might be important. Like the laptop, and all the counters in here. I packed away boxes of things. I used gloves when I injected the poison into the wine bottles. But I only had a couple of hours before Freddi showed up to blackmail me. I planned on clearing out more today, but it's a lot of work. And I couldn't be sure it would be enough if you got in my suite before I left—or what you might have already seen."

"You had the nurse lock up your belongings because of me." Why hadn't I suspected? At least I understood now why the chairs around the firepit had held no significant imprints.

"Of course. Then I realized this morning as I was deciding what to do about Freddi that I could use her to make sure you didn't rat me out. So after I gave her the pills, I texted you. Like I said, I'm good at improv." She leaned forward and tightened my other cuff with one hand, the other still steadily pointing the gun at Freddi. "For what it's worth, I'm really sorry. I know it'll make Shannon sad, and I like him a lot."

I winced at how firmly her finger lay on the trigger. If I twisted to grab her with my legs, Freddi might not survive. "What about Micaela's boys?" I pressed. "If it's pills, maybe you could still call the ambulance. There's time, right?"

"They'll go to England to their grandmother. She's a nice

person, I hear. Who knows, maybe they won't grow up to be like me." She seemed to find that amusing.

"Where is the new will?"

Lyndia laughed. "Gone. Down the disposal."

"What about Nigel's cap? Did *you* put it by Frontier Cabin?"

"Of course. A little misdirection never hurt. I thought they'd look into Tyrus and find out about his adoption, and it would get some of the heat off Holt. I didn't want him going to jail before I sold the inn. I hoped he'd give up on the disputed land first. Luckily, I was wearing gloves when I put the cap there. Or maybe you would have figured that out before. And yes, before you ask, it was me who called in the tip about Holt meeting with Nigel. My next step was to mention Nigel blackmailing Holt about shooting Deanna's kid, but that won't be necessary now. I only need two days. Still, you never know." She paused and stood slowly. "Now, don't move. I'll be right back."

She walked to the other entrance where I'd seen the blue raincoat, dipping out of sight only for a second to grab the handle of a canvas wagon. "These come in quite handy around here," she said. "They hold a lot of stuff for a beach outing. Or to bring food inside when I come back from shopping. I had two of them actually, but I got rid of one when Nigel disappeared. Good thing, too. If you had touched it, you might have found him by now."

"So you shot him and then put him in a cart. And then what?"

Ignoring me, she parked the cart by Freddi. "Get up!" she ordered, kicking at the unconscious woman. When Freddi barely fluttered her eyes, Lyndia swung the gun in my direction. "You get her inside."

I succeeded in getting Freddi into the cart through sheer determination and a hope that Lyndia would take us to wherever she had stashed Micaela.

"Now turn around. I need your phone." She slipped it from my back pocket, powered it down with her gloved hands, and put it inside a teal purse I knew had to be Freddi's. She tucked the bag into the cart next to Freddi. "This is another way they'll connect you. Now pull her out to the garage."

I rolled the cart out to a ramp in the garage and repeated the effort of getting Freddi into the front passenger seat and the cart into the back trunk. "Hope you can drive with those cuffs on," Lyndia said, opening the driver's door for me. "I'll be in the back watching."

She waited until I was seated before slamming my door, climbing in herself, and opening the garage with an automatic door opener. Then she extended a set of keys. "Go carefully. If you hesitate or get in an accident, I'll shoot her and then you."

I put my hands on the wheel, and immediately found an imprint.

I stared up at the side of Magnolia Inn. The extra copy of the will that I'd hidden in the magazine at Haven Retreat was my security if Lyndia reneged on the deal later. But even the ten thousand down payment she promised me today would be enough to keep the wolves at bay for a little while.

Guilt crept into my heart, and I tried to push it away. Sure, Welby might have decided to give his inn to his grandson instead, but Lyndia had been with him all these years, and what the grandson had never expected, he wouldn't miss. And I needed this money so much after all that Nigel took from me.

The imprint had been less than an hour ago. In that short time, so much had changed. But it was something I could use.

More imprints followed, and I pushed them away, trying to focus on my driving.

The car was an automatic and even with the cuffs I could steer, especially with how slow I had to go in the increasing storm. The sky was dark, trees were bent over in the wind, leaves and debris flew through the air, and the roads were almost deserted.

Lyndia laughed softly. "I couldn't have planned this better. I might come home after instead of staying with you to call the police. Let them figure out what happened between you two. I could be in Mexico before they even find either of you. In fact, until they realize Freddi's missing, they won't even search for her phone and purse, which I'll leave for them to find."

That didn't sound good. Maybe Micaela wasn't at the end of this little trip as I'd hoped.

I drove, following Lyndia's directions. To my surprise, we stopped in the deserted parking lot by the Jacksonville Beach pier.

"Freddi? Are you awake?" Lyndia poked Freddi with the gun. Freddi stirred and Lyndia slapped her face. "There's coffee in that mug," she told me. "Wake her up!"

I looked at the covered mug in the cupholder between the two seats. She'd thought of everything, it seemed. The first mouthful dribbled down Freddi's shirt, but she drank the second as I pressed the mug to her lips.

"Just in time," Lyndia cooed. She pulled on her blue raincoat, zipping it all the way up and tying the hood tightly so only her eyes and nose were exposed. When she hopped out of the car, the wind nearly ripped the door from its hinges.

Terror came into Freddi's eyes as she tried to focus on me. "Lyndia," she whispered.

"She has a gun," I said, my voice low. "Just do what she says. I'll get us out of this. But have you seen Micaela?"

"No."

Lyndia had opened my door and was standing there, a small blanket over the gun. "Get out!" she screamed over the wind. "And get her out too."

I'd have to act before Freddi was in the line of fire again. I climbed out of the car, pretending to be unsteady with the wind. Lyndia's voice cackled a laugh that sent new shivers through my body.

I turned to face her, the wind pushing between us. I needed to get her closer so I could control her gun. "It's too bad no one will ever know how brilliant you are," I shouted. "But I guess you don't really want people to know. Especially Tyrus."

A flash came to her blue eyes. "Oh, but I do want people to know. Everyone thinks I'm stupid." Her voice rose as if mimicking someone. "Lyndia doesn't do this well, or we can't trust her to do such and such. They never stop to think that I just don't *want* to run an inn. I want to travel and have fun, to do things I can't do here."

"What?" I said, putting my hand to my ear. "I can't hear you."

She took a step closer. "I said they think I'm stupid, but I'm the one with the last laugh. Five million plus all the money I've been funneling off the inn. Grandpa had no idea."

"What?"

She took another step closer. "Forget it."

"Okay." I grabbed the edge of the door in a pretended attempt to wrestle it shut. I needed her eyes off me, and the door was all I had. I stepped on the other side of it. I was closer to her now.

"Leave it!" she shouted.

I gave a final shove and the door slammed shut, drawing her gaze. I leapt toward her at the same moment, grabbing her gun hand and wrenching it to the side. A shot fired harmlessly into the air. She tugged away, but I tightened my grip. I was in control now, even with the cuffs.

I jabbed my elbow upward, slamming it into her chin, then brought her arm down hard on my knee. She released the gun. I had it now, pointed at her chest.

"Where's Micaela," I gritted.

She didn't answer. "I'm not going to tell you. Go ahead and shoot. She won't have him."

She turned, and I knew she was going to run. I couldn't shoot her without knowing where Micaela was, nor could I let her go free to maybe finish the job.

I jumped at her, slamming my body against hers. We tumbled to the ground. Her fists hit my face, but there was no energy behind the blows. She tried to scramble away on hands and knees. Pulling her foot out from under her, I laid her flat, face down on the pavement. I dropped the gun and jumped on top of her back.

"Where is Micaela?"

She bucked. I hit her with my joined hands. The cuffs dug into my skin, but the satisfying crack stilled her instantly.

I looked back at the car. "Freddi!" I shouted, hoping she could hear me over the wind. I needed to call the police so I could get back to the inn and check Lyndia's place for imprints. That thought had me scrabbling for her gloved hand to see if she wore the ring Bonnie had mentioned. She wasn't. Maybe she hadn't put it on since the hospital. There also no imprints on the gloves. Not a single one.

I didn't dare leave Lyndia there, since I was sure she was faking unconsciousness. "Freddi!" I shouted again.

Freddi's wan face finally appeared in the driver's window. Would she help me? Was she too drugged? Or would she only look out for herself as she'd done ever since this mess started? Even as I watched, she laid her head against the window and didn't move. I'd have to figure something else out, but moving from my position of advantage wouldn't be wise.

An instant later, a car zipped into the parking lot at top speed, bringing me back to full alert. When Shannon popped out of the car, I sagged in relief. He ran toward me, shouting something the wind carried away.

He skidded to a stop on his knees next to me, arms going around my body.

"Why are you . . . how did you know?" I asked, pushing into his warmth.

"You didn't show up at the precinct. And I couldn't trace your location on my phone, so I knew it was turned off, which I knew you wouldn't do during a case. I put in a call to Paige to ping the chip we put in the phone after the last time, and while I waited, I came here to make sure your idea wasn't to go looking for that bullet in the storm. I thought maybe whoever it was tried again."

"You weren't far off. It was Lyndia all along."

Shannon glanced at the back of Lyndia's head, his jaw clenching. "That explains a lot. Mom's been talking to Micaela's mother on Facebook. They're five hours ahead in England, and she was texting Micaela at about three-thirty when the texts suddenly stopped. The mother thought it was odd, but she figured Micaela went to sleep or the storm had pulled down a cell tower. But right before that, they were talking about her date with Tyrus and about working at the inn because of the poisoning. The last thing Micaela texted was, 'Speak of the devil.' We thought she meant Tyrus."

Shannon helped me off Lyndia, turning her over onto her back. Her eyes popped opened. "You won't find her in time," she taunted. "I've been careful not to touch anything without gloves, which I've changed four times in the past day. And there's no proof. I'll be out as soon as my money can hire the best attorneys."

"That's going to be a little hard," I said, "when there's still a copy of the new will at Haven Retreat."

"No!" Lyndia gasped. She darted a glance at Freddi's car, where the woman still rested against the glass. "I'll kill her."

"Go ahead—try," Shannon taunted. Lyndia shot him a glare full of hatred.

"I'd better check on Freddi," I said. "I bet the keys to these handcuffs are in her purse." Sure enough, that's where I found them, along with my phone, which I pocketed. While Shannon kept Lyndia on the ground and called the police, I gave Freddi more of the coffee to keep her awake.

"I'm sorry," Freddi murmured when she could finally keep her eyes open. "I should have told everyone about the will and that Nigel was blackmailing Lyndia. I just . . ." She shrugged. "I didn't know what else to do."

"We'll get the will to Tyrus now." I was also going to owe that man an apology for all my suspicions. "But are you sure you have no idea what she might have done with Micaela?"

"No. I'm really sorry. If I had talked before, maybe she wouldn't be missing." A tear dripped from the corner of her eye.

She was right, so all I did was pat her arm. "You're going to be okay."

At last sirens filled the air, and Detective Wallace showed up to take Lyndia into custody. An ambulance arrived for Freddi. I went back to Shannon, who put his arms around me and held me close. A surprisingly warm rain had begun while I was in the car helping Freddi, but I was freezing cold as if some unseen thing pushed at me.

"I'll need you to come down to the station," said Detective Wallace. She was in surprisingly good spirits, but why wouldn't she be since I'd solved her case for her? Or most of it.

I shook my head. "Not yet." To Shannon, I added, "Take me back to the inn. I need to see if Lyndia left any imprints. I don't think Micaela has much time." We had no way of knowing how much of the drugs she'd ingested.

"I'll bring her down later," Shannon told Wallace over his shoulder as we hurried toward the rental car.

He drove like a maniac, not pulling to a stop in the inn's parking lot but driving up on the walkway to nearly the front door. Once inside, I headed toward Lyndia's rooms, wondering if we'd have to break the door down, but the cold urged me in another direction.

"What is it?" Shannon asked, seeing my hesitation.

"All this time, I've been trying to get the cold to imprint again, but maybe all I really need is to follow it." It had led me to the hat, toward Lyndia when I'd been out by her firepit, and to safety on the beach.

Moments later, we'd scaled the now-closed pool gate and stood in the wind and rain next to the fire pit. *Why this place?* I thought.

"Well?" Shannon said.

"I don't know." I looked around, my eyes fastening on the firepit. The firepit Lyndia had put in just before her grandfather died—after Nigel threatened to expose her. The firepit she had bought herself and placed. The same firepit where she'd replaced all of the chairs after learning about my ability.

If she'd shot Nigel by Frontier Cabin, it would have been an effort to drag the cart with him all the way down to the pier by herself—and even if she'd used a car, without a storm to cover her tracks, she could have been easily spotted. Besides, his body had never been found. While that might be possible, with so many swimmers and boats, it wasn't likely. And what was it Detective Wallace had said about water wells and bodies tending to end up in them?

Maybe there was a well on Magnolia Inn property—or something similar—but hidden in plain sight.

"Give me a hand!" I yelled into the wind, reaching for the stone edge of the firepit.

Shannon bent to help. Strangely, the cold had vanished now, and I felt an imprint on the stones. Not words, but a sense of satisfaction and warmth before the rain washed it all away.

Under our assault, the firepit came up with surprising ease, revealing a flexible gas line that allowed us to tip it all the way on its side. Underneath, the ground wasn't paved with flagstone or cement, and it wasn't even dirt, but a huge metal disk.

"It's a lid," Shannon said, feeling the edge with his fingers. "It should have a lever lock somewhere. Over here looks like the only place wide enough. Yep, I've got it." He opened the lever, but the lid came up only an inch before hitting a cement ring that had supported the firepit.

He laid it back down, and we both pulled on opposite sides at the same time, lifting it straight up. The gleefully malevolent imprints on the lid had me dropping it as quickly as possible. There would be enough time later to read those, if needed.

We peered inside the hole but could see nothing under the weak light coming from the inn. Shannon had his phone out before I did, shining it into the darkness of a metal drum that seemed to extend down forever. Then the light hit something. Or someone.

"It's her!" he shouted.

Tossing his phone to the side, he fell to his knees and bent down into the hole until his top half was almost completely inside. "I got her," he said, his voice echoing inside the drum. I reached inside to help as he drew her high enough for me to grab. Together, we pulled her limp form out onto the flagstone. I knew for sure then the presence I'd felt had been Welby, that he'd wanted us to find Micaela. Whether for her sake or for Tyrus's, it didn't matter.

I held my breath as I checked her pulse. "She's alive. But her pulse is faint. Better call an ambulance."

Shannon did as I cradled Micaela's head.

"We're here," I told her. "Hold on."

No response.

Silver duct tape covered her mouth, and more tape secured her hands in front. I worked the tape from her mouth so she could get more oxygen, all the time slapping her face lightly and talking to her, trying to bring her back. I didn't stop until a faint groan escaped her lips.

"That's it," I said to her. "Please stay with me. Your boys need you."

Where was that ambulance?

A strange smell wafting up from the hole made me pause to pull out my own phone. Down, down, I angled its light inside the metal drum that was easily taller than my entire height. My breath caught in my throat as it landed on a heap of charcoal briquettes that covered everything except the top of a bald head and a glimpse of pale, wrinkled fingers. Micaela wasn't the only one inside.

We'd also found Nigel Carr.

Chapter 19

Two days later, early Wednesday evening, Micaela came home from the hospital. The doctors had recommended staying at least another day after her near brush with death, but she wanted to be with her boys. Bonnie and Holt had installed her in the fold-down couch bed in their private sitting room, where they could keep an eye on all of them until she was feeling stronger.

Micaela didn't remember being in the metal drum with Nigel's body—and everyone was glad for that. She did remember Lyndia taping her hands before being forced to ingest the pills. By all accounts, we'd found her barely in time. Micaela had been at risk not only from the pills but from suffocation. She'd survived as long as she had only because the barrel was old and the edges of the metal lid severely bent.

Lyndia had been meticulous in her plans, buying the used, two-hundred-and-ten-gallon drum from a private seller on the Internet for cash and having the company who put in the flagstones bury it. When questioned by the police, the contractor admitted to thinking it was odd, but Lyndia had told him she wanted the barrel to hide valuables, and it wasn't by far the strangest request he'd had from a customer.

Nigel had died from blood loss due to the single gunshot. It hadn't been an easy way to die, but the medical examiner said he was likely unconscious after the first hour. The charcoal surrounding him had done a lot to mitigate the smell of decomposition, and Lyndia had planned to use her tickets to Mexico long before any construction began on the property.

More investigation uncovered that Nigel had poisoned both of Freddi's old boyfriends, one fifteen years ago and the other only last year. The first had died, clearing the way for Nigel to marry her. The second had been the only man she'd been serious about after their breakup, and he'd recovered only because the dose had been off.

Imprints on Lyndia's ring, discovered in her bedroom safe, revealed that her mother had tried to poison her husband but had ended up an unwitting victim herself when he'd had a violent reaction in their car while driving. The mother might have been clinically mad, but Lyndia's actions had been her own choice.

No charges were being brought against Freddi, and now that Nigel had been found, she was eligible for widow benefits, which had brought her to tears. She'd be staying another day at the same hospital where Micaela had been treated.

Shannon and I joined Holt and Bonnie in their private sitting room to welcome Micaela home, and also Tyrus, who hadn't left her bedside the entire time she was at the hospital. He sat on the edge of the couch bed, as close to her as he could without actually climbing into bed with her. It was clear to everyone that neither of them planned to be separated ever again.

"Here," Bonnie said, handing him a copy of the handwritten

will I'd found in the main sitting room, exactly where Freddi had left it. "I already made a few extra copies for our files."

"Freddi promised to testify on your behalf if the copy isn't enough," I added. "Once she gets out of the hospital, of course."

We'd told Tyrus about the will, but this was the first time he'd actually read the words. His eyes scanned the page eagerly. "He really did leave the inn to me."

"That's because before he died," I said, "he found evidence that Lyndia was stealing money, and that's what started his suspicions." I didn't need to tell Tyrus I'd learned this from imprints left at the inn. "Welby believed you would take care of Lyndia even if you received the entire inheritance. He knew she'd run through anything he left her far too fast. Of course, once he began to suspect she was poisoning him, he didn't want to reward her at all."

Tyrus shook his head. "It's all so much to take in. But no wonder he kept needing money." Tears filled his eyes, and he struggled a moment before gaining control. "I should have done more."

"You did what you could." Micaela grabbed his hand. Half a dozen pillows supported her on the couch bed, and she looked like a beautiful princess holding court. Tyrus smiled at her, his eyes latching onto her face as if he were afloat in an ocean and she were his lifesaver. I'd run into many imprints from him over the past two days—mostly at Magnolia Inn and at the hospital—and I understood that the infatuation and regret he'd harbored for ten years were well on the way to becoming real love for both Micaela and her boys.

"The good news is the stolen funds will be returned," Shannon said.

"But you should figure out what you want to do with the

inn sooner rather than later," Holt said. "In the meantime, we've asked Deanna to step up and manage the inn, and we loaned the inn the funds to pay the staff. She's already hired two new people. I've looked at the books, and without Lyndia draining the profits, there should be a profit coming in from here on out with Deanna managing." Holt paused and sighed. "Or I suppose you could sell it after all. Welby would understand, I think. He knows how you feel about your work."

"Thank you," Tyrus said. "I guess I have a lot to consider." Silence met the words because none of us could make the decision for him.

"I still can't believe Lyndia did all this," Micaela said after a while. "When she came to the inn that morning, she was like a person I'd never met." Her gaze shifted to me. "Thank you for finding me. I didn't get a chance to tell you before, but I'm so grateful."

Tyrus brought her hand to his lips, his eyes meeting mine. "We are both grateful."

Maybe I wouldn't have to apologize to him after all. I caught Shannon grinning at me knowingly. "I'm glad it worked out," I said, winking at my husband.

Husband. That was still so strangely new.

"Vovó, Vovô!" High-pitched voices from somewhere inside the house drifted to us urgently. *Grandma, Grandpa!* Heartbeats later, the boys skidded into view in the hallway, peering into the room from the open door.

"Two men are here," Dimas said importantly, looking pleased with himself. "They want to see you." He climbed up on the bed next to his mother, and the smile they shared was worth everything Lyndia had put me through. That and the joy on Bonnie's face.

"They look like rich people," Lucio added. "They're wearing suits. Even though it's so hot."

"We don't have new guests arriving until tomorrow." Bonnie rose from a chair she'd dragged next to the couch bed. "Guess I'd better go see what they want."

But before she reached the sitting room door, two men appeared behind the boys. They were indeed wearing suits, and all of us recognized them at once: the two real estate investment attorneys. Both men were flushed from the outdoor heat, and the taller one with the slight double chin mopped at his brow with his handkerchief.

As before, the tall man took the lead. "I'm sorry to barge in like this. The boys said it was okay to come in."

"What do you want now?" Holt said, going to stand by his wife, his fists clenched at his side.

"We wanted to inform you that we have recently purchased Magnolia Inn from Lyndia Carr." He opened a new-looking leather folder and took out a form, holding it out to Holt. "We also have a sworn affidavit from her stating that her grandfather allowed you to use part of his property for a cabin. This is land that our backers will be reclaiming as we go forward with construction. In good faith, because of the ongoing dispute, we're prepared to offer you one hundred thousand dollars to reimburse you for the cottage on the land, even though technically, we are not obligated to do so since we have already purchased the land from Miss Carr."

Utter silence met the man's obviously prepared speech. I'm sure I wasn't the only one who noticed the vast reduction in their offer, though that wasn't the worst of it.

Holt didn't take the paper. "No," he said. "You can take your hundred thousand and shove it."

"I guess you didn't hear that Lyndia has gone to prison," Bonnie added, "and that she doesn't own the land. There's a new will."

The man smiled with false benevolence. "I assure you that you won't be able to fight this in court. As I told you last time we talked, our backers have deep pockets. You're only wasting your money."

Tyrus jumped from the edge of the bed and rushed to the door, shoving his copy of the will into the man's face. "No. You're wasting our time. I'm the new owner of Magnolia Inn. Here, you can have this copy of the will—we have others. But since Lyndia didn't inherit, she couldn't have sold you anything. As I'm sure any judge will tell you."

"You'll also find that the land my cottage is on is no longer in dispute," Holt said, "It's all right there in black and white in Welby's own handwriting."

Tyrus lifted his chin. "Even if it were in dispute, it wouldn't be anymore. My grandfather wanted Holt and Bonnie to have it, and they will. We'll be adjusting the property records this week."

The tall man's eyes fixed on the document, his heated face becoming even more flushed. "Well, this can't . . . we've already paid for the property. We helped Miss Carr get through probate."

"Sorry," Tyrus said. "I'll be filing an injunction in the morning."

The attorney took a breath, glancing at his partner. "Well, then maybe we need to change gears," he said to Tyrus. "What if we offer you the same price we offered Miss Carr? Even without the extra land?"

"No," Tyrus said without hesitation. "It's not for sale. Not ever." He turned to Micaela. "I may be a writer, but I'm not always traveling, and I need a home base. It might as well be here on the property my grandfather loved. Will you help Deanna and me run it?"

She nodded with a bright laugh. "Yes, I'd love to."

It wasn't exactly a marriage proposal, but I was sure that was where they'd end up. And from Bonnie's ear-to-ear grin, I guessed she didn't mind finding another employee for Haven Retreat.

"The first thing we'll do," Bonnie said, "is change the whole firepit area."

"Agreed," Tyrus said a little too emphatically.

Holt focused on the men with an insincere smile. "Sorry. Guess you'd better start using those deep pockets to get your money back from Lyndia."

The men's pleasant grins turned into grimaces as they pivoted on their heels and strode into the hallway without another word.

"It's all decided then." Shannon met my gaze with those sexy eyes that had wooed me from the beginning, even when we were at odds. I didn't need an imprint to tell me what he was thinking. We'd done what we'd come to do. Now we still had two and a half more days here to eat wonderful food, visit estate sales, walk on the beach, and spend long afternoons curled up in each other's arms in Rose Petal Cottage.

Except the boys had other plans. "It's time for hide-and-seek." Lucio dove for Shannon's hand. "You promised."

Dimas shot from the bed to grab his other hand. "That's right. You did promise."

Shannon groaned. "Well, in case you haven't noticed, we've been a little busy helping the police wrap up this case."

"Well, it's all over now," Dimas countered. "You just said so."

Shannon looked at me. "Okay, let's play," I answered for both of us. I didn't figure they'd last long in the heat.

"You know what?" Holt raked a hand through his hair, stretching his back a little. "I think I've got a mind to play too." The boys cheered.

Bonnie walked us out to the back lawn, where we were surprised to see Deanna coming down the path from Magnolia Inn. We waited in the muggy heat for her as the boys began wrestling on the grass, still layered with leaves and blossoms brought down by the storm. Their high giggles punctuated the air.

"Is everything okay?" Bonnie asked when Deanna was only a few feet away, her loose blond hair hanging limply around her face.

Deanna smiled. "Oh, yes. Without Lyndia there mucking things up, everything is going perfectly." She shrugged a little in apology, though we all understood the sentiment. On some level, everyone still felt sorry for Lyndia. She had played the helpless child for so long and so well, it would take time to begin thinking of her as the cold-blooded murderer she really was.

"That's good." Bonnie thumbed at the house. "I'm about to put a fresh batch of chocolate chip cookies in the oven if you'd like to stick around. I thought today I'd make ice cream sandwiches with them for the boys."

"I would. Thank you. But first, I'd like Autumn to look at this." She held out the brown journal I'd seen her reading at the inn on Monday.

"What is it?"

"It belonged to the boy who I believe was with my son

when he was shot. He died in prison himself not long after my son, but his sister and I have kept in touch—Brysen dated her for a while." Her eyes strayed to Holt. "She's one of the reasons I finally came to terms with what my son was doing and stopped blaming Holt. Anyway, she was moving and found this and decided she was ready to part with it. It's mostly dates and names and addresses and columns of numbers. She knows I'm connected with Holt and Bonnie and thought it might be of use, even though it's been so long, so she brought it to me while she was here on vacation."

She shrugged as she met my gaze again. "I've looked through it, and there are some pages from around that date and my son's name, but not a lot of detail. I thought maybe you might see something more."

She looked back at Holt, and the rest of her words were for him. "I was so awful to you right after it happened. I'd lost him all over again. And then—"

"It's okay," Holt interrupted. "You had every right to mourn him. I will regret that day for the rest of my life."

"But that's just it." Tears formed in Deanna's reddened eyes. "You shouldn't have to. After I learned what Autumn can do . . . I thought maybe if you knew for sure what happened that day, you would be at peace like I am now."

Bonnie, Holt, and Shannon all turned expectantly in my direction. Reluctance filled me. Maybe I'd find an imprint on the book, or on one of its pages. Maybe it would free Holt from his private torment. But there also might not be an imprint, or maybe the imprint wouldn't reveal what they hoped. I didn't trust that I was a good enough liar to hold back the truth.

"It might not make it better," I warned.

Holt understood at once. "Please try. It's worth the risk."

"Okay." To Deanna, I added, "Why don't you set it over there?" I motioned to the closest table on the back patio, currently empty of guests.

Deanna did as I requested, then seated herself across from me. Everyone else gathered around and remained standing, except Dimas and Lucio, who had accepted the delay good-naturedly once they learned of the ice cream sandwiches. They ran into the pool area and began splashing water on their hot faces.

I set a finger on the cover of the journal. Imprints tumbled through me, taking me back through the years. Impressions of wistful sadness mostly, and I guessed they were left by the woman who had kept the journal belonging to her long-lost brother.

More imprints followed, some vivid with violent outbursts and others dulled by substance abuse. I didn't catch a glimpse of anyone that looked like the picture Elliot had sent me of Deanna's son, Brysen.

"I'm sorry," I said. "It's not here on the outside, at least. There are plenty of imprints, though. None of them good. This gang was violent. I can still try the individual pages. What was the date?" I'd rather not go through them all. I was already feeling shaky inside.

Deanna took the book and opened it three-fourths of the way through. "There's not a date on every page, but there are about ten pages between dates that might match up."

I began touching the pages. It was more of the same, or nothing at all, snatches of places and people like a kaleidoscope of images. The brother hadn't been the only one to use the notebook, it seemed.

When what I was looking for appeared, I almost missed

the importance of the imprint, dulled as it was by substance abuse.

I made a big X over the tally of numbers. We weren't ever recouping what we lost today because of those stupid cops. Now we'd have to find another place to open up business. All our current plans to expand at the middle school were off after today.

I was still staring at the X when a thin man with a scruffy beard and long hair came into the bedroom, kicking aside trash and clothes lying on the floor. He peered at the book. "Shake it off, man. Brysen knew the risks, just like the rest of us. He was a hothead anyway. A ticking timebomb. We all know it. At least you got his gun. With any luck, that nosy policeman will be fired for shooting him." He laughed. "Poetic justice."

Grabbing Brysen's forty-five from the floor as it skittered away from his hand after the shooting was all I'd done before running out the back and through the alley. I hadn't stopped Brysen from pulling his weapon or yanked him away from the window. I'd saved my own skin. And now he was gone. Before he could even get off a shot.

I couldn't let myself care. That was business. That was life.

"Right," I said.

"Your sister and Brysen were a thing, right? I bet if we tell her he wasn't carrying, she might tell his mom. Brysen was always saying how his old lady loved him no matter what, right? Now she can go on a rampage. That cop will be out on his ear, and the attention will be off us."

"They broke up weeks ago," I said. In fact, I'd ordered Brysen to stay away from Jilly, and he'd agreed as long as I gave him a promotion. "But I'll tell her anyway. It might give us a break."

The imprint ended as he slammed the journal shut. In the

pages that followed, there was nothing more about Brysen. It didn't matter. I'd seen enough.

"Well?" Holt asked eagerly, obviously noting something in my expression.

"Eighteen years ago on June fifth, the person who imprinted on this was with Brysen. They both had guns. Brysen's was a forty-five. When the police showed up, Brysen pulled the gun. He was going to shoot. After it happened, his buddy grabbed the gun and ran. He told his sister, Jilly, to tell Deanna that he wasn't carrying. They were hoping to make life difficult for you and get the attention off their gang." I paused a heartbeat before adding, "You stopped them from expanding their business in the middle school."

A choked gasp escaped Holt's throat. "So I didn't imagine the gun."

"No. You didn't," I said.

Deanna reached for the book and handed it to Holt, tears glittering in her eyes. "I should have known it was a lie. I shouldn't have gone after you so hard. I shouldn't have accepted money from you before I really needed it."

Bonnie bent to hug her. "We were happy to help."

"You are a good friend." Deanna hugged her back.

"There's more," I said.

"Oh." Deanna drew away from Bonnie, her expression lost. While she might have come to terms with her son's death, I could tell this had cost her.

"Your son bragged that you loved him and would do anything for him," I said softly. "He went there that day knowing he was loved unconditionally."

Deanna lurched forward in her chair and hugged me tightly,

her hair brushing my face. "Thank you," she whispered. "I'm glad he knew that, even though he caused a lot of heartache." She drew away, looking steadier.

"This really calls for ice cream cookies." Bonnie pulled Deanna to her feet. "Come on. By the time they finish their game of hide-and-seek, we'll have them ready." The women went off together, arms linked.

Holt wiped his eyes. "Let's get this game over with. I think my allergies are acting up, and my back could start hurting again at any minute. I'd like to put on more of that salve Autumn bought. Good stuff, by the way." He called the boys from the pool, locking the gate behind them. "Go hide, everyone. I'll count."

Shannon and I ran to hide, ending up crouching behind the same bush. "Thank you for that," he whispered. "I think knowing there was a gun will help Dad finally be able to talk about it."

"It was the truth."

"I know." He rubbed one of my hands between his, sending off all kinds of delicious sparks. "But I also know those imprints weren't all that fun." He kissed me then, pulling me into his arms. "I know a better place to hide," he said thickly when we finally drew apart.

I laughed. "The boys have really been waiting a long time."

"So have I." His groan was only half teasing.

"I promised Lucio I'd help him hide."

In the distance, we heard giggling. Holt must have found one of the boys. They'd be coming for us soon. Time to move to another bush.

"About that thing with my mother?" Shannon said, catching my hand.

"What thing?"

"The kid thing."

"Right." I waited for more because he obviously had something to say.

"One part of me doesn't want to share you—ever. But this?" He indicated the bushes and the screaming laughter coming now from close by. "I think I'm almost ready for all this."

"Good to know," I said, kissing him again. "I think I am almost ready too."

TEYLA BRANTON has worked in publishing for over twenty years. She loves writing women's fiction and traveling, and she hopes to write and travel a lot more. As a mother of seven, it's not easy to find time to write, but the semi-ordered chaos gives her a constant source of writing material. She's been known to wear pajamas all day when working on a deadline, and is often distracted enough to burn dinner. (Okay, pretty much 90% of the time.) A sign on her office door reads: Danger. Enter at Your Own Risk. Writer at Work.

Under the name Teyla Branton, she writes urban fantasy, paranormal romance, and science fiction. She also writes romance, romantic suspense, and women's fiction under the name Rachel Branton. For more information or to sign up to hear about new releases, please visit www.TeylaBranton.com.